Experimental battle tank XM-F3—
"No Slack":
the ultimate in mechanized death

"Its monopolar carbide armor is tougher than anything on tracks. Twin turbine engines give it a top speed of more than eighty miles per hour. A full complement of armaments, including War Club missiles, make it a match for anything on the ground or in the air. Radar, laser aiming devices, and on-board computers give it a technological superiority that devastates the enemy!"

TANKWAR

WORLD WAR III COMBAT ZONE

TANKWAR

LARRY STEELBAUGH

BERKLEY BOOKS, NEW YORK

This book is dedicated to JAMES and KERRY ALEXANDER, for the time and friendship and support they have given, and for the country comforts.

The author would like to thank Mr. Gordon Rottman for his time and generosity in providing information crucial to the composition of the books in this series. He is responsible for many of their virtues and none of their faults, which are the author's alone.

1

For Staff Sergeant Max Tag and the crew of the XM-F3 tank No Slack, it began with the slaughter of pigs on the little iron bridge across the River Main, just upstream from Bamberg. If he had been doing everything by the book, Tag later thought, they would probably all be dead, the pigs *and* the men of No Slack.

The night before, a radio glitch and a balky hydraulic servo unit had given him an excuse to reinterpret their ordered withdrawal toward Mannheim and maneuver the surprisingly agile XM-F3 beneath the bridge abutment, where the tank's loader and unofficial electronics whiz, Specialist Four Francisco "Fruits" Tutti, muttered in his Bronx brogue while hunched over the battle-frequency module, and Sergeant Robert E. L. "Wheels" Latta, Tag's driver, tinkered with the servo unit. But that all suited Tag just fine. He was already pissed about being called away from where they all knew it was going to happen—and soon.

"It" was Situation Firebreak, the code name for a So-viet-bloc invasion of northern Europe. The buildup of forces in Czechoslovakia's 15 Guards sector just across the border was no secret. And it was no secret what would happen to the Allied Forces nearest the border when the fire storm broke: Their orders were to hold until they were overrun or ordered to fall back. This was Tag's fourth tour in Germany, and he had never been on a field exercise to rehearse for a retreat. To make sure he didn't get the word, he hadn't even set a radio watch.

At 0430 on August 2, Tag was just struggling up into the shallows of sleep when the wailing *freeeesh* of rockets brought him to. In the moment before he came fully awake and registered the salvo of flashes and explosions ripping across Bamberg, ten kilometers away, he confused the sounds of the rockets with the panicked squealing and skit-tering of the hogs being driven across the bridge above him.

"Incoming!" he bellowed, and the ground around the tank came alive as Fruits, Wheels, and Ham Jefferson, the black gunner of the No Slack, scrambled out of their in-flatable bedrolls and into the deck hatch behind the turret. Wheels already had the turbine engines humming when Tag dropped through the commander's hatch and slammed a helmet over his ears.

"Shit and git, Sarge?" Wheels's voice came over the integrated headset in the helmet.

Tag adjusted the microphone in his CVC. "Wait one, Wheels," he said. "Fruits, can you still receive ComNet now?"

"You got it, boss."

There was a hum and pop as the Command Network's coded frequency came up. A voice as monotonous as a recording was repeating, "All units, all units, initiate Firebreak sequence. All units, initiate Firebreak sequence."

"Shit," Tag shouted through the intercom. He slid into the pistol harness draped over the back of his seat and grabbed his 8×40 day/night binoculars out of their cubbyhole.

"You people stand by," he said. "I've got to go naked and see what the fuck is coming down."

Tag came up through the hatch, glancing in disgust at the empty War Club missile racks on either side of the turret, and almost at once the throaty *thock-thock-thock* of approaching Hind-D rotors drowned out the melee on the bridge above him. Then came the wild chatter of heavy 12.7mm machine-gun fire raking the iron-planked bridge. The darkness was filled with the howl of ricochets and the fear-shit stench of the hogs. He heard a voice above scream out, *"Nein,"* then strangle in a thick, wet sound. As the helicopter passed, Tag more felt than heard the snarl of approaching armor.

The Soviet battle unit of six T-80 tanks and a dozen BMP armored personnel carriers tore across the bridge in rapid file, through the roiling mass of hogs, forcing blood, guts, and savaged pork through the gaps in the bridge like sausage through a colander, spattering Tag with gore and excrement. It was 0445.

Five minutes later Tag low-crawled up the embankment and surveyed the carnage on the bridge. Gut-shot and mangled hogs dragged their broken bodies, squealing through the bloody hash, as a single unharmed piglet snuffled at the wound on the drover's neck. Tag scanned the far bank, where the tanks had come from, the red cast of his glasses melding with the blood on the bridge, then turned toward the sound of the armored column as it swept along the arcing road in the direction of Bamberg.

Flanking movement, Tag thought, trying to block the back door out of town. Thanks, God, thanks.

"Fruits, Ham, lock and load, all guns, AT rounds!" Tag was barking his orders even before he settled the commander's helmet on his head. "Wheels, key in the bridge coordinates for the LandNav." As Wheels and Ham checked out their electronic equipment, Fruits stacked five shells in the autoloader of the 75mm gun and rammed a sabot round into the breech of the 120mm cannon, while Tag double-checked what he had in mind on his maps.

"All right, you bad asses," Tag announced over the intercom, "in case you haven't guessed, we're in Firebreak. We're also behind the lines, with no War Clubs and no ground support and one whole shitpot of bogeys between us and wherever we need to be. In other words, we got Ivan right where we want him. The jokers that just rolled over look like they're on their way to set up a blocking force on the back side of B-berg. But Wheels here is gonna take us cross-country, so we can be there to welcome the boys to town. The brass wanted us to shake down this rig, and that's just what we're about to do. Any questions?"

"Yo." Ham's voice came over the headset. "I got a question, Sarge. How come you smell like pigshit, man?"

"'Cause I'm choosing my company better. Roll it, Wheels. Beeline for these coordinates. . . ."

The terrain wasn't made for conventional tanks, but the XM-F3 was anything but a conventional tank. Its one-piece monopolar ("slick-skin") carbide armor was tougher than anything on tracks and fifty percent lighter. Its twin turbine engines would run on everything from av-gas to cheap perfume. One of them alone would carry the No Slack along at a solid fifty miles per hour, and both gave it a top end of more than eighty. With its full complement of armaments, including the missing War Club missiles, it was a match for anything on the ground or in the air. And its radar, laser/IR aiming devices, and on-board computers for fire direction and land navigation gave it a technological superiority that the Soviets (and some NATO allies) had yet even to guess.

The ground that Tag and his crew had to cover between the bridge and the agricultural suburbs of Bamberg was in places cut by mazes of gullies as rugged as any in the Teton River breaks of Montana where Max Tag had been raised. Even using the IR periscope, he couldn't be sure he would see a washout in time. But that was only a passing reflection as Wheels sailed the No Slack over ruts and hummocks at speeds over fifty miles per hour, sending thirty tons of machine airborne as they leapt ditches and came down in a *whoosh* of compressing air-torsion suspension. Even the oil dampers on their seat pedestals couldn't keep the shocks from banging the bases of their spines like licks from a Louisville slugger.

"Goddamn," Fruits Tutti exclaimed in his nasal Bronx whine. "Don't tell me we ain't in no friggin' cavalry."

"Shoot, boy," Wheels Latta drawled as he worked his joystick and pedals furiously, "this ain't nothin' more than a Carolina washboard. You ever see me put a tank in a four-wheel drift?"

With that he locked alternate tracks through a series of switchbacks in the gullies, snapping their heads from side to side.

"Hey, soda cracker." Ham Jefferson snarled in mock belligerence. "You can let me out at the next bus stop. You hear? I may be a po' boy from Saint Louie, but I don't deserve to die like this."

Good, Max Tag thought. Good. They had shaken off whatever initial shock they felt and were sounding again like the bitching, whining, ball-busting bunch they were: the best fucking tank crew in Europe.

Dawn was just breaking gray when Wheels spun them out of a final turn and into a bowl-shaped depression behind a low hill that had once been worked as a gravel quarry.

"Hold up," Tag ordered. "Ham, air radar. We got Hinds somewhere. Fire on sight. I'm going to have a look over the ridge."

Tag clambered out of the hatch with his binoculars in hand and pawed his way up the loose gravel slope to the top of the rise. The road looping into Bamberg lay three hundred meters away. The Soviet column was just entering an outlying township populated by local farmers, some of whom Tag could see fleeing across the fields to the south. Two of the T-80s broke off to skirt the edges of the village, while the others and the BMPs continued their relentless course along the road. By the book, Tag thought, knowing that the last tank out of the village would be the command vehicle. He knew Soviet tactics as well as he knew his own, and this was a classic, just like a punk street fighter telegraphing his punches.

He looked right and left until he saw a place where the slope flattened, then moved quickly back to the No Slack.

"Okay," he announced to the crew, "they're in your basic flex-and-run sweep. We got their flank. Wheels, move us up onto that bench about a hundred meters dead ahead. Ham, we're gonna take the flanker on our side while the others are still in the vil. When the others come out, pop number four. That'll be the command tank. Move."

The low-slung XM-F3 slewed up onto the flat below the lip of the rise. Ham screwed his face against the eyepieces of his sight and activated the range finder.

"Target," he said.

"Shoot," Tag ordered, feeling the moistness at the heels of his hands.

"Shot," Ham said.

The recoil of the 120mm cannon rocked the No Slack on its loose footing as the armor-piercing sabot round screamed from its tube. Through his periscope Tag watched as the Soviet tank blossomed in flame and black smoke. The explosion lifted it off its near-side track and pried the turret back like the lid of a tin can, smoke pouring from the gap.

"Splash one," Tag said.

Fruits was locking the cannon breech behind another integral-propellant sabot round as the first of the other T-80s emerged from the village, its gun twisting toward the position of the No Slack like a hound hunting for a scent.

"Wait for number four, Hambone," Tag said softly over the intercom.

Then came the second tank, rushing to come abreast of the first.

"Steady," Tag said.

Just as the third tank's snout broke into view from behind a steel warehouse, an explosion erupted behind it, then a second explosion in its rear drove the T-80 forward and left it to settle in a smoldering heap in the middle of the road.

"Whadda fu—" Fruits began, only to be cut off by the blare of the air-defense horn and a blast that knocked the No Slack from its precarious footing and sent bushels of gravel whanging off its slick-skin armor.

Tag regained a grip on his scope and, from their cock-eyed position with the rear of the tank off the low side of the bench, saw the profile of the Hind against the lightening sky, while his radar screen blipped wildly.

Silently cursing the rear-echelon assholes who had nixed the inclusion of the War Clubs on the No Slack, Tag ordered, "Air defense. Evasive tactics. We got us a Hind."

Wheels threw the gears in reverse and dug dirt in a sharp arc as a second rocket from the massive helicopter passed inches over the turret and erupted in a cloud of fine dust and rock. Wheels jammed the tank into a bootlegger's turn as Ham and Fruits swung the turret around to bring the 75mm rapid-fire gun to bear.

"Get us back in the gullies," Tag said. "We got no cover in this damn bowl."

The tracks spun as Wheels punched the throttle wide open, jerking the No Slack forward and away from the impact of the third rocket.

Firing manually and to the rear, Ham pumped rounds from the 75mm as fast as Fruits could stack them in the autoloader, hot brass clattering in the shell hopper.

Wheels cut left into a narrow defile, seeing too late that it was blocked by an abandoned dredge.

"Freeze it," Tag ordered. "Ham, you better take your best shot."

The Hind hove into view, nose down, searching. Ham triggered two rounds. The first one smashed through the windshield of the cockpit and went off directly beneath the main rotor, which spun away like a child's whirligig as the flying tank came apart at its fiery seams, showering comets of hissing magnesium alloy over its quarry as it fell.

What happened to the second round would forever be a mystery to Hamilton Jefferson.

A column of inky smoke boiled from the wreckage of the Hind, and its ordnance cooked off in high-explosive tattoos, filling the air with wild rounds and renegade rockets.

With the dredge to the rear and the Hind erupting in the quarry, Tag had but one choice: "Charge. Run and shoot, boys. Gunner's choice."

Wheels gunned the turbines, and the No Slack responded with a leap, clawing up the low, steep rise more like a motocross cycle than tracked armor. It crested the rise to face a phalanx of three T-80s and six BMPs rumbling toward it across the fields between the ridge and the village.

Ham swiveled the turret to the left, locked on the outside tank, and touched off the 120mm sabot. The XM-F3 rocked back from the recoil, but no one inside had a chance to see their target shudder from the internal explosion or its commander struggle in flames from the turret hatch. Another of the T-80s had fired at the same moment, its shot caroming off the armored track-skirt of the No Slack and flying back up the narrow defile to their rear, striking the rusted dredge and blasting it from its base. A round from the third T-80 exploded directly in front of the Americans, tipping their tank up precariously on one track. When it settled, the Soviets were almost on them, less two of the BMPs that, unaccountably, sat belching smoke and wounded troopers in the middle of the field.

"Back to the gullies," Tag barked.

Fruits reloaded the cannon as they jolted back over the rise and raced in reverse through the defile, narrowly clearing the teetering boom of the dredge.

Tag was grinning, showing a wedge of clenched teeth, as he remembered a game he and his boyhood friends used to play in Jeeps and dune buggies among the Teton River breaks.

"Wheels," he said, "you ever play Rat Race?"

"Used to give lessons to the revenuers," the Carolinian replied.

"Well, let's see if Ivan knows the game."

Wheels changed gears and sped into the eroded maze as the two Soviet tanks paused at the top of the rise to survey the terrain and the smoldering wreckage of the Hind.

Taken out of their prearranged battle plan and with their unit commander dead, the Communist tankers were not prepared for the improvised tactics of the No Slack and its lunatic crew. After a few minutes of anxious chatter over their radios, the two Soviet tanks split up, one edging down into the gully and the other racing along the ridge in what they hoped was an enveloping action.

While the enemy tankers were puzzling out what to do, the crew of the No Slack had been organizing a surprise for them. On the inside bend of a wide washout, they had found a deep recess dug in the dirt face where quarry equipment had once been stored. The low-profile XM-F3 just fit, even the muzzle of its cannon hidden in shadow.

"Okay," Tag said over the intercom, measuring his voice against the adrenaline swelling in his chest, "here's the drill. I'm going to go pop a smoke grenade just around the bend, let them think we're stalled, then nail 'em by opportunity. Questions?"

"Yeah," Fruits said. "Who da fuck's whammin' doze guys besides us?"

"Soon as you find out, tell me, Fruits," Tag said. "Stand by your guns; I'm going naked."

Tag piled out of the hatch and stood at the edge of the shadow in the mouth of the recess, listening. He heard the keening Communist turbines, one at high speed moving away to his left, the other prowling through the maze to his right. He moved quickly along the vertical dirt face until he could no longer see the No Slack's cavern, then heaved a white-smoke grenade twenty meters farther ahead and scatted back to his tank.

Standing in the turret with the XM-F3 turbines at idle, Tag could easily hear the approach of the questing T-80 as it revved up for a run at the smoke. He twisted down into his seat and buttoned up seconds before the Communist main battle tank passed.

"Scoot and shoot," he ordered.

The No Slack wheeled out into the wash, going wide for a clear shot around the bend. The T-80 paused in confusion when it saw the source of the smoke, and that was when Ham nailed it. The armor-piercing sabot tore through the rear exhaust grille, and the resulting explosion blasted back through the entry hole with enough force to scorch the markings off the nose of the XM-F3.

When the smoke cleared, Wheels said, "Can't get past him, Sarge."

"Well, get us the fuck out of here. We got another one somewhere on the high ground."

"One o'clock high." Ham's voice came sharply over the crew's headsets.

Tag swiveled his scope as the turret moved, then jerked to a crawl.

"Yo' mama's fuckin' servo unit, Wheels," he heard Ham say.

"Go to the 75mm," Tag ordered.

The 75mm's limited coaxial cone of movement was just shy of enough for Ham to draw a bead on the underside of the T-80 that loomed on the rim above them, nose up, unable to see the No Slack or to direct its own fire on it.

"Back the sonofabitch up, Wheels." Ham's voice was calm but deafening in the tank's momentary silence.

Fruits mumbled something that could have been church Latin but was lost in the No Slack's sudden lurch to the rear.

They all knew that the 75mm couldn't be counted on to puncture the forward belly armor of a T-80 and that the lame turret didn't give Ham many choices for a shot. Every one of them could smell his own sweat.

The turret gave a sudden jerk as Ham fired, causing the shot to fly wide, at almost point-blank range. "Yo' mama's—" the gunner began, only to be cut off by a blast on the side of the T-80 that shelled track off its drive cogs like a snapped string of beads. The Communist driver engaged his other track but managed only to swing in a short arc, exposing the lighter rear armor to the No Slack. But even as Ham triggered his 75mm again, another blast ripped through the rear of the T-80, toppling it down the back side of the embankment.

"Now this is some weird shit," the gunner said in amazement.

"May be, Hambone," Tag said, "but it ain't no act of God. Wheels, let's go find out who our buddies are."

The No Slack screamed back through the labyrinth toward the bowl of the quarry, until Tag spotted a slope they could traverse.

Not lingering on the crest to silhouette themselves against the now-bright sky, Wheels leapt over the top and brought them down into the fields at full throttle. It took the crew of the No Slack a long moment to take in what they saw.

A hundred meters ahead of them, a skeletal vehicle bristling with recoilless rifle tubes was careening across the fields. One figure stood in it, manning a heavy machine gun as it rushed toward the rear of a Communist skirmish line strung out among six BMPs. Four other Soviet personnel carriers were in smoking ruins nearby. Beyond them, other figures advanced from furrow to furrow in four-man rushes toward the Communist line.

Hot damn, Tag thought. "Fruits," he almost shouted, "AP rounds in the 75mm. Hit it, Wheels. We got us some light work." And he jacked a belt into the coaxial 7.62mm machine gun. "Give me their flank."

The No Slack fell on the armored infantry company like a lion on a pack of lapdogs. Ham walked rounds down their line, the 75-mm gun ripping through the thin armor of the personnel carriers but failing to disable one remaining BMP, while Tag and the gunner on the strange vehicle raked the line with automatic fire. The Soviet soldiers nearest the surviving BMP scrambled back into it. The rest died as it sped away between converging small-arms fire from the two Allied vehicles and the troops advancing from the village.

Tag kept the BMP in his scope, the corners of his grin bending toward his chin.

"You wanna show your shit, Ham?" he said. "Moving target. Mark."

Ham keyed his computer. "Mark, bark, and spark, boss man," he said.

"At your leisure, Mr. Jefferson."

"HE round, Mr. Tutti," Ham said to his loader, who replaced the sabot with a solid 120mm high-explosive.

"Make up your friggin' mind," Fruits whined.

Ham remained impassive as he loosed the shell, following its trajectory in his mind until the laser-guided shot ripped through the side of the BMP, disintegrating it in a cloud of dust and smoke eight hundred meters away.

Tag yawned audibly over the intercom. "Okay, boys," he said, "let's get out and stretch our legs."

The tankers tumbled out of their hatches and milled around the No Slack, examining its dents, scorch marks, and gravel pings.

"Hell," said Wheels, gnawing a cud off a plug of tobacco, "I had an old '63 Chevy that useta look worse'n this after runnin' a county blockade. Sombitch would do a hunnert and forty with a hunnert gallons of white whiskey in the tanks."

"Yeah?" Fruits said. "Well, next time I'll take the A train, thanks."

Ham clapped him on the shoulder. "Don't be too hard on the cracker, Toots. He can't help it if he's a Baptist and a bootlegger. All that inbreedin' softens they heads, you know."

The attack vehicle that from a distance had looked like a pile of mobile scaffolding slid to a stop next to the No Slack. Except for the belly and nose armor, the .50-caliber machine gun on a naval mount, and the three recoilless rifle tubes on either side of its roll cage, it was a dead ringer for a stretched dune buggy. The West German officer who had been manning the machine gun stepped out, snapping his goggles up onto his forage cap, and came up to Tag wearing a broad grin.

"What's your matter?" he bawled. "You can't find a nice beer garden to bust up?"

"Rick!" Tag blurted in amazement as he rushed forward to embrace Oberlieutenant Heinrich Holz. "You crazy bastard. What the hell are you doing in B-berg?"

"Saving your butt, it looks like," Holz said as he pumped Tag's hand in both his own. "Same as always."

"Yeah, yeah," Tag said. "I guess I do owe you one for that little disagreement in Koln."

It had been during Tag's second tour in Germany, in '88, that he had met then Cadet Holz in a beer garden in Koln, where Tag had overmatched himself against three brothers of a Fräulein who understood his intentions only too well.

"You packed a mean beer stein in those days, Rick. But what's all this?" Tag waved his arm to include the troops swarming over the Soviet dead, as well as the other vehicles that were similar to Holz's and were moving toward them from the village. "Don't tell me you're a sponger."

"*Ja,*" Holz said, standing a little taller. "Jagd Kommandos. The best, we are."

The Jagd Kommandos were motorized antiarmor troops, armed with recoilless rifle vehicles like Holz's and mobile missile stands. Billeted in suburbs and agricultural townships, their strategy was to allow superior enemy forces to pass unopposed, absorb them like a sponge, then strike from the rear and be gone before the Warsaw Pact invaders knew what hit them.

"You'll damn sure do in a pinch," Tag said. "But we may not have much time here for all this mutual admiration. We've been a little busy this morning, and I haven't even had time to get a sitrep. We've got to find out what the skinny is, get us some fuel and some—"

"Wait, wait." Holz stopped him. "The forces moving up from the south are at least two hours away, and the Bamberg bridge will hold for almost that long, I think. For all the rest, we can provide. But first you need to eat and talk with me some strategy, *ja?*"

"*First,*" Tag said, "I need to get up with my people. See, I was supposed to be halfway to Mannheim by now. I kinda bent a few orders and, well, it's a long story."

Holz's face went solemn. "Max," he said, "I'm sorry, but you are your people here now. Second Armored, they stopped transmitting just before these others arrived here. To you, ComNet would not respond. They also are having a busy morning. Come with me and I will show you my maps. I think now we are the field generals. Come."

Tag turned to his crew. "Sorry about introductions, gents. You heard the man. Let's saddle up."

"Max," Holz called to him, "you should meet my driver, who suggested we lend you a hand."

"Glad to," Max said, walking toward the gun buggy.

The tall, slender driver got out, removing a helmet that released a cascade of ash-blond hair.

Tag froze, his hand half extended and his mouth agape.

"Staff Sergeant Max Tag," Holz said, a mischievous smile playing across his face, "I would like you to meet my sister, Giesla—the one I told you of who drives the rallies."

"Pleasure," Max mumbled as he took Giesla's strong, slim hand awkwardly in his own. Beneath the dirt and grime on her face, she was as beautiful a woman as Tag had seen.

"Glad to please," she said, releasing Tag's hand and climbing back into her seat.

Standing in the turret of the No Slack, Tag watched the gun buggy race down the furrows toward the village. "Wheels," he shouted down the hatch, "follow that car."

At 0630—fed on omelets, black bread, and coffee—the crew of the No Slack gathered in Holz's headquarters in a warehouse basement to look at maps and review the situation in northern Europe two hours into World War Three.

2

Holz's sand table was a hasty model shaped in an old fruit-sorting bin, but it told the story from the Fulda Gap south to Austria. The Group of Soviet Forces in Czechoslovakia (ZGT), headquartered in Milovice, had already swept unchecked more than fifty kilometers into West Germany on a line for the River Main to the Donau. North of the Main, Schweinfurt had already fallen, though Fulda itself was proving a bottleneck, clogging the Soviet advance. Bamberg, on the south side of the river, had its eastern flank protected by the rugged hills where the headwaters of the Main formed in the Wagnerian forests above Bayreuth. But with armor and mechanized infantry pouring down from Schweinfurt and the line advancing from the southeast, the town had no more than a couple of hours before it was pinched off—and that only if the Bamberg bridge held.

"Shit," Tag spat. "That bridge, the one where we saw

them cross the Main, I hadn't even thought of it. We should have taken the sonofabitch out before we left."

"It's taken care of, along with the old ferry," Holz said. "And the militia have patrols scouting for pontoon bridges. Not that there is a lot we could do."

"Y'all sticking around here?" Wheels asked, lifting the heavy coffee mug to his mouth with both hands. He and Fruits and Ham stood against one wall of the basement, just out of the light, wolfing down the last of their bread and coffee as Holz outlined the situation.

"No," the German replied, stepping back from the table and into the edge of shadow. He pointed with the blade of his saw-backed sheath knife, sweeping it through the cone of light. "There, Nürnberg, your armored cavalry headquarters; and there, Würzburg, the Third Infantry headquarters, that will be the line. That is as far as they can go . . . for now."

"What's to stop them?" Giesla asked as she leaned into the light, bracing her hands on the rim of the table and peering intently at the crude contours studded with colored flags.

"Logistics," her brother said.

"And the U.S. Army, thank you," Tag added from his end of the table.

Giesla looked levelly at him, squinted, and stood out of the light.

"*Ja*, you're right, Max," Holz said. "By then the U.S. Five and Seven Corps and the French Two Corps will have organized well enough—and the Soviet resupply will have become so crucial—that they must regroup, prepare for the counterattack."

"And meanwhile," Tag said, "they're gonna be moving hell and Georgia to get their asses on line. Can you tell anything, Rick, from the radio traffic? What's holding? Who's falling back?"

Holz bellied back up to the lighted table. "Come in close, all of you," he said, beckoning to the No Slack crew and his own NCOs. "My people already know most of this," the German commando continued, "so don't worry about translations. I've been thinking, and here is our best plan—for us and for you. We both must be out of Bamberg soon."

Giesla moved aside for the two Kommando NCOs and stood next to Tag at the end of the table. He tried to ignore her as she leaned in to listen to her brother; tried to ignore her scrubbed, fine-boned face turned in quarter profile to him, her hair tied now loosely back, the ess of her lithe body twisting inside the jumpsuit. He wasn't having much luck.

"Max," Holz continued, "your last orders were to withdraw to Mannheim, *ja*?"

"Uh, right."

"Okay. You might make Würzburg from here"—with his knife he traced a route in the sand westward along the Main—"and that would put you halfway to Mannheim. But with the troop concentrations moving down the river and the forces already in Schweinfurt, maybe not. Your better route would be through here"—Holz trailed the blade through a hodgepodge of contours that Tag supposed were meant to be the forested hills northwest of Nürnberg —"and you will still need some help. Our own orders, Max, are to scatter, scrounge whatever we can, and rendezvous in these hills, at a place we think will be behind the lines. If the field-exercise supply depot here"—Holz tapped negligently with the point of the knife—"is still intact, we'll have plenty of fuel and ammunition."

"Have you been in contact with them?" Tag asked.

"*Nein*," Holz said, "but they are part of our standing Firebreak drill. Still, who knows? Between now and then . . ."

"Yeah, Sarge," Fruits Tutti said, motioning across the

table at Tag. "And now dat de balloon's gone up, who knows what bets are off?"

"We *got* orders, Fruits," Tag said. He turned to Holz. "Rick, it's your show, if you think you can get us out of here. But we gotta have some go-juice. If you got maps of where we're going, we can scan 'em into the No Slack computers. That'll help."

The sound of dry hinges and the flat rasp of boots on the stone stairs into the basement caught the attention of those at the table. Out of the corner, lit by an open door at the top of the stairs, an FRG commando spoke in German to Holz, who replied, then turned back to Tag.

"We can do all of that, Max. If we are agreed . . .?" He let the question hang in the air a moment. "Good, then we must make ready."

Holz spoke to his own men, who turned and hustled up the stairs.

"You heard the man," Tag snapped to his crew. "Shag ass."

At the foot of the stairs, Max spun around at a crash behind him. Holz had upturned the sand table and was dusting off his hands with an air of grim satisfaction.

The angle of morning light was not right—too soft, too golden—to illuminate the scene on the street outside the warehouse. In front was the still-smoking carcass of one T-80, an oil slick spreading like blood from beneath it, creeping toward the lunar-like pockmarks in the asphalt where bits of burning metal landed. Behind it, just beyond the warehouse, was the remains of the command T-80, one side ripped open to expose the turret cog and the churned, grisly interior of the crew compartment.

Across the street, the six Kommando gun vehicles were already lined up and gassed. Behind four of them were towed racks of antitank missiles, with twenty-four tubes each. In addition to the six 106mm recoilless rifles, each attack vehicle also had a .50-caliber machine gun naval-mounted on the roll cage and two 9mm MP25s for the crew, as well as grenades and individual sidearms. The Jagd Kommandos were scrambling over the vehicles, securing spare tires and gear, replenishing ammo boxes.

Holz turned to Tag. "Have your men fuel up down there," he said, pointing out a tractor garage a hundred meters up the street, where several civilians were gassing up motorcycles and Fiats and Volkswagens. "Meanwhile, I'll see what we can do about your ordnance."

"Wheels," Tag said to his driver, who was sitting up through the driver's hatch, talking to Fruits and Ham as they leaned on the No Slack glacis, "take our baby down where you see those cars and get her a drink. Ham, you and Fruits come with us."

As the No Slack's turbines settled into a tenor hum, Holz asked Tag, "You don't care what fuel we have?"

"No, sir," Wheels put in. "Right now I'm pumping all our JP4 into one tank, and I'll put whatever you got in the other. If it burns, we can run on it. But baby don't like to mix her drinks."

As if seeing it for the first time, Holz watched the No Slack accelerate backward toward the tractor garage. "What is that tank, Max?" he said to Tag. "A new model, *ja*?"

"Newer than that, my friend. That is the one-and-only-in-Europe XM-F3 tank, No Slack. Rick, this is the damnedest machine you've ever seen. It'll run with one of your VW hot rods, outshoot a T-80, bust Hinds like clay targets, and go through a nuke without a scratch. We've been with her for six months, and we're still finding out things she'll do."

"Like get her turret stuck?" Holz asked blandly.

"Yes, you asshole. But that wasn't new design stuff; that was a servo unit from an Abrams. I'm more worried about the radio. We can still receive, but we can't transmit except on the TAC frequencies."

"If we hurry," Holz said, glancing at his watch, "we can use our base unit."

"Fruits, Ham," Tag said. "Go over in that building and see what ammo you can scrounge. How long do we have, Rick?"

"Lots of time; perhaps fifteen minutes."

Tag could hear the pitch of battle around Bamberg changing, from the swooping tympani of artillery and rockets to the ragged crescendos of small arms marking the movement of foot troops into the city. Tag followed Holz into the ground floor of the warehouse and through a maze of sandbagged vehicle bays until they came to a concrete room in the center, where the Jagd Kommando operations center had been. A radioman was tearing pages from codebooks and crumpling them into a fuel barrel outside the door.

Holz spoke rapidly to him in German.

"Nein," the radioman replied.

"We're in luck," Holz said. "Come."

Tag seated himself in front of the radio, dialed in the ComNet frequency, and keyed the handset.

"Queen Bee, Queen Bee, this is Butcher Boy. I say again, this is Butcher Boy. Do you read me? Over." There was only static and a whispered babble of ghostlike transmissions. "Queen Bee, Queen Bee, this is Butcher Boy. Do you read me? Over."

When a voice did come through, it was as clear as if it had been next door.

"Butcher Boy, this is Queen Bee. Where are you? Position from any brew."

"Queen Bee, this is Butcher Boy. From Budweiser, down one-five-zero-zero. Be advised, this is our last, I say again, our last transmission. We have radio problems, and I'm sending on a borrowed transmitter. Over."

A different voice came over the handset, this time that of Colonel Menefee, the officer in charge of the No Slack's evaluation.

"Butcher Boy, this is Queen Bee Actual. That Bud's not for you. Are you still operating under last orders? Over."

"Affirmative, Queen Bee Actual. Over."

"Butcher Boy, listen up. Proceed with all due dispatch toward your objective. Under no circumstances will you allow your hardware to be compromised. You are to terminate your hardware, if necessary. Do you copy? Over."

"Queen Bee, this is Butcher Boy. I copy: Haul ass and burn the trash. Affirmative? Over."

"Butcher Boy, this is Queen Bee Actual, do it now. Over."

"Queen Bee, this is Butcher Boy, roger and out."

Tag put down the handset and swiveled in his chair to face Holz. "Did you get all that, Rick?" he asked.

"Most of it, I think."

"What old Satin Ass didn't say was that we're on our own. If we're about to buy the farm, we gotta compost the No Slack."

Holz grinned and slapped him on the shoulder. "Let us get away from all these farmers, then."

Out in the street, Wheels had the No Slack back from refueling, and he, Fruits, and Ham were lashing crates of rations to the rear deck. Nearby, the Jagd Kommandos were loading the last of their ammo and gear. Giesla came out of the building across the street carrying a can of belted .50-caliber ammunition in each hand. The day was beginning to heat up, and Giesla had shucked the top of her jumpsuit and tied the arms around her waist, leaving her in an olive drab green T-shirt that clung to a sweaty patch between her high, full breasts. As she leaned across the driver's side of her vehicle, straining to set the two cans of ammo between the seats, her jumpsuit rode up, sculpting the inverted heart of her ass against its fabric.

Tag saw two commandos with reserve insignias on their sleeves lounging against the wall of the building near Giesla, smoking cigarettes and eyeing the blonde as she struggled with the ammo cans. One of them stepped forward and spoke to her. She said something. The man shrugged and turned, paused, glanced over his shoulder, then executed a backhand grope of Giesla's round behind.

Faster than it takes to tell, she whirled on the man, taking his wrist in her near hand and driving his elbow forward with her other. At the same time she brought her knee up into the base of his spine and drove her shoulder into the middle of his back. Confused by being hurt in so many places all at once, the man careened headlong across the sidewalk and into the stone wall where he had stood. Tag could hear the wind go out of him as his head thonked hollowly against the rock.

Before his knees hit the ground, the three tankers from the No Slack were there, followed by Tag and Holz. Giesla turned, and her death's-head grin froze them all. Her mouth was as grim as a rictus, revealing two rows of strong, small teeth as regular as tombstones. Even as he stopped, Holz was barking at the two men in Teutonic fury.

The dazed man's friend helped him to his feet, keeping a wary eye on Giesla and the three tankers, who still stood on the balls of their feet, knotting their fists and straining like leashed pit bulls. As the stunned reservist began to grasp what Holz was saying, he dropped again to his knees and let pleas and apologies—plain in any language—pour out of his mouth.

Giesla let her face relax and looked at her brother and Tag. "No, Heinrich," she said in English. "It was only a training accident. This soldier and I were studying . . . self-defense. And you may tell him I will be glad to show him the technique again, anytime he wishes." With that she walked erect across the street, shoving her arms back in the sleeves of the jumpsuit.

"What the hell?" Tag said.

"*Ach*, nothing," Holtz told him. "I was going to shoot him, but Giesla is right. That would be pointless. But excuse me while I talk to him." And Holz, his voice now a metallic hiss, brought the two men to attention before letting the anger of his words fall on them like lashes.

"Oo-whee," Ham Jefferson said, watching Giesla sashay into the operations center as the crew strolled back toward their tank. "That mama be bad to the *bone*, Jack."

"What you say," Wheels added. "And her brother the CO too. That sumbitch has got to be crazy."

"Okay, okay," Tag said, tearing his own eyes off Giesla's figure. "I'll see if I can arrange a best-two-out-of-three match. Anybody want to be first?"

"I'll hold your coat," Fruits said.

"Fuck you, Tutti. Are we loaded?"

"Gassed and ready," Wheels replied.

"Ammo?" Tag asked.

"Sorry, boss," Ham Jefferson said. "We got all the machine-gun ammo in the world, but no 75mms and sure nothing for the main tube."

"So how do we stand?" Tag asked his gunner.

"We got ten rounds of AP and fifteen HE left for the 75mm. For the 120mm, nine sabots, four HE, and all five beehive cannisters."

Tag shook his head. "Shit," he said. "I hope this field supply dump is all Rick cracked it up to be. What about thermite or some C-4?"

Fruits cocked his head and looked at Tag. "Whadda we need dat for, Sarge?" he said.

"Orders, Mr. Tutti, strict orders from Queen Bee Actual his own self."

The crew smiled. Tag had a special relish in his voice when he got to call Menefee "Queen Bee."

"Under no circumstances, gentlemen," Tag went on, "under *no* circumstances can we allow the No Slack to be taken intact by Ivan. Our orders still stand to hiako back to Mannheim. Only difference is, now we got to do it catch-as-catch-can. Holz says his spongers can spring us. Anybody think we got a better shot?"

"What do we do after the supply dump?" Ham asked.

"Head west-southwest, either through the forest in the hills or through those farm roads that run down to the Mannheim highway." Tag traced figures in the air.

"Uh, yeah, Sarge," Fruits said, clearly still pushing some adrenaline, "but what about *contact*, you know?" Wheels and Ham drew serious faces and turned them from Fruits to Tag.

"If you numbnuts had read the Firebreak manual," Tag drawled in feigned impatience, "you would recall Chapter Two, Engagement, Article three, Subsection C, the part about 'engaging all targets of opportunity at the commander's discretion,' and you wouldn't be asking me these dumbfuck questions."

The two FRG reservists came slinking past the No Slack, one abashed and the other guilty by association, as Holz walked up to Tag and his crew.

"Start your engines, my friends," he said jauntily. "I'll confirm the radio is down and get my driver and we can be off."

"Your driver?" Tag said. "Do you mean your sister?"

"*Ja*, of course she's going with us."

"Is that really a good idea, sir?" Wheels said.

Holz looked at them. "You Americans," he said wearily.

"Giesla is the best driver I have, the best I've ever seen. She also holds a reserve commission in intelligence, speaks seven languages, and, well . . ." He turned to Tag. "Would *you* want to tell her she cannot come?"

"Right," Tag said. "Let's go." And he scrambled up onto the turret.

"Our other solo vehicle will be coming with us, Max," Holz said. "I'm sending the ones with the missile launchers to the rendezvous."

Holz turned away just as Giesla emerged from the warehouse, a Sauer 9-mm automatic pistol strapped beneath her arm, her helmet and goggles in one hand. She hurried toward her brother.

"Heinrich," she said urgently. "An entire motor battalion. Three kilometers and coming fast."

"I'll see to the radio."

"It's done," she said, and the first rounds from the T-64Bs accompanying the motorized Soviet infantry crashed into the last buildings at the end of the village's main street. Civilians scattered from the tractor garage in a frenzy of motorbikes, frightened four-cylinder acceleration, and pedestrians bolting toward basements and shelters.

Tag paused on the turret and turned to Holz.

"What's the drill?" he said.

But Holz was already coughing orders to his battle crews. The two reservists that he had disciplined were the first in their vehicle, the flat *whap* of its exhaust slapping the air. Holz spoke to them above the rising blare of motors. They both nodded in acknowledgment, then wheeled the gun buggy out of file in a wide turn and accelerated down the street toward the incoming Soviet rounds.

Holz turned back to Tag. "Max," he said, "we've got too many civilians here to stay and draw fire on them. Just follow me for now." And he sprinted for his vehicle.

Tag was through the hatch and in his fighting seat before he thought it, running on reflex and adrenaline.

"Wheels," he said, "stay on Rick's six. Fruits, rack the
75mm with AP. And Ham, just be ready on the main tube.
I don't know exactly what our German ally has in mind."

The ex-bootlegger from Grandmother's Gap booted
open the throttles of the turbines and slung divots from the
asphalt as the No Slack leapt on its tracks and raced after
the tank killer.

The FRG reservists who made up the local infantry that
had attacked the initial Soviet assault squadron now were
dispersing in a skirmish line southeast of the hamlet to
meet the second wave. Underground concrete silos became
their bunkers, drainage ditches their trenches, even as their
homes, barns, shops, schools, and churches were being
blasted to rubble by walking salvos from the advancing
Soviet armor. There was haste but no panic in everything
they did, Tag thought: the ground-towed missile rack has
preplotted coordinates for defense; Rick has a grip on his
AO; we got our orders; and all is right with the world.

At the second left off the main street—an unpaved but
level farm road on a bed of crushed stone—Giesla power-
slid the gun buggy and accelerated southwest, perpendicular to the Soviet line of advance, followed by the No Slack
and the second antitank vehicle and the creeping carpet of
Communist gunnery, while the three remaining Kommando
vehicles sped away with their missile racks in tow.

Wheels slammed the No Slack into a hard left turn and
muttered, "Fuck," over the intercom. "Where the hell's he
goin'?"

"Just stay with them, Mr. Latta," Tag said. "Let's get
the passive air systems up."

He screwed his periscope in an arc toward the Soviet

forces. He could distinguish the T-64Bs from the BMPs, now fifteen hundred meters away at their nearest flank. Two of the Communist tanks broke from the formation, crashed over low stone walls, and came at the three vehicles in a cloud of dust across the harrowed fields. Scanning a hundred and eighty degrees, front and sides, Tag could see that the road they were traveling at nearly one hundred kilometers per hour ran past a silo and some farm buildings set in a dell to the right and ahead of them a half kilometer away, then on to a low, wooded hill and out of sight. Even though the T-64s were the souped-up models with electronics that allowed them to shoot on the move, Tag doubted that they would chance a shot while pitching and yawing over broken ground. And he didn't want to give them a chance to get set. At a thousand meters, the 125-mm cannons on the refitted T-64Bs were murder.

"Sabot in the main tube," Tag ordered. "Ham, we have two at nine o'clock. Fifteen hundred meters and closing."

Fruits Tutti dialed the loading carousel and seated a 120mm armor-piercing sabot round in the breech of the big gun. As Ham Jefferson swung the turret and watched the screen of the No Slack's unique TAD (target acquisition device), the concentrated silence of the crew compartment was rent by the high-frequency horn of the passive air defense, signaling low-flying aircraft.

Tag immediately keyed his scope to the radar, thinking even as the two Hinds appeared in his eyepieces: *We're all the air defense we got.*

He watched a moment longer as the heavy helicopters lumbered higher above the Soviet formation, and one of them dipped its nose and peeled off to cover the T-64Bs that were advancing toward Tag and the German antitank commandos.

"Air defenses up, radar-controlled fire, manual overrides on," Tag rattled to his crew. "Fruits, you take the flyer; Ham, stay on the T-64s and—"

"Bumps!" Wheels's voice broke in over the intercom just in time for Tag to grab the padded tubes on either side of his commander's seat as the No Slack, following Heinrich Holz's command gun buggy, swung violently to the right and down the embankment above the farm. Its off track left the ground while the low-side track clawed for purchase in the soft sod and shredded wire fences in its cogs. In an instinctive and useless gesture, Tag threw his weight back in the seat to counter the lift and momentum that felt as though it would send the tank ass-over-teakettle down the hill. All that saved them was the counterweight of the cannon pointing left. The spine-slamming jolt when Wheels brought the off track down came as a relief.

Regaining the focusing forks on his scope, Tag panned the dell and could see it had been a dairy farm—there were stone milking barns and a feed lot on either side of the concrete silo. Beneath the embankment opened what looked to be an arched brick culvert. Tag puzzled for a moment before it hit him. Of course. An underpass for cattle and equipment moving from field to field across the road.

"Cannon rear," Tag said to his gunner.

The barrel seemed to move with the force of the slide Wheels threw them into as he braked left and shot into the mouth of the tunnel less than a second behind Holz.

Tag could see a long rectangle of gently sloping light beyond the speeding gun buggy, perhaps a hundred meters ahead. Whatever Holz had in mind, Tag thought, it would still mean they'd have to stop and arm their tubes.

"Wheels," he said over the intercom, "pass that turkey first chance you get. All defenses up, boys and girls. We're going to come out smoking."

The Kommando vehicle slid to a stop in the verge of the rectangle of light. Holz and Giesla were out of it before it quit rocking, stuffing armor-piercing rounds in the 106s as the No Slack howled past, its turbines echoing through the tunnel like the keening of banshees.

Tag had muted the passive air-defense klaxon, but the radar screen was the first to come alive as they emerged into the sunlight, blasted up the incline—constructed for tractors and complacent dairy cattle—and sprang out of the chute almost immediately between the two Soviet T-64Bs. The Communist drivers were totally befuddled, uncertain whether to charge, shoot, shit, or go blind. The final option seemed to suit them as they rumbled steadily past the XM-F3 that came racing between them. The pilot of the Hind had more presence of mind.

Yuri Kalnikov had swung his huge helicopter out ahead of the two tanks, hoping for an easy shot at the Jagd Kommandos he imagined were huddled in desperation behind the roadbed. The small tank reported with them he assumed to be a Sheridan or some similar light-armored vehicle—certainly nothing to pose a serious threat to the MI-24D. But when Kalnikov—himself from a farm near Smolensk—saw the tunnel, he knew at once what had happened. Immediately he communicated with battalion headquarters, which, in keeping with the Soviet practice of centralized control on the battlefield, would inform the commanders of the two T-64Bs that the pesky FRG spongers were bottled up in the underpass.

That was all happening as the tank erupted from the earth, baffling the Soviet tankers who were expecting Jagd Kommando vehicles that would be vulnerable to machine-gun fire.

Even Yuri Kalnikov was taken unprepared, releasing a burst of fire from the Hind's rotary nose-cannon before he realized it was a tank.

The swarm of 40mm HE rounds exploded on the No Slack's slick-skin armor, scattering lashed rations from the deck, and not without effect inside.

"Piss me off," Ham Jefferson said with a snarl, and he began triggering 75mm rounds, aiming manually on the radar screen before the lasers' parallax, locked in on the hovering Hind. His third shot caromed off the heavy belly armor of the helicopter and blossomed as black flack just aft of the tail rotor; every other round went wide.

"Fire locked," Tag ordered as Fruits dropped a fresh pan of ammunition into the 75mm's autoloader. But something was happening to the Hind.

Kalnikov hadn't intended to touch off the shaped-charge antitank rocket, but the sudden lurch of his ship and the stick becoming like a live thing in his hand had caused him to mash the trigger in panic. He watched the smoke from the rocket with horrified detachment, keenly aware of the red system-failure lights throbbing on his console and feeling more than hearing the howl of his rear rotor out of control and the metallic finality of the rotor seizing in a sick-making contusion of gears. Everything seemed to slow almost to a stop— the rocket's explosion away and below in the open field opened like a time-lapse flower; the shudders running through the helicopter were a slow pulsation. Then Yuri Kalnikov saw a blur and felt the force of gees and counter-gees and of something that struck him black.

*   *   *

Instead of spinning crazily, the Hind had lurched and hung for a fraction of a second before it shot up and appeared to leap down to the ground, like some suicidal toad. The terrific crash scattered doors and shattered glass for a hundred meters, but when the dust settled, the Hind was perfectly still, save a thick coil of smoke rising from the tail, where a dime-sized piece of casing from Ham's one near miss had perforated a hydraulic line and cut through wiring harness.

I'll be damned, Tag thought. "Gun front," he ordered. "Wheels, bring us around to the right, assault speed. Laser Doppler sights, Hambone. Manual trigger, at my command." Tag was still chafed at his gunner's five shots at the Hind.

As the turret spun into the turn, the No Slack appeared to reassemble itself, settle back into its lines, and gather speed. A high-explosive round fired by one of the tanks back in the Soviet column threw up a geyser of plowed earth fifty meters behind the No Slack.

With their new orders from the column headquarters, the two T-64Bs were converging on the tractor ramp even before the Hind hammered in. Its crash alerted them that the tank was also still a threat, but not quickly enough.

"Shoot," Tag spoke.

Even quartering across broken ground at attack speed, the No Slack was running at almost plumb level when Ham triggered the sabot less than three hundred meters from the T-64B. The accelerated round penetrated the engine before exploding at the back of the crew compartment in an inferno of hyperheated diesel that left the men inside no air with which to scream before they ignited.

Two more 125mm rounds came in from the Soviet column and ripped up the fields near the No Slack.

Fruits locked another sabot in the main tube.

Wheels juked through the furrows, trying to keep the dead T-64B between himself and the other tank.

Tag wondered what had happened to the Jagd Kommandos.

As the second T-64B rushed forward past the mouth of the tractor ramp, an explosion ripped the forward drive cog of its near-side track, sending the tank rearing sideways, only to be hit again in its thin belly and crash over on its side in a roar of cooking ordnance that blew the hatches loose in gouts of bristling flame.

"Shit and git, Wheels," Tag said. And Robert E. L. Latta, hugging the curtain of smoke that blew from the burning tank, raced back toward the ramp. One of the 125s fired by the distant Soviets hit near enough to rock the No Slack's suspension before Wheels cut back left and down into the tunnel.

"Whoa, hoss," Tag ordered at the bottom of the ramp. He hauled himself up into the turret and opened the hatch. He scanned the sky for the other Hind that had been hovering over the column. Decided not to risk it, he thought. Tag could see the flank of the advancing Soviet battalion, now only five hundred meters from the village. Silently, above the smoke and dust and rumble of Communist armor, a daisy chain of white bursts began to creep across the face of the advance, followed by the drum thuds of their sound.

Instinctively Tag looked toward the village for the source of the fire. A second and a third salvo rained death on the Soviet forces, and then Tag saw the second Hind, hanging like a hawk on a lazy thermal as it passed, strafing, over the reservists' skirmish lines. The white traces of two rockets slithered from the Hind's pods toward something on the ground, something that went up in a triphammer sequence of secondary explosions.

"Max!"

Tag looked down at Heinrich Holz. "It looks like your two bad boys bought it. From goats to heroes in half an hour."

"*Ja, ja*, Max. At the end we are all good soldiers. It is a universal consolation. Now follow me, please."

3

Being a good soldier—or any other kind—was a long way from Max Tag's mind when he was a boy growing up on the family ranch in the Teton River country of northwest Montana. There weren't many soldier-heroes in the seventies and early eighties, and none so near at hand as the cowboys who drifted on and off the Tag spread from April until November each year. To Max, these men were not icons of the Saturday matinee; they were living emblems of the only world he knew, the only America that mattered.

They were many different kinds of men who called themselves "cowboy." There were Indians—Sioux and Blackfeet and Nez Perce—and Chicanos from Denver and Bakersfield and two black brothers from Wichita. There were local boys whose brothers Max went to school with, and there were lean, laconic drifters who blew in from who-knew-where to work a day or a year before they disappeared. There were men with no Social Security Numbers, and family men with wives and kids and satellite dishes and mobile homes drawn behind four-wheel-drive trucks. There were drinkers and preachers, gamblers and cowards, bar fighters, and one overly familiar cook, whom Max's father had to save from a serious ass whipping by a highly exercised crew of line riders.

Cowboys were his heroes, but they were heroes he could touch. They, as much as his father or his older brother, Fred, taught him the first things he ever thought worth learning—to ride and rope. At the age of six, during spring branding, Max went into the pens on foot with a cowboy named Lonesome Ted and learned the trick of scooping a calf's hind legs up in his loop. At age eight, Max could do it from horseback. And at eleven he began signing his school assignments "Teton Max Tag," against a saw-toothed silhouette of mountains.

As a man, Tag would not think of his growing up as happy or unhappy; to him it was always *full*. In the summers he worked on the ranch like any other hand. He herded cattle, hauled hay, mended fences. He also fished for trout, went swimming with his friends, played American Legion ball (hitting .391 and covering the gap between second and third like a fence), and would drive twenty miles to the county seat on Saturday night on the outside chance of getting to talk to a girl at the video arcade, where he once set the still-standing record for "kills" on a game called Tank Attack.

In winter there was school, elk hunts, and the ubiquitous chores that piled up during the seasons when the temporary range hands all went south to work the feed lots in Colorado or the big dry-land spreads in Texas.

Max didn't care for his chores any more than any other boy, but he did them, with only two memorable lapses.

Once, when he was twelve, Max became absorbed in a book on the battle of Hastings and forgot to feed two dozen new heifers, until his father came in from a Cattlemen's Association meeting well after dark. He saved himself a hiding by fessing up but was terrified for days by the hot rebuke he received from his usually taciturn father. The second, less than a year later, caught Max in a pointless lie; he denied backing a tractor into a corner of a shed. His father exposed the lie—and Max's backside—to a leather belt.

Those two events stood out in Tag's memory for their incongruity. Most of his recalled boyhood was a collage of horses and men, on high plains and mountain meadows, frosting the air with their breath; of trout streams and baseball in summer; of noisy school buses and the institutional echo of halls in the County Cooperative School; of rodeos and barbecues; of skiing and the reassurance of his mother's fried rhubarb pies.

Max did not mythologize his life or his heroes. Rather, he developed a deep, abiding *faith* in them. Even when, at fifteen, he almost simultaneously discovered girls and that life held options for him other than being a cowboy, Max maintained his fascination with what he saw as the virtues of the range: self-reliance, stoicism, and bone-deep integrity.

In high school Max mixed A's and B's in the classroom, lettered in three sports, and revealed a knack for mechanics and trouble. People in the county seat at Choteau still talk about the day all that conspired to make Max Tag locally famous—or, as some might say, infamous.

It was at the end of Max's junior year, and he and Celestina Nunez were County Coop's junior-class delegates to the Student Leaders Day held each year just before graduation at the county courthouse. Max was on the honor roll and co-captain of the football and basketball teams; Celestina, a gawky, blushingly shy girl with two of her three brothers in prison, was class valedictorian. The trouble started almost as soon as they hit town.

The previous winter, working with his father and a friend in the ranch shop, Max had built what he called "the ultimate dune buggy." With two souped-up VW engines on an extended frame, full-time four-wheel drive, oversize off-road tires, and the body from a Triumph GT-6 (one engine sat in the backseat), the Montana Mudster, as he called the machine, was like a loud piece of surrealist sculpture tooling into town. Police stopped them twice just to get a closer look, causing Celestina no end of anxiety. But things got a little more than curious when they stopped for gas.

Among the small crowd of teenagers, kids on bicycles, and men with nothing better to do who gathered in front of the Exxon station to inspect Max's strange vehicle, there were two of a local bunch who rode stripped-down motorcycles and wore sleeveless denim jackets with "Death's Darlings" stenciled across the backs. While Max was inside paying for the gas, these two waded through the crowd and elbowed their way to the passenger side of the car, where Celestina sat staring at her folded hands.

Max saw something was wrong the moment he turned from the counter toward the door. People were stepping away from his car, while two men in Levi's jackets leaned on its roof, their heads hunched toward the passenger-side window. Max took off his tie and put it in a pocket of the jacket that he shed before going out the door.

Max was already a six-footer, lanky and strong. But the bikers were both older than he, men with coarse faces and ragged beards. He held the jacket thrown casually over one shoulder as he approached them, his muscles tensed the way they were just before the first snap of a football game, anticipating that first good lick that would dispel all the butterflies.

"Come on, baby," Max heard one of the bikers say to Celestina, "get shed of that shit kicker of yours and we'll have us a real party."

"Yeah," said the second, shorter biker, stroking his crotch. "Wouldn't you like to feel that big . . . bike of mine pounding between your legs?"

Celestina balled her hands in her lap.

Max stopped two paces from the car.

"Friends of yours, Ces?" he asked.

Celestina made a worried motion with her head, and the two men looked up at him.

"Hey, now," said the taller of the two as he turned, stood, and leaned with his elbows on the streamlined roof of the GT coachwork, "here we must have your basic boyfriend. How you doing, boyfriend?"

At the corners of his vision Max could see a rank of men and boys; it was like walking onstage.

"Fine," Max said. "Ready to go, Ces?"

Celestina nodded anxiously.

Max started around the car.

The bikers both stepped toward him.

The summer before, Max had had to wrestle every man on the hay crew. One day, when he was feeling quick and good, he threw a Sioux day hand named Tom Strong and went for a pin.

Tom Strong snapped a kick up from the ground and bloodied Max's nose. Tom apologized at once, but Max wouldn't give in until Tom taught him the technique of whipping a kick from the hip.

Max turned and in one motion swept his twill blazer

into the face of the tall biker and snapped a penny loafer into the gut of the other.

The tall biker clawed the jacket off his face, just to have his jaw stroked smoothly twice each by Max's left and right fists and to hear the nightingales sing.

Something heavy shied off Max's kidney, catching at the fabric of his shirt. He spun with it, to his left, and dropped into a peekaboo crouch.

The short biker winged a fistful of lead knuckle duster at Max's head. Max slipped the punch and nailed an elbow to his attacker's cheek. It moved the man back enough that Max could cock and deliver another kick, this time to the balls. Max barely had his leg out of the way before the biker jackknifed and puked between his feet.

Max got back in the car and, reassuring Celestina all the way, drove them to the Student Leaders gathering. She clutched his arm almost painfully as they walked through the ceremonies and were introduced on the shade-dappled courthouse lawn.

They ate lunch beneath tent pavilions stretched on the grounds. The lieutenant governor and the state representative from the district both spoke, along with the director of the Department of Education, the county school superintendent, and a senile judge. Celestina said two or three funny things and made Max uneasy with her restrained but blatant infatuation.

After the tours of the courts and the county offices, the announcement and reading of the winning essay "On Democracy," and an inspirational lecture by a muddled anthropologist who once hosted a PBS series, Max wanted nothing more than to get Celestina back home and himself over to a friend's house, where there were rumored to be no parents and all the cheerleaders in the world from County Coop High.

Trailing Celestina from his arm, Max walked across the courthouse grounds toward the parking lot, where his ultimate dune buggy was parked. Leaning on their kickstands around it were a half dozen customized motorcycles, each attended by at least one denim-jacketed rider and a friend or mama. The biker Max had smooth-stroked at the Exxon station stood from his hunker and walked to the front of the Montana Mudster.

"Hayseed," the biker said, "you have fucked up, bigtime. And now we're gonna stomp you."

The others formed lines on either side of the Mudster, facing Max and Celestina.

"Ces," Max said to her, "go on back to the courthouse. Find a cop." He faced the bikers.

"You want to go to jail?" Max asked the tall one. "Jumping me here on the courthouse square! You're nuts, all of you. The goddamn sheriff is less than fifty yards from here."

The biker stared silently. Max could see there was no backing down in his eyes.

"Tell you what," Max went on quickly, "give yourself a break. You let me get in that car, and then if you can catch me outside town . . . well, we'll see what we'll see."

The tall biker was looking at something behind Max. "Yeah, won't we?" he said, turning to his cohort. "Let's roll."

As the Darlings kicked their choppers to life, rupturing the air with their exhaust, Max looked over his shoulder and saw Celestina and two county deputies approaching from the courthouse. He went to meet them.

It took a few minutes, but he finally convinced the deputies that the incident was over, also convincing Celestina to catch a ride back with some other students from their quarter of the county. He walked with her to find them, and while he did he also talked to several other friends, boys who shared his enthusiasm for off-road vehicles. Then he walked back to the Mudster, shucked his coat and tie, connected the secondary carburetor linkage on each engine, and cranked up.

Max cruised town slowly, in second gear, until he saw the gaggle of bikers drinking beer from cans outside the dark garage they called their Chapter House. He gave them a wave and smoke from all four tires.

Max slowed to the speed limit until he reached the edge of town, the Darlings running in formation a block behind. He crossed the river and took the county road west out of Choteau, jacking his speedometer past ninety, until the fence posts blurred into pickets. The cyclists filled both lanes of the road behind him, fifty feet from the Mudster's bumper and closing. Max topped a low rise, braked, downshifted into second gear, and threw the car shuddering into a hard right turn across a cattle guard made of railroad tracks. His four tires threw rooster tails of dust as Max careened over the pasture on the faint truck trace that led to the river and its eroded basin.

Max could see nothing in his rearview mirrors through the dust, but he was sure the Darlings were still with him, hanging back at the edge of his dust trail. He didn't exactly have a plan, just a confidence that once down in the breaks he could elude the cyclists—and with a little help from his friends, maybe a little more.

The flat field dropped off nearly sheer where the twin tracks Max was following turned to follow the cutbank of the river. He bent with the trace, glancing back around the hook of his dust wake to see the Darlings turning in echelon to quarter across his course.

Hot shit, thought seventeen-year-old Max Tag. The familiar exhilaration he felt playing rat race among the breaks burned through his veins. A broad gully cut into the bank in a swale of the field. Max wheeled down the steep bank, braking with his gears but still going airborne across the red-clay erosion gutters and scuffing both sides of the main gully before turning into his slide and regaining control of the Mudster as it bit into the chat-shot earth and hurled itself down into the maze of gullies, marooned islands, willow thickets, and sand banks that made up the floodplain.

Max roared into the gravel flat at the mouth of the gully and spun the Mudster one hundred and eighty degrees, facing back to watch the Darlings bounce in single file down the rocky, eroded vee. He waited until the first of them reached the bottom, then Max gunned the car in a tight arc and showered the bikers with a fusillade of river rocks, sending the first two of them veering into skids on either side, tumbling over their high-rise handlebars.

Max came out of the spinning turn and accelerated through a willow brake, riding down the saplings with his belly pan. He knew this stretch of the riverbed—not as well as some of the breaks but, he hoped, well enough. His mind was whirling as he grasped for a plan. He knew that outrunning the Darlings was no trick, but Max was hot. He didn't want to hurt the bikers; he wanted to humiliate them. His self-important, teenage sense of gallantry even let him believe it was because they had frightened Celestina. Nothing makes a man or boy meaner than self-righteous indignation, real or imagined.

When Max broke from the willows, he slowed until he was certain that the Darlings had found a way around, then he sped away again, dodging among brush- and tree-topped patches of high ground that became islands when the river was up, always allowing the bikers to stay just close enough to keep from losing him. He ran this way for a quarter mile, until he came to a narrow, open stretch of bottom, a half mile gravel bar, where he opened both throttles on the two 110 HP motors and screamed away from the choppers that were skittering in the loose stones.

The low-slung bikes, with their chopped frames and extended front forks, plowed through the deep gravel, pounding their riders and sending dry sparks flying from the frames. But the tall rider whom Max had KO'd at the Exxon was a local boy himself, and he knew what was around the bend where the long bar disappeared.

The Mudster sat up past its hubs in a bog below a big stock pond that drained into the riverbed. Cattle—lots of it—had found the bog and churned it with their legs and bodies as they mud-bathed as contentedly as hogs, making the bog a rich mix of mud and manure. Max was ten yards into the bog, with another twenty to the other side, his motors idling, when Death's Darlings wheeled up in rank at the near edge.

In his rearview mirror Max could see six cycles carrying nine men and two women, some of them scraped and bloodied from spills and lashing branches. The tall leader of the Darlings kicked down his stand with his heel and swung his leg over the tank to dismount, leaving a gumcracking girl in denim shorts and orange hair perched on the sissy seat of the idling Harley.

"Shit kicker," the biker shouted, "this is it. It's stomp time, fucker. And if we have to come in there and stomp you in that shit, you ain't never coming up."

The Mudster's engines screamed, and all four tires erupted in geysers of bog, spinning in place and hosing the rank of Darlings. Max reversed, cut his wheels, and sliced off a wave of mud that broke like a tsunami over bikes and bikers alike, drowning engines and sending Darlings a-sputter to their knees.

Max completed his turn almost where he began, but now facing the edge of the bog. He threw back the moon roof he had installed in the GT, stood in the seat, and leaned out, unsmiling.

The tall biker pawed sludge from his eyes and began walking toward the bog. "You're dead, shit kicker. Dead," he shrieked.

"Look again, buffalo breath," Max said evenly, pointing to the rim of the cutbank and the narrow gravel bar behind the bikers, where more than a dozen Baja Bugs, dune buggies, and assorted four-wheel-drive trucks had suddenly materialized. Up on the bank, a man—young but well past a teenager—got out of one of the trucks and walked to the edge. Max and the Darlings all recognized him as Doody Howell, Teton County's hero of Vietnam and youngest deputy sheriff. Few people could say they knew Doody well—and Max not at all. He was a distant figure, like one out of history, of whom people always spoke with a certain reverence. No one, as far as Max knew, had any idea what he had done in the war to merit this respect.

"What's going on, fellas?" Doody asked casually.

"These boys were having them some trouble getting across this little wet patch," Max answered in kind, "and I was just fixing to give them a tow."

"That's neighborly," Doody said. "All of you," he said evenly to the Darlings, "get back, now, and give him room."

"Bullshit, Howell," wailed the tall, filth-covered biker. "Them's our scooters."

"Axelrod," Doody said, "I know you boys don't have any sense, but if that fella wants to help you get across that mess, you ought to be damn grateful.

"Go to work, son," he said to Max.

Using a thirty-foot braided lariat he kept beneath the

seat, Max stood in the open roof and looped a floating noose over the handlebars on three of the choppers. He tied the rope to the roll cage and put the Mudster in reverse. The bikes crashed together as the noose tightened and dragged them in a heap into the bog. Max backed through the deepest part of the wallow, where the manured mud came up into his wheel wells, pulling the three motorcycles into it before he loosed the rope. The cycles settled in the slime under a single, thick bubble, with one protruding sissy bar to mark their spot.

Max changed gears, slopped back across the bog, and stopped on the dry margin, facing the other three motorcycles and the eleven mud-smeared Darlings standing in a group twenty feet away.

"Hey, Max!" yelled one of the boys on the cutbank above him. "Here, you need another rope."

Max stood in the roof and caught the coiled rope the boy tossed down to him. He shook it out, made a couple of false passes to test its feel, and dropped his loop over the remaining bikes.

"Hey, shit kicker," shouted the tall biker called Axelrod, "I know you now, fucker. Remember that."

"And we all know you, Axelrod," called Doody Howell from the bank. "You better pray that nothing ever happens to that fella. If he so much as catches cold, I'll personally be on you like stink on shit. 'Sides, I know about Otto Tag, and you don't want nothing to do with any kid of his."

Max backed the Mudster across the bog again, dropping the bikes he was hauling along with the others. He gunned his car down to the river and into some rocky shallows, where he flushed his tires and spun sprays of fresh water to wash out the wheel wells, then scrambled up a negotiable slope of the bank and pulled in among the trucks and dune buggies parked there.

"Sorry about your rope," Max said as he got out.

"Hey," said the boy who had thrown him the lasso, "I'da paid cash money for this show. Are you done with 'em? I mean, is that all?"

"I'd say it's enough, son," said Doody Howell, stepping over and extending his hand to Max. "I'd like to shake your hand . . . Max, isn't it?"

"Yes, sir. Max Tag." Max took the deputy's hand.

"Well, I'm Doody Howell. That bunch has been like the weather for too long, Max; everybody talking about them, but nobody ever doing anything about them. All the same, don't let me catch you going out of your way to get in theirs. Understand?"

"Yes, sir," Max replied.

"All right, let's break this up, boys," Doody said at large. "I know you all got places you need to be. And, Max, would you give my regards to your dad? I never met him, but if you could just tell him that someone sends regards from Ksor Blok in Cheo Reo, I'd appreciate it."

"Sure," Max said. "Ksor Blok in Cheo Reo. Who's that, anyway?"

"Just somebody I met one time who thought a lot of your dad. Give him the message, will you?"

"Yeah, I will. And thanks—for coming out here, I mean."

"That's my job," said Doody with a wink, "to protect those citizens from the likes of you boys."

Max made it to the party that night, the story of the bikers made the rounds, and he made out with a blond cheerleader named Sandi. It was several days, however, before it all got back to his dad. And it was only then that Max remembered about Ksor and Cheo Reo.

Like the cowboys, Max's father was ordinarily a tight-lipped man. Patient, even kind, there was always something about him, though, that made Max think he must have some deep sorrow in his past. Otto Tag never talked about any past beyond a year or two, and then only to recall the snow or the drought or the flood. So when the strange names of Ksor Blok and Cheo Reo came up, Max was surprised at his father's reaction.

"Dear God," Otto said in amazement, dropping onto the hay bales that he and Max were loading onto a flatbed trailer. He didn't even look at Max as he went on speaking, almost as though his son were not there.

"Cheo Reo. Christ, almost twenty years ago. And just like that"—he snapped his fingers—"it all comes back. Memory is funny that way, Max."

"What's Cheo Reo, Dad?" Max asked innocently. "Is that some kind of Spanish name?"

"It's the place I came up here to get away from, son," Otto told him.

"In Missouri?"

Otto Tag flashed one of his rare smiles. "No, son, not Missouri."

"But that's where we moved here from, isn't it? After Grandpa died?"

"Yeah, but it was a long time after your granddad died, Max, and his death had nothing to do with it. I'm surprised you even remember Missouri; you were just—what, two? —when we left. And Frederick not yet four."

"I remember it was in town. I could stand at the door and see lots of houses, and the people next door had a big brown dog that I always wanted to pet."

"That's the one," said his father, nodding absently. "You say it was Doody Howell that told you to send regards from Ksor?"

"Yes, sir."

"Tell you what to do, Max. You go ask Doody Howell

to tell you what he's heard about me and Ksor Blok and Cheo Reo. Then come back and tell me what he said and I'll tell you whatever else you want to know, you and Fred. I was going to, someday. But right now let's get this load out to the south feed shed and call it a day, okay?"

It took Max almost a month before curiosity overcame his reluctance and he finally talked to Doody Howell.

It was after a Sunday baseball game against a team from Billings, in which Max went three for five and assisted on two double plays. Max came out of the showers in the Community Center and saw Doody leaning against the backstop, talking to the coach, who called Max over to congratulate him on his game.

Max was feeling good, exuberant on youth, all his senses keen, but he accepted the praise modestly, waiting for the coach to go. Then he halted Doody Howell as he began to walk away.

"Mr. Howell," Max said, "can I talk to you a minute?"

They sat in the bleachers, in the shade of tall cotton-woods, and Max told what his father had said.

Doody sat silent for a while, chewing on a splinter he'd peeled from the bleacher seat.

"Max," he said at last, "did you know your dad was in the Army?"

"Yeah, I guess so. I mean, I don't really remember, but Fred—that's my brother—he says he remembers Dad in his uniform one time."

"But your dad never talked about it?"

"No, sir."

Doody tossed the splinter away and faced Max, but his eyes seemed to focus on something a thousand yards away. "Well," Doody said, "he was. Back in the sixties. Special Forces, you know, Green Berets. In Vietnam."

Doody's distant stare and telegraphic delivery knotted

Max's throat in apprehension. He nodded mutely.

Doody cleared his throat and went on. "Anyway, when I was in Vietnam, I was six months at a place called Cheo Reo, working with a bunch of Montagnards, mountain people, training them to fight the Vietcong, same as your dad had done eight years before me. Your dad was damn near a legend there, Max, and not just to the 'yards. We'd all heard of him, all of us in Special Forces.

"Well, the leader of the 'yards was this Ksor, a tough little bastard. But there were also some South Vietnamese troops there, and the 'yards and the Vietnamese hated each other. Ksor Blok was so sure they were going to try to kill him that he wouldn't even sleep in the compound. Every night he was off in the jungle somewhere, hanging in a hammock in the trees, the way he said he and your dad used to do.

"Ksor Blok said your dad saved his life, but that happens in combat. Nothing special when you get right down to it. No, what made your dad special was making Cheo Reo the safest enclave in the highlands. After he and his teams—he was there with two different ones—after they had been there less than a year, every Vietcong in his right mind gave Cheo Reo a wide berth. He taught the 'yards weapons and discipline and tactics, and they taught him the jungle and the people. The 'yards even adopted him into their tribe. Cheo Reo was a perfect model of how to win that war, Max, but the Army wouldn't let your dad stay there and do it. So, the story goes, he just packed it in, quit the army, and disappeared."

"And that's it?" Max asked.

"Oh, there's lots of other stories, but they're his stories, Max. By the time I heard them, they'd been told and retold so many times, it was hard to know what was true. What I do know for sure is that your dad was one hell of a soldier. He didn't get the respect of a fighter like Ksor by being a fool, and he damn sure didn't win two Silver Stars and the DSC kissing ass in Saigon."

Doody stopped abruptly. "That's it, Max. It didn't dawn on me for weeks after I got to Cheo Reo that the Otto Tag everyone talked about was your dad. And I've never said a word to him, never even met him. Until I got to Vietnam, all I knew was that he was a good rancher who'd moved up here from someplace and kept pretty much to himself. I figured he had a good reason, and it wasn't any of my business. Anything else, he's going to have to tell you himself."

Max drove back to the ranch with his imagination afire. He had seen the puckered scars on his father's back and legs and always assumed they were from some sort of accident. Now he envisioned wild, close-quarter firefights in steaming Asian jungles, his father wounded and bawling orders to small, brown, frightened soldiers while firing a machine gun with one hand. He thought about such things hard, trying to believe his father had actually done them. Max loved and respected his father, but he had to work to picture that quiet, industrious man as a soldier in battle. And in Vietnam—a Vietnam that Max knew only from hearsay and high-school history, both of which had told him that the war was some sort of national shame, like having a deranged cousin locked in the attic.

Max's brother, Frederick, was back from his first year at the University of Nebraska, where he was studying animal science. There was no mistaking that Max and Fred were brothers; they shared the same lean jaw and even walked alike. But where Max's eyes were alive with kinetic energy, Fred's held a more contemplative focus, one suggesting thoughtfulness and reserve. All he ever wanted to be was a veterinarian.

They sat together after dinner, dangling their legs off the

wide back porch, talking about baseball and watching the summer sun go down behind the mountains. They could hear their mother putting away the dishes they had washed and their father getting something from the pantry.

In a minute Otto Tag backed through the screen door and came out carrying an unlabeled wine bottle in one hand and three orange-juice glasses over the fingers of his other. Max took the glasses from him, and Otto sat down between his sons.

"Frederick," Otto said, "your mother and I are really proud of the year you've had at school, just in case you didn't know. And, Max, you may surprise me yet, if you'll just learn to wait on that hanging curveball."

Max grinned; he knew he was his father's favorite.

"Anyway," Otto continued, working the corkscrew into the neck of the bottle, "I think you're both old enough now that we can have a drink at home together—uh!" The cork popped loose from the bottle. "This is some of Mrs. Morgan's dry elderberry," he went on, putting aside the cork and screw and picking up a glass. "You may recall that this is the wine she used to get the Reverend Trout drunk with at the county fair wine judging last year, so treat it with respect."

He handed glasses to his sons.

"You talk to Doody Howell yet?" he asked Max.

"Yes, sir. Today, in fact, after the game."

"Uh," Otto grunted. "Thought you might. I saw him there as your mother and I were leaving. Well"—he raised his glass—"here's to the ones that do."

"And here's to the ones that don't," Frederick put in, before anyone could drink.

"But never to the ones who say they will . . ." his father recited, picking up the verse.

Max held his glass and listened eagerly as they went on.

"And then again they won't."

"But the girl we'll toast from break of day..."

"...to the wee, wee hours of night..."

"...is the one that says she never has..."

"...but, of course, she always might."

"Hear! Hear!" Max said as they all laughed and drank.

"Otto," Max's mother called from the kitchen, "I hope you're not out there teaching my boys dirty drinking songs."

"Frederick started it, Mom," Max said. "It's all his fault."

"Hush," Marjorie Tag said as she stepped out onto the porch. "I'm going over to take Mrs. Morgan some Mason jars, if any of you drunkards care."

She leaned down and kissed her husband and went back into the house.

"Mom just took Mrs. Morgan a bunch of jars yesterday," Max said.

"I know," Otto said, stretching back to lean on his elbows. "I asked her to make up an excuse to be gone, so I could talk to you two alone."

"What about, Dad?" asked Frederick, turning to lean against a porch post and look at his father.

"Why don't you start, Max," Otto said.

Haltingly at first, then with gathering confidence, Max explained to his brother about Ksor Blok and Cheo Reo and what Doody Howell had told him.

"Dad," Max concluded, "I'd like to know about Vietnam and everything, but how come you quit? What happened, I mean?"

"Why'd you never talk about any of that stuff, Dad?" Frederick added.

"Whoa, boys," Otto said softly, staring off as Doody Howell had when Max talked with him in the bleachers that afternoon. "I can't tell you everything at once, but there are a couple of things.

"I was in the Army for nine years, seven of them in Special Forces, and nearly two in South Vietnam, mostly at the Montagnard camp in a place called Cheo Reo. At that time I was a captain, in command of a Special Forces A-team. I was wounded. I won some medals. But none of that's really important."

Otto emptied his glass and put it aside.

"War is horrible, boys," he continued. "It's the worst thing man can do against man. But however savage and terrible that is, once you're in one, the consequences of losing it are even worse. And the really appalling part of it is that because a war is so terrible and its loss so devastating, it requires the best people to fight it. Not just the bravest—most men are equally brave and frightened in combat—but the best minds, the best *souls*, as the Reverend Trout might say. In that regard, there's no higher calling than to be a soldier."

Max had never heard his father speak like this before, not with such words or such a timbre in his voice. Together they filled him with feelings he had no name for, only a tightness in his chest and a rush of blood to his cheeks.

"That's the way I felt about it," his father said. "Despite anything you may have heard or read about Vietnam, and regardless of the wisdom of our being there, we had ways to win. When we didn't use those ways—when we weren't allowed to use those ways—a lot of those good people—those *best* people—got killed. And when I couldn't keep them from getting killed, I got out."

Otto Tag rolled up on one elbow and busied himself with pouring and sniffing and drinking from another glass of wine, avoiding his sons' eyes. Max was the first to speak.

"I . . . I kinda understand, Dad," he said, not wanting to ask too much. "But what about Ksor Blok? Will you at least tell us about him? Doody said you saved his life."

"Huh!" Otto snorted. "No more than he saved mine, Max.

"No, I don't mind telling you about Ksor Blok. Here, have another glass of wine, and then that's it for tonight."

He poured them each three fingers of elderberry, leaned forward on his knees, looked out into the darkening sky, and began. "Ksor Blok was a Montagnard, one of the mountain tribes of Vietnam. He went to a French school run by nuns until he was twelve, then he went to work with his father as a charcoal maker in the Montagnard village outside Cheo Reo. But he liked to read, and the nuns continued to give him books and magazines and newspapers. By the time he was sixteen, he could read French, English, and Vietnamese. He wrote letters for people, read letters to them, and finally became an indispensable man in the whole complex of Montagnard villages around Cheo Reo. He never held any formal office, but the provincial governor and the village chiefs all paid him for all sorts of reports and commissions he prepared for them. Then the Vietcong came.

"At first, Ksor Blok said, there were only the political cadres, propaganda preachers, who slipped around from village to village, trying to convert the 'yards. Ksor Blok was about twenty at the time, just a little older than you boys, and he didn't have any particular stake in a conflict he saw as being strictly between Vietnamese. Any obligation he felt toward the local Vietnamese officials was completely commercial—mercenary, you might say—and he felt none at all for these bullying outsiders with their willingness to shed his blood to win their war.

"But the Vietcong wanted Ksor Blok. They recognized

that he was a leader, a kind of prince among his people. So when persuasion didn't work, they turned to terror. Thinking they could buffalo Ksor into cooperating with them, the Vietcong began killing his family. First a cousin, then a brother-in-law, then his own brother.

"The night the Vietcong came to kill his father, Ksor Blok and his girlfriend and two others ambushed them with crossbows—with *crossbows*—against four men with machine guns and grenades. After that Ksor Blok could no longer remain an anonymous clerk. After that there was no stopping the people from making him a legend.

"When I first met him a few years later, he was a major figure in the Montagnard liberation movement, called FULRO, as well as the de facto military chief of the area, coexisting uneasily with a South Vietnamese garrison in the province. My team's job was to train both these groups and somehow get them to work together.

"The Vietnamese turned out to be worthless, mostly city boys—conscripts—who had no stomach for soldiering and no love for the 'yards who populated most of the countryside they had been sent to Cheo Reo to defend. Their captain was a prissy little shit who had a Peugeot car flown in by helicopter so he could make regular trips to see his mistress, who lived a few miles down the road.

"The yards, on the other hand, were terrific soldiers, and they were fighting for their own ground. But *who* they were fighting were the Vietnamese, and Montagnards made little distinction between north and south.

"While Ksor Blok and his troops were kicking some serious butt out in the boonies, the South Vietnamese troops were pulling perimeter duty at the compound, diddling the village girls, and getting three hot meals a day. But the worse part was supplies. All supplies for the camp, for the 'yards and the Viets, came through the Viet commander, who was selling what he wanted on the black market and giving his troops enough to keep them quiet. It was the 'yards who got the dregs—the guys who were out there in the bush, keeping South Vietnam safe for hypocrisy.

"Near the end of my first stint at Cheo Reo, it all came to a head. FULRO had decided to mutiny, and Ksor Blok was responsible for taking the camp at Cheo Reo. He had orders to kill as many South Vietnamese as necessary.

"He came to me and told me all this, told me to get my team out of camp for a day or two, because our hooches were in the Vietnamese section of the compound, and he feared some of his people might identify us with them and kill us along with them. He said I was his friend, but once the shooting started, there was nothing he could do.

"I argued with him, told him it was crazy, suicide, that the Saigon government and the U.S. Army couldn't afford to let something like a mutiny, especially an armed one, go unpunished.

"We talked and talked, but it finally came down to the choices of my staying put and taking the chance of getting my entire team killed, or of going along with Ksor Blok, or of telling the Vietnamese commander. I didn't like any of them. So since I didn't have any specific orders to cover the situation, I tried to split the difference. I sent half the team to the orphanage run by the nuns, on the pretense of civic action, as we called it. Then I convinced Ksor Blok that he and a platoon from his strike force should leave the camp with the rest of us, to make it look like a regular patrol. I was afraid that the Vietnamese captain might sniff something fishy if only Americans went out—we were forbidden to—and especially if the whole team went. If Ksor Blok and his troops got lost in the jungle and had to come back to camp—well, those things happen. What I didn't tell Ksor Blok was that I had contacted Saigon and informed my HQ about the mutiny, not that it mattered. Lots of people told them, but no one did anything.

"Forty-eight hours before the mutiny was scheduled, I got choppers and took five men from my team, Ksor Blok, and a platoon of 'yards about fifteen miles up in the mountains, into an area where we had never encountered any VC activity. It was understood, but never said, that sometime during the first night in the field Ksor Blok and his troops would slip off and hiako back to Cheo Reo.

"But that didn't happen. About two hours after we were inserted, while we were working our way up an old trail, trying to get to some high ground, we got hit. It wasn't an ambush, but it was stupid on our part, never should have happened. Our bunch and a VC patrol just blundered into each other. We pushed them back and pursued them along the trail. That was our second mistake—my second, really.

"One minute we were in a running firefight, with thirty or so 'yards spread out in the jungle chasing five or six VC, then all at once there were mines and machine guns going off all around us, right on top of us. It was a nightmare. We were scattered, outnumbered, and pinned down. Couldn't see more than twenty or thirty feet through the undergrowth. I was hit in the legs, couldn't move, and there were wounded all around me.

"Somehow Ksor Blok managed to rally a dozen or so of the 'yards. They hooked up with three of the men from the team and fought themselves into a sort of perimeter around me. We were in the middle of a bunker complex that no one had even suspected, with no telling how many bad guys running around in it.

"There was no way we could go back the way we came; our only chance was to get off the ridge through the jungle. But Charlie knew that too. He had sent out about a squad to get between us and the way down. I saw them moving up from below us, and I threw a hand grenade that may or may not have done any damage, but it did make several of them get up and move in the open.

"There were shots over my shoulder, and two of the Vietcong fell. I turned and saw Ksor Blok aiming past me.

"He said, 'Again, *dai-uy*. Again.' I was a little goofy from the morphine, I guess. When I threw the next grenade, the Vietcong scattered again, all right, and Ksor Blok got off some shots, but there was no explosion. I dug in my pack and grabbed what felt like a white phosphorus grenade. But when I looked at what I held, it was a C ration can.

"'Throw, throw,' Ksor Blok was yelling. So, I did, and the Vietcong moved again, and Ksor Blok shot them again. And again there was no explosion.

"This time I did find a grenade in my map case, and I threw it, and Charlie didn't run. It exploded. Then I threw another C rat can. Charlie ran; Ksor Blok shot. We went through a half dozen ration cans and four or five grenades that way, until we had fought our way into good cover, with me being dragged by my team medic and one of the 'yards.

"I called in artillery and air strikes on the bunker complex all that day as we slowly moved farther and farther away. But there were still Vietcong in the jungle all around us, sometimes close enough for us to hear, and no chance of getting to a landing zone where the choppers could get to us. We had to leave half our 'yards dead on that hill, and the rest of us were all hurt.

"That night, I passed out. Next morning, Ksor Blok and his men were still there. They stayed with us all day, until we finally made an LZ just before dark. Ksor Blok missed the mutiny, which may have been as well for him. It was not a success, and many of the leaders were jailed or shot by the Vietnamese.

"But that's the kind of man Ksor Blok was; when the chips were down, he couldn't betray a friend. It was people like Ksor Blok that made me convinced I was doing the right thing in Vietnam."

And as he sat there in the dark on the porch with his brother and his father, Max Tag first became convinced that being a soldier was the right thing for him, and he set himself on a course that eventually led him to be in command of the XM-F3 tank No Slack, which now roared away with the two Jagd Kommando vehicles, away from the battle of Bamberg.

4

None of them looked back to witness the fall of Bamberg as they regained the road beyond the dairy farm and raced into the concealment of the lightly wooded hills. None spoke; none cried. Their senses were keen as mystics', their throats swollen with adrenaline. Tag could hold steady even his most tumbling thoughts as the No Slack rushed at eighty kilometers per hour through the ruts and bends of an unfamiliar road, with Wheels never farther from Heinrich Holz's lead vehicle than the edge of its dust trail.

In his mind's eye Tag spread out the map of Europe, its recent changes representing less political boundaries than conflicts, the ideological struggles that had quietly, almost unobserved by outsiders, gutted and discredited the reforms of Gorbachev and Svetlov. "Openness" and "restructuring" had been allowed to wallow along in the trough of bureaucratic incompetence and indifference in most of Mother Russia herself, as well as in the Baltic republics and some cities of Siberia—all places where it could be easily displayed for the foreign press and equally easily controlled and repressed. But when the government-elect of Czechoslovakia unveiled its democratic program, called the New Charter, tanks thundered in amid echoes of 1968. The antiquarian generals and ponderous bureaucrats who controlled the Politburo and the Kremlin displayed their will, their slavish and intractable devotion to the dismal dialectics of Marxist-Leninist thought with a force that rocked the entire Warsaw Pact to attention.

In a bloodless coup, Soviet armor swarmed into Czechoslovakia in overwhelming numbers. In less than a month, all but a handful of Czech regular army units had been disbanded, their personnel dispersed to Soviet divisions, even their equipment repainted and incorporated into the Red Army. The Soviets then sent these mongrel units into Hungary and Romania, repeating the process, leapfrogging through the flaking Iron Curtain alliance, hammering it back into temper. Only in Poland, where Soviet garrisons had become a fixture in the wake of successes by the labor union Solidarity (successes that brought about its suppression), and in East Germany, more Soviet than ever, were the armed forces spared this massive impressment that, at the end of three years, had put a half million Soviet-commanded soldiers in a face-off with about a third that many NATO troops.

Like many others, Tag had seen it coming. First were the troop-reduction treaties that drained NATO strength; then came the trade agreements that bolstered the artificial Soviet economy; and even after the rearming of the Pact, a minority bloc of Greens in the German assembly and a liberal labor coalition in London had scotched sufficient redeployment by the Allies in Europe to make the shuffling bears of the Kremlin believe that the West still had its resolve.

The Firebreak Manual, Tag reflected, was a galling document. On the face, its intent was to outline a strategy that would allow the Allies to fall back, taking a minimum of casualties, and establish a line—a firebreak—that would slow the Soviet advance until reinforcements could be brought in. In fact, it was choreographed suicide for most NATO units, a kind of mass (and not altogether voluntary) seppuku. Tag knew it; the generals knew it. But no one discussed it except in grim jokes, like those told by people who live on a fault line or beneath an active volcano. And now it had happened, and the ground shook.

After twenty minutes the No Slack followed Holz off the rock roadbed and down a muddy gash in the trees into a hollow and a thicket of pine, the second gun buggy close behind.

Holz got out in the thicket and told Giesla to kill their engine, motioning at Tag to do the same. He was sorting through his map case when the American slid out through the commander's hatch and joined him.

"Hey, mister," Tag said, "you got a radio frequency for a veteran?"

Holz looked at him blankly, then cracked a feeble smile.

"Oh," he said. "A yoke, *ja*?"

"No goddamn joke not being able to talk to my sweetie there," Tag replied, nodding across the seats toward Giesla as she unfolded herself from the roll cage. "For a while I was afraid you'd left us to play tag with those two T-64s."

"*Ach*, radio. Of course. I had forgotten," Holz said, turning his attention nonchalantly back to the map case.

Giesla circled behind the vehicle and leaned against one of the tri-tube pods of 106mm recoilless rifles. "And you,

Sergeant Joker," she said with saccharine contempt, "you, not knowing our strategy or your orders, charge through pig-eyed in that iron warthog of yours. You disregard commands, recklessly endanger everyone—and you call yourself a soldier?"

"Giesla!" Holz snapped.

Tag interrupted him. "No, Rick," he said. "That's what I'd call a little practical, professional criticism. Point taken, ma'am."

He touched the rim of his commander's helmet and smiled.

Giesla stared impassively.

"Max," Holz said crisply, "get your driver and let's have a look at these maps."

"Wheels," he called back to the tank, "you and the rest of you, come here."

The crew of the No Slack joined Tag, Holz, Giesla, and the two men from the second gun buggy, all circled around where Holz sat sideways in the seat of his vehicle with a grease pencil in his hand and an acetate-covered map spread in his lap.

"We are here," he said, tracing lightly with the pencil. "From this place we will follow the fire trails and the footpaths to this point"—Holz marked where the hills turned farther west and an agricultural valley fell away to the south of them—"and from there we have two choices . . . maybe. Our safest route is probably to continue through the hills, away from the line of advance. But if we can, it will be faster this way." He drew a dark line down the valley, then back west one inch. "This road is new—not opened, in fact—but the tarmac is all down, and we have used it before. Okay?"

Holz searched the faces around him, his expression

pleased that he saw professional concentration in each one, then went on.

"Max, you scan these maps into your computer, and Sergeant Betcher"—Holz indicated one of the men from the other gun buggy—"will provide you with radio frequencies and our call signs. How is your German, Max?"

"Bad."

"*Gut*. So you stay close to me, Jan," he said to the driver of the second vehicle, "take the wire antenna up one of these trees. I want to try to raise our others." Holz grinned as he handed the maps to Tag.

While Wheels scanned in the maps and Ham and Fruits tied down the mangled remains of ration crates on the deck, Tag went over the radios with Sergeant Betcher, taking as his call sign Butcher Boy, after Holz's handle, Meat Grinder One. Depending on the terrain, the tactical-frequency radio would carry up to eighteen kilometers, and Tag figured that if the No Slack and the spongers were that far apart, he was up shit creek, anyway. He'd just have to keep the ComNet channel open and hope to pick up something, anything.

"Anything?" he asked Holz, walking up to the gun buggy.

"A little," the German said. "Three of my towed units made it away from Bamberg; that's the good."

"And the other?"

"There is another motor battalion, supported by a company of armor, out there somewhere, probably scouting for the main divisional thrust, I would guess."

"Then we don't have a lot of time?"

"Perhaps more, perhaps less. It will depend on their approach. The ridges east of the new road are low but very steep. BMPs and tanks would have to stay in column on the roads. Farther south, it's easier. What do you think, Max?"

"You're right. But if it was my show, I'd send one flank recon unit in from the east while my main body moved in formation from the southeast. That's if I was Ivan."

"I agree. The road, then . . . maybe."

"Maybe."

"We'll take ten minutes here, then. If your men want to eat again, it may be their last chance for a while."

"Take ten," Tag called to his crew. "Eat it if you want it."

Turning back to Holz, his eyes met Giesla's. She stood behind the vehicle, unwrapping a sausage she had taken from the possibles box in the rear. She held it in one hand, poised at her lips. When she saw Tag, she bit the end off viciously and walked away carrying ration boxes toward the other gun vehicle.

"Rick," Tag said, "what is the deal with your sister? And don't tell me it's because she likes me."

"Jan," Holz said to the young driver who was recoiling the wire antenna. "Take the handset for a while. Let's walk," he said to Tag.

"You know," Holz continued as they stepped out of hearing of the others and into the shadows of the thicket, "that might not all be untrue—that is right English, *ja*? 'Not be untrue'?"

"What are you driving at, Rick?"

"Three years ago Giesla married an American, Bobby Ruther. You've heard of him?"

"I remember he won Indy one year."

"That's the one. They met at the Monaco rally, the first one Giesla drove for Audi. Bobby was there for the road race the following day."

"And he crashed. That's right, I remember reading about it. Put him out of racing, didn't it?"

"He was not badly injured—a broken wrist, I think—but Giesla stayed with him until he was released from the hospital and talked him into being her navigator for the rallies in Spain and the Italian Alps, since he could not drive. When his wrist healed, he gave up road racing and married her. Together they were Audi's number-one rally team. It was all very romantic and dashing."

"So what's the point?"

"About a year and a half ago they were among the teams entered in the Pan-African rally."

"Oh, sweet Jesus." Tag whistled. The Pan-African massacre. At a checkpoint near the Tanzania-Zambia border, where crew trucks and officials were gathered, terrorists had ambushed or hijacked more than twenty of the rally teams, killing nearly everyone—eighty-six people all told. Reports that Russian and East German advisers were involved with the terrorists had contributed to a final breakdown in East-West relations.

"Yes," Holz went on. "She and Bobby were the last car taken. The animals made them drive out into the bush, where they killed Bobby and . . . did what they did to her."

"I see," Tag said.

"No, not entirely, my friend. You must understand, Giesla has always been a woman who likes men. She liked working with men, competing with men, but she did *like* them.

"When she came back to Germany, she gave up driving. She applied for a reserve commission and for six months devoted herself to training, excelling in all her classes. She was even offered a regular commission and a billet in counterintelligence, which I encouraged her to accept. But something happened in her training, something to do with a man, and she resigned. She somehow arranged for orders to work with our Jagd Kommando group, as G-2, and for the past six months she has been in Bamberg.

"She is very driven, very fierce, Max. I don't quite know how to say it. She was always very strong but warm. Our mother call Giesla 'my happy baby.' But now all there is, is that bitter strength. Don't push her, Max. She is pushing herself hard enough already."

"Roger, wilco," Tag said. "And thanks, Rick. I wish now I could say it was just me she didn't like."

"Don't pity her, Max. She has some respect for you, and that, I think, would lose it."

"Respect? For me? Huh." Tag snorted.

Holz shrugged. "You're probably right," he said, adding before Tag could respond, "Let's go." And he walked directly back to his vehicle.

Tag rode "with the top down," standing in the open turret hatch, one shoulder against the .50-caliber machine gun. For almost an hour the small column had been creeping through weed-choked trails at idling speed, stopping frequently at Holz's command to run up the wire antenna, hoping for some clue to what was swirling around them. Twice they heard jets pass overhead, once too low and fast, and once too high to be identified. There were occasional distant thuds of ordnance, but nothing to signal an organized battle.

Holz stood up through the cage and signaled them to halt. Giesla got out and walked back to the No Slack.

"Sergeant Tag," she said, "you can still receive on your primary radio, that is correct." It was not a question.

"Right," Tag said.

"I want to use it to scan for Russian traffic."

"Be my guest," Tag said. "Fruits," he called down the

loader, "open the commander's hatch for . . ." He paused. "What do I call you?" he asked Giesla.

One corner of her mouth twitched, but the eyes remained unchanged—blue pools in the pale patch where her goggles had been.

"You may call me . . . Lieutenant Ruther."

"Open the hatch for . . . Lieutenant Ruther, Fruits." Tag nodded at Giesla, deadpan. She returned it.

Tag heard his loader mutter "Ballbuster" as he knocked back the dog on the hatch.

"At *ease*, Mr. Tutti," Tag said softly, with menace.

Fruits threw out the hatch, and Giesla slid through into the commander's seat.

"Who knows this set best?" she asked, craning her head back toward the crew.

As Tag started to step down, he heard, "Uh, dat's me, ma'am. That is, Specialist Fourth Class Tutti. Ma'am."

Tag bit his knuckles and leaned over the rim of the hatch, trying to keep from laughing. Up close, a beautiful woman baffled Fruits, all his barracks bawdiness notwithstanding. From the belly of the tank he heard: "Please, *ma'am* makes me feel old. I'm called Gies, Specialist Tutti. And you?"

"Geese?" Fruits asked incredulously.

"Yes, almost." Giesla's voice held the promise of a titter. "And you?"

"Uh, Fruits, ma—Yeah, Fruits Tutti. Whatcha need?"

It was more than Tag could bear. He hauled himself over the lip of the hatch, held one of the empty War Club racks, and vaulted over the side, knees bent, into a textbook parachute-landing fall. Twice a winner of the Fort Benning Best Ranger competition, Tag was an exception to the rule that real tankers didn't jump out of perfectly good airplanes.

Heinrich Holz barked a short laugh. "Feeling your oats, as you used to say?"

"Just easing the kinks," Tag said, dusting off his knees. "Tell me something I don't know."

Holz shrugged. "If Giesla does not hear otherwise, we proceed as planned. Just through these trees and we will be on the trunk road to the new highway."

"How far?"

"Perhaps two kilometers. Quiet! Listen!"

Tag found himself holding his breath and released it slowly, clearing his ears. At first he heard what was closest to him: the contractions of cooling motors, a cough, the deceptive rustle of leaves. Then, like the gathering roll of kettledrums at the opening of a symphony, an approaching wall of sound began to thrum through his chest.

Tag turned at the crash of two hatches banging on the No Slack's armor. Giesla was climbing out of one, and Wheels Latta was calling to him from the other.

"Max," the driver said, "better come here. We got some weird shit on the radar."

Giesla had to dodge to clear Tag's way as he bolted feetfirst into his seat and grabbed his helmet.

"What have we got?" he asked, swiveling around to the air-radar display.

"Lookee there," Ham Jefferson said, pointing to his own screen. "The mutha shows to be comin' and goin' all at once. *The!* Shit, look at 'em."

The blips on Tag's screen began to jump like fleas on a griddle, the digital readouts all flashing green zeros.

"Max!"

Tag looked up to see Heinrich Holz's face staring with urgent concern through the open hatch.

"We have armor moving parallel to us," the Jagd Kommando said. "A heavy column, maybe two hundred meters inside the woods, and headed for the trunk road."

Tag dismissed the stippling radar screen with a quick shrug. "Wheels," he said, "call up your LandNav maps and see if we've got a place to fight from inside those woods. Rick, is there any way past them?"

"Not once they are on the road. We would not make the supply depot then."

Standing in the hatch as he talked to Holz, Tag froze in mid-thought at the approaching sound of low-level jet aircraft—which meant the planes must be on them. Before Tag could pass an order, a concussion he at first confused with a sonic boom struck him from the left, followed by more a roar than an explosion, and then a wall of searing heat.

"Napalm!"

As Holz ordered his troops into the lee of the No Slack, away from the boiling ridges of fire that raked the trees, Tag and his crew buttoned up for full NBC (nuclear/biological/chemical) defenses, omitting only their bulky protective suits and visors.

The radar screens continued to flicker incomprehensibly as the napalmed earth shook from the tremors of five-hundred-pound bombs, then was cauterized again with jellied gas.

Burning debris—metal and flaming tree chunks—hailed down in the forest, starting dozens of small fires, and flames leapt across the tops of the pines that lined the trail, fanned by their swaying. Tag came up through his hatch in time to hear, this time for certain, the distant, Dopplering concussion of three sonic booms.

"What was that?' Holz called to him.

"Stealth," Tag said, almost to himself.

"What?"

"Stealth assault bombers," Tag said, turning toward

Holz. "Our radar was going crazy with them. Just be glad
we were shut down and standing still. If those zoomies
thought we were the flank of that column—*whoosh*. We'll
be crispy critters."

"Will they be back?" It was Giesla who asked.

"I'd guess not—not on this run, at least. I say we have
a look at their work and see how we stand with the road. If
whatever the sky jocks hit has been neutralized, it may be
our day. Rick?"

"No, Max. We must move more quickly. Listen! There
it is again."

Through the smoke and dust and crackle of flame, Tag
could again hear the growl of an approaching tank. "Get
back there," he said to the Kommandos. "It's right here,
there in the smoke."

Tag eased his hatch cover down as he spoke. "Thermal
sights. Sabot. He's right on us, Ham. Maybe fifty meters at
ten o'clock."

The target was so near that Ham at first thought his
thermal sight/range finder was malfunctioning; all but the
corners of the screen was rippling with green.

"Confirmed," Ham said.

At that moment a shifting breeze fanned the smoke from
the clearing, allowing the scorched Soviet commander
standing in the cupola of his blackened T-80 just a glimpse
of the No Slack, a frame frozen in his brief memory of the
muzzle of the 120mm gun as it recoiled into the turret,
away from the cone of smoke. Then he was lifted into
blackness.

Through his scope Tag saw the kill and the Communist
tanker blown from his hatch, before the wind stalled once
more and the smoke fell even more thickly over them.

He looked again at his array of commander's screens. "You see anything else out there?" he asked Ham.

"Too damn many fires, boss," the gunner replied. "But nothing close."

Tag opened his hatch, crawled out, and slid to the ground over the No Slack's glacis.

"Rick," he said to the Kommando leader, "can you get your vehicles somewhere safe, near the road but not on it?"

"*Ja*, I'm sure."

"Okay. We're gonna pull a quick recon through the strike zone, try to see what's what. If it looks good, I'll be with you on the radio, and we can regroup on the road."

Holz shook his head. "The time, Max," he said. "We should go now. All of us."

Tag hardly paused. "No, Rick. I can't do that. I got orders. We don't know how good a job those invisible birds did. They missed at least one that we know of. If there're others that scattered toward the road, I damn sure don't wanna go roaring up their six, with them all pissed off and everything."

He grinned. "See you on the road, Rick."

Tag dogged down his hatch, turned his commander's chair, climbed up into the turret, and through the hatch. He plugged in his helmet.

"Ham, Wheels," he said, "keep all your screens up. I'm going to be on the fifty with the top down. Wheels, take us in where that one came from."

Away from the small pines, the smoke was less dense but more acrid with ozone. Tag put away thoughts of strapping on his NBC mask, willing to barter stinging eyes and a slurping nose for the security of the mask's suction cup on his face. His cheeks fanned red with the heat.

The path that the No Slack followed toward the strike

zone passed through a leafy swale of mixed hardwoods, many of their tops now broken out by boles and limbs and trunks blown from the explosions. Small fires congregated all across the forest floor, and sunlight broke through the smoky, shadowed air in gray shafts. As the tank came over the far side of the swale, it was almost at once in the fiery perimeter of the strike zone, where for fifty meters the trees graduated from colossal torches to carbonized skeletons as they approached the axis of the zone. Tag halted the No Slack in a skeleton thicket that hissed with heartwood boiling inside its blackened branches, mixing green steam with the smoke.

Tag scanned the strike zone with his binoculars. Roughly a hundred yards wide, it lay in scorched desolation for a kilometer or more. Through the smoke and heavy air rippling with heat, Tag could make out the smudge-pot gouts of at least three burning tanks and several charred rhomboids that he took to be BMPs. The bomb craters were immense and, at this end, almost overlapping. Everywhere between and beyond them, smoldering stumps studded the strike zone.

"Wheels," Tag said to his driver, "we're gonna have to go around to the right. That'll keep us closer to the road. Put your head out, and be ready to put us back in the woods.

"Ham, keep all the screens up. Sabot in the main gun, and free the 75mm for Fruits on manual.

"And, Wheels, remember: This is a *quick* reconnaissance. Move."

The No Slack plowed out of the thicket, through a turn, and leveled off at twenty miles per hour, the best it could make through the stumps. There was no movement in the zone. Beyond the first cluster of bomb craters, the stick of five-hundred-pounders had fallen in two perfectly staggered rows. The last layer of napalm had annealed the scene into something like the ruins of Pompei. Tag coughed and pinched his nose, trying to keep a clear eye for movement, or signs that anything might have escaped the strike zone.

"Wheels," Tag said after they had traveled about four hundred meters, "cross to the other side here, between these next two holes."

Looking down into one of the craters, Tag could see the grotesque remains of two BMPs slid end to end, spilling out crews into a puddle of fire fed by the napalm mixed with their own fuels. Got 'em with the top coat, he thought, and shuddered.

On the other side of the strike zone, Tag found two disabled and abandoned T-80s in the woods and four more break trails heading west. The incomprehensible babble on the frequency Giesla had been monitoring before the attack was a lot less and getting weaker. As Tag reached to dial in the TAC frequency and radio Holz to rendezvous on the trunk road, he watched as a third derelict tank, sitting less than three hundred meters away at the end of the strike zone, elevated its cannon and turned its turret slowly in the direction of the No Slack.

"Target!" he barked. "Stationary tank. One o'clock. Free fire."

The two 75mm high-explosive rounds that Fruits Tutti splattered against the T-80's armor went off just in time to give Ham Jefferson his sight picture and to spoil the aim of the Soviet gunner.

"Shot!" Ham said.

"Splash!" Tag echoed as the Communist tank's shot went wide like a dying sob and a jet of fire blew out its ventilator grille.

"Okay," he said. "To the road, Mr. Latta."

As Wheels started back across the charred no-man's-land, Tag spoke to Holz.

"Meat Grinder One, this is Butcher Boy. Over."

"Butcher Boy, this is Meat Grinder. Go."

"Meat Grinder, meet me about two klicks down the road. It may be our day."

"Butcher Boy, roger. Out."

The Jagd Kommandos made better time down the macadam trunk road than the No Slack did through the woods, so Holz was waiting when the tankers arrived.

"We can be on the highway in five minutes," he said, "if that rhinoceros of yours can gallop."

In four minutes and forty-one seconds they were barreling down a German autobahn at more than seventy miles per hour. Only once before, on the test track at Ft. Hood, had Tag felt the exhilaration of riding the No Slack with the top down at full throttle. Here, now, at the mild end of summer, it was hard to realize that just beyond these tree-covered hills, the Third World War was raging. He could hear nothing through the wind. Never relaxed, Tag somehow rested during the time it took to cover twenty kilometers like that. Then Holz slowed them and pulled into the shade at the side of the road, just below the rolling crest of a hill.

"Max," Holz called to him, jumping from his vehicle, "come with me for a look."

Tag got his binoculars, slid down the front of the No Slack, and followed Holz through the trees to the top of the rise. From there they could see the half-cloverleaf exchange across the autobahn at the bottom of the hill.

"That is our road, to the right," Holz said.

"Uh-huh," Tag muttered, screwing the binoculars to his eyes, feeling the pine needles on the forest floor prick through the fabric of his jumpsuit. "And there're men down there, Rick."

"Are you sure?"

"Shit, one of them just walked across the road. That's U.S. Army, mister. Here, have a look." Tag held the binoculars up to Holz.

"Yes," Holz said, focusing, "here he is, coming back. There is a vehicle of some sort, too, back in the trees."

"Okay," Tag said. He was up and brushing off his sleeves. "Let me go in first, and you cover me from the top?"

Holz shrugged. "They are your people, *ja*?"

With the turret reversed and the gun at trail arms, Tag tied a Stars and Stripes to the main antenna and ordered the No Slack over the slope at thirty miles per hour, while he stood in the open cupola beneath the snapping flag watching the trees and the ramps and exits through his glasses as they approached the traffic exchange. He was sweating through his eyes. He ordered Wheels to slow to twenty at the exit, and made an exaggerated arm signal for a right turn. They even stopped at the sign where the exit merged with the road, the same place Tag and Holz had seen the American GI cross. Now Tag could see the glint off the windshield of the truck in the woods opposite him.

Tag turned on the exterior speaker and cleared his throat. "Ah-hmm. Listen, don't shoot. We're Americans. We know you're looking at us, and we need your help."

Immediately to his right, out of the nearest woods, came two GIs armed with Ml6s that they held tentatively at high port.

"Who goes there?" one of them said, shamefaced, knowing even as he said it how ridiculous it sounded.

Tag killed the speaker. "Where's your CO?" he demanded. "Who's in charge here?"

"Who's wanting to know?" the soldier said, liking that better.

Tag stifled his anger at the soldier's stupidity. "I am Staff Sergeant Maximillian Tag, and I command this, the XM-F3 tank, No Slack. We're under direct command of Group, and we've got some Jagd Kommando buddies with us, and we all need what you got in that depot. Savvy? Who do I need to talk to? Now!"

The boy came almost to attention, stopped only by a hand placed on his shoulder from behind by a third soldier who emerged from the woods. Tag's voice had stirred a kindred spirit.

"I'm First Sergeant Weintaub," said the older soldier, brushing the boy aside. "You'll have to pardon my clerk's manners. New Army, I guess, huh?" The first sergeant laughed breathlessly as he approached the tank, even bending to support himself on his thighs as he stepped across the ditch and climbed the few steps up to the road. He leaned one hand heavily on the fender of the No Slack and looked up at Tag. When he did, he raised a cocked Colt .45 pistol along with his gaze, both steady and leveled at Tag's head.

"Now," said First Sergeant Weintaub, "I want you out of there, and I want to see some wholesome American faces in those hatches."

Tag stepped out and stood on the turret. "Showtime," he shouted to his crew.

"Larry!" Fruits Tutti shrieked, popping from the turret hatch.

"Moe!" Wheels Latta boomed, slamming back the driver's hatch.

"And Curley Joe!" Ham Jefferson cried in triumph, standing in the commander's hatch.

"What about it, Top?" Tag pleaded. "Can you give us some slack?"

Weintaub holstered his piece, laughing breathlessly again. "Pull over here in the shade, Sergeant," he said. "Come talk to me."

As quickly as he could, Tag outlined their situation to Weintaub, who sucked his teeth and tutted.

"I'm afraid you're a little late, Sergeant," Weintaub said. "Our lieutenant and the EOD man are laying charges right now. Expect them any minute, then we're history."

"How far?" Tag asked.

"How far's what?"

"The depot, Top. I've got to stop them."

"About two klicks, but . . ."

But Tag was already scrambling back through his hatch and firing orders to the crew.

"Call and tell 'em I'm coming, Top," Tag yelled as they leapt away and cut down the two-lane blacktop.

The gun was still at trail arms—and Tag in his commander's chair contacting Holz and the Jagd Kommandos —when the No Slack, slewing around an unbanked turn, was rocked by the explosion of a 75mm HE round against the rear of its turret, now the leading edge.

By reflex, Tag shouted, "Target! Sabot!" and Wheels threw the No Slack into an accelerating turn as Fruits dialed in the sabot and Ham swung the turret.

"Stand down," Tag said, eyes glued to his optical scope. Through it he saw an American soldier walking toward them from a Type-4 Bradley Fighting Vehicle, waving his arms above his head. "Wheels, let's go check out the pedestrian."

The Bradley, Tag could see, was one of the new "muscle" models, with an extended body, a 75mm turret-mounted cannon, as well as twin .50-calibers topside and a 7.62mm machine gun mounted coaxially in the nose. They were damn lucky that the Bradley hadn't hit a track.

Tag came up through his hatch and heard the soldier from the Bradley say, "Goddamn, sorry about that, fellas. Weintaub just called. Anybody hurt?"

"We're all right," Tag said, waving off the GI's concern. "But we've got to get some of your fuel and ordnance before you smoke this place. Who do I see?"

"Lieutenant Prentice, but he's with first squad and the powder man. Just wait one and I'll get him on the horn."

Finally, Tag thought, *finally we get one on* our *side*.

5

In the next hour a lot happened. Lieutenant Prentice was stopped in time. Holz and the Jagd Kommandos arrived shortly afterward, and a hasty strategy conference among Holz, Prentice, Tag, and the other senior NCOs gave them a rough plan of action.

Not only had they found 120-mm sabots and 75mm AT and HE rounds, the depot also revealed a cache of the latest-generation War Club missiles. These could be directed by wire or by infrared, laser-Doppler, thermal, or radar sights. Worried by a couple of puddles he had found in the slick-skin armor, Tag even had the crew now bolting shaped-charge "reactive armor" to the hull of the No Slack. Low-velocity rounds with nozzle charges designed to burn through conventional armor still posed some problems for the No Slack. The reactive charges would explode at first contact, blasting away the incoming. With its Art Deco contours and monopolar carbide armor, the No Slack was virtually immune to any conventional HE round, regardless of size. The tracks, of course, were still vulnerable, but even the top of the turret and the rear deck had more armor than an M-1A.

The confab with Holz, Prentice, and the "leg" NCOs scotched some of Tag's plans, but especially given the No Slack's crippled communications, the alternative didn't look too bad. With the addition of the garrison force at the depot, the Allies' order of battle now included one XM-F3 experimental tank and crew of four; two tank-killer gun vehicles, with six 106mm recoilless rifles and a .50-caliber machine gun each; two Type-3 Bradleys; one two-and-a-half-ton truck; a replacement lieutenant; a quartermaster first sergeant; and thirty very nervous teenagers who made up the two squads left to scuttle the supply depot.

At Tag's insistence they had moved one squad of infantry into the truck and loaded spare ammo and fuel into the back of one of the Bradleys—no point in exposing their most valuable asset to small-arms fire. Prentice was a nervously subdued lieutenant, anxious to do the right thing, fearful of being wrong and having to defend it. Nevertheless, he at once saw the rationale in Tag's proposal, as well as the danger. Prentice announced in a voice something like a command that he would ride drag in the transport Bradley; last, save for a gun buggy that would trail the column by a kilometer or so. The other of Holz's vehicles —his own—would take point recon, followed by the second Bradley, the infantry in the truck, and the No Slack, each at intervals of fifty meters. Their goal was west-southwest through the wooded hills toward a fan of folded gullies in the headwaters of two streams, where the Jagd Kommandos had established their prepared rendezvous. The troops from the supply depot had orders to withdraw as best they could, once the depot had been destroyed.

Lieutenant Prentice seemed to like strength in numbers and elected to convoy with Tag and the Germans, "until the situation becomes less fluid," he said, as though Firebreak were some basic school exercise waiting to be resolved. Tag had his doubts about the green lieutenant and his supply troopers coming along but could think of no clear reason why they shouldn't. Besides, there might be a need for some infantry before the fat lady sang.

Whatever their effectiveness as infantry, they were now more than well armed. In addition to their M16s, Tag saw a bristling assortment of .223 Squad automatic weapons, M-60 machine guns, 60-mm mortars, Stinger missiles, and Dragon and LAW antitank weapons. Even Top Sergeant Weintaub had added another .45 to his belt and was supervising the loading of the Bradleys with an M-203 grenade launcher draped over his forearm.

Tag saw Lieutenant Prentice and the demolitions man coming from the fuel tanks toward the transport Bradley, and he walked over from the No Slack to meet them. Prentice was at the radio in the cab of the Bradley when Tag arrived.

"Okay," he heard the lieutenant say, "bring 'em in, and lock the gate behind you."

Prentice turned to him. "Sergeant," he said, "how is everything here?"

"I think Top has a handle on it, sir."

"Good. Our people back at the traffic exchange are reporting sounds of heavy motorized movement coming up the road. As soon as they get here, we're out the back gate. Sergeant Dunn here"—Prentice indicated the powder man—"will stay with me to shoot the charges and ride shotgun. I want everybody else outside the wire."

"No argument from me, sir. But what about the rearguard vehicle?"

"About three hundred meters outside the back gate

there's a tank park. It can wait there. But the rest of you need to keep moving. There's not much cover out the back gate until you hit the ridges, maybe two klicks."

"I'll pass it on, sir."

At least, Tag thought, the lieutenant was on top of his detail. But Tag was still apprehensive about Prentice assuming the habit of command too much. As far as Tag was concerned, Holz had command of the column, and he and the crew were just straphanging until they got to their stop. Prentice was his own problem.

With the column formed and ready at the back gate, Tag stood in the cupola of the No Slack, sweating and anxious to be gone. News of the Soviet column advancing up the highway had made him think of air cover. The War Clubs were the only thing they had for defense against fixed-wing jets, the infantry's Stingers notwithstanding, and there was that long, open stretch Prentice had mentioned. Bamberg and breakfast seemed a long way away, but water was all that Tag could force through the knot in his stomach. Air strikes and explosives both made him a tad edgy. Not to mention a butter-bar supply lieutenant with aspirations.

Tag's fretting was broken by the blare of exhaust from Holz's vehicle as it shot out ahead of the column. The first Bradley, with Weintaub in the cab, lumbered to life, followed by the deuce-and-a-half full of troops. The No Slack, its slippery profile blurred by the explosive blocks of reactive armor, wound up its turbines and scattered gravel up to the gate, where Tag halted them for a moment.

Lieutenant Prentice, Sergeant Dunn, and a private holding a spool of wire that led back into the depot all stood next to the transport Bradley. Tag leaned out over the War Club rack on the left of the turret.

"Be happy to stick around for backup, sir," he said.

"No. No," Prentice said. "Keep moving."

Just checking, Tag thought. "Yes, sir," he said.

Wheels caught up with the deuce-and-a-half just past the tank park and slowed to keep the interval—the truck was straining its main bearings just to squeeze out forty-five miles per hour. A minute later Tag felt the shock wave a nanosecond before the roar of the exploding ammo and fuel collected his head. Following the eyes of the soldiers in the truck in front of him, Tag turned and saw the black billow of oily smoke spreading at the top into a blunt mushroom, growing with the crackle of secondary explosions ripping through the earth from underground igloos and storage tanks, rimming the smoke with fire. It was an awesome and spectacular sight.

To the Soviet officer who commanded the recon force just entering the depot from the autobahn, it was spectacular as well . . . and awful. Assuming the place deserted, he had sent three of his six T-80s inside to scout the depot and was watching from his command BMP when the explosion blasted the three tanks to cinders among the gushing flames of fuel oil and munitions. Someone would have to pay.

Two minutes after the initial explosion smoke was still boiling and belching from the depot as Tag came into sight of the cover in the sparsely wooded hills. Prentice had been right: Field exercises and tracked vehicles had pretty well demolished any effective tank cover for a couple of klicks behind the depot, and even this ridge, with its trees widely spaced, like a park's, wasn't ideal, especially now with the sun straight overhead and no shadows to work with. A hundred meters inside the trees, the deuce-and-a-half growled to a halt. From where he stopped the No Slack, Tag could still see the road clearly. After one of the longest minutes he ever spent, Tag finally heard the *whap* of a gun buggy's exhaust. In a shorter minute it and the second Bradley were in the trees.

Tag spoke over the radio, "Meat Grinder One, this is Butcher Boy. All aboard. Over."

"Roger," Holz replied. "Out."

The column jerked itself into motion and began to creep through the forest.

The Soviet commander who had allowed the three of his tanks to blunder into the supply dump just before it went up was torn by a host of competing emotions. Most of all, however, there was fear. Not fear of battle or death itself —oh, no, something much worse. He had a political officer with his battalion. Even when his scouts had circled the inferno and found the back gate, the road, and the fresh tracks, the commander was reluctant to pursue. What if it were an ambush? If the road were mined? His orders were to take the depot. He had done that. But the three tanks!

"Comrade Major," the political officer said to him, "how do you plan to retaliate against this attack?"

Thinking quickly, feverishly, the commander said, "We cannot desert the objective, Comrade Secretary. We must consolidate our gains and—"

"Gains!" the political officer burst out. "What have you gained, Comrade Major, aside from a rubbish fire and twelve martyrs to the Revolution?"

"Who died gloriously in the attack on, and destruction of, the imperialist supply depot." The major made it sound like a question.

"Perhaps." The KGB political secretary eyed him narrowly. "Though there is still the matter of those escaped vehicles."

"We do have second priority for close air cover."

"Then perhaps, Comrade Major," the political officer

said, lighting a cardboard-filtered cigarette, "you should call. It would be much better, believe me, if those vehicles were found and destroyed."

Holz closed up the column and halted them in a thick copse of fir on a commanding ridge that ran rocky and barren away from them to the west.

Tag had the crew out pulling a camouflage net loosely over the No Slack when Holz and Giesla came up to him.

"Don't tie down, Max," the German said. "Let everybody eat, so we can be away from here in fifteen minutes. I want Giesla to monitor on your command set, and we need to talk as well. From here things are a little more—what do you say?—tricky."

"Okay," Tag said, nodding toward Giesla. "But let me throw our crew shelter over the back of that deuce-and-a-half; there's too much steel shining back there. Ham, Fruits, get a couple of those legs to help you."

They collected Lieutenant Prentice from his Bradley and gathered around the acetate-covered map that Holz spread on the possibles box on the back of his vehicle.

"We are here," Holz said, tapping with his grease pencil, "and our objective is here. If we can travel this ridge, it will take us here, to this road, then back into these hills and to the rendezvous point. Otherwise—"

"Just a minute," Prentice said sharply. "Are we just going to park somewhere at the end of some road? Box ourselves in?"

Holz was indulgent. "The map," he said, "was not made yesterday. There are . . . features it does not show. *Ja*?"

"Yeah, sure," Prentice said.

"Sir," Tag said to him, "this is the Oberlieutenant's backyard."

"If we do not travel the ridge," Holz continued, "we must

traverse some very steep country, hills we believe the Soviets will want to take. I suspect that the unit dispatched to the supply depot was a reserve battalion, just there to secure the site, because its location is of no strategic importance. The major thrust will have been south, to take command of these ridges facing southwest, here"—Holz beat a light tattoo on the acetate as he thought aloud—"making our question: Do we risk artillery and air by taking the ridge, or risk time and armor traversing the hills?"

"Hell," Prentice squawked. "You're leaving us behind the lines."

Holz turned slowly toward him. "That," he said evenly, "is correct. Unless you have an alternative, Lieutenant?"

Tag could see that Prentice was getting rattled. Once released from the absorbing protocols of the demolition detail, he was confounded by the disarray war had thrown his world into, even before he heard the first enemy shot. Tag could tell that not knowing or being able to define his place in the command structure, Lieutenant Prentice was torn between giving orders and taking them, between command and leadership. Tag had seen it before, the face of indecision and failure on men who would snafu key problems in Ranger School.

"Lieutenant Prentice," Tag said, "sir. I've been with the Oberlieutenant and his people since dawn. They're the only reason we've made it this far, and I'm inclined to go on with them."

"But go *where*?" Prentice waved his arm at the map. "Into a free-fire zone or into a regimental assault? Oh, boy."

Tag saw Holz's rising impatience. "What," he said quickly, "does the lieutenant have in mind?"

"Well, what's wrong with staying put, letting the situation catch up with us?"

"Enough," Holz said icily. "If we stay here, the only thing

to catch us up will be the Soviet Army. If you convoy with me, Lieutenant Prentice, you will travel under my command. In about ten minutes we are going to leave this place and travel by the ridge, vehicles staggered on either side of the crest, in the same column order. I hope you will join us."

Holz snapped his maps shut and walked away toward the No Slack.

Prentice looked at Tag and said, "Sergeant, have your men retrieve their crew cover and get ready to leave."

"Yes, sir," Tag said, and followed Holz to the No Slack.

Giesla was sitting with her head through the commander's hatch, talking to her brother, when Tag walked up. "Stow the net and the crew cover," he called to his men. To Holz he said, "Any news?"

"*Ja*, a fierce battle for the supply depot." He grinned wickedly. "Three tanks lost."

"No shit?" Tag said. "Whaddaya suppose?"

Holz shrugged. "Why does one ever tell lies?"

"Anything else?"

"No," Giesla said, pushing herself up and out of the hatch. "There is a lot of traffic, but much of it is weak. There is nothing I can make out."

From somewhere to the south they heard the punctuated thunder of a bombing run. The scent of evergreen in the copse was as sharp as cordite.

"Ready when you are," Tag said.

"Of course," said Holz. "Giesla, would you mind informing Lieutenant Prentice? We don't need to linger here."

"That's pretty cruel, Rick," Tag said, once Giesla was out of hearing.

"What?"

"Siccing your sister on him."

Holz grinned. "Psychology," he said.

The ridge was rocky, with a wide crest and steep sides

falling a hundred feet or more into brush-choked ravines. Hooking to the left, it ran unbroken and unprotected for more than five kilometers, until it disappeared into the corrugation of streams and gullies near the rendezvous. Even with the wheezy deuce-and-a-half, it would take no more than twenty or thirty minutes to negotiate the rubble and washouts along the military crest. That was what Tag thought as he watched the truck pull out of the trees and sway heavily to its downhill side.

The Soviet pilot leading the flight of three MiG-21s that had just dumped their load of ordnance on a reported anti-tank redoubt also saw the truck lumber into view. From three miles away and a mile high, it was just a wink of motion, but in a place where there shouldn't have been one. After a brief radio conversation with his ground headquarters, the flight leader banked into a tight turn, his wingmen following in a shallow vee. If what headquarters said were true, these could be the survivors of the devastating attack on the supply depot. The flight leader smiled, the gee forces flattening his cheeks.

Tag licked his lips and tasted sweat at the corners of his mouth. This was all going too slowly, turning into a tanker's nightmare. There was not a prayer of cover for as far as he could see, only the ridge shearing off into impossible gullies. The schist crown of the ridge was tricky for the tracked vehicles but absolutely perilous for the deuce-and-a-half, which rolled and yawed over the rocks and narrow crevasses as though about ready to sideslip off its crumbling purchase. After five minutes of following the truck, the No Slack was no more than a hundred meters from the copse of trees. There was no place to fight from, and the crazy angle of the tank forced the crew to fight gravity as well as the clammy funk that overtakes tankers who find themselves slow, exposed, and feeling vulnerable in battle.

Tag was standing in the turret hatch, trying to locate the antenna mast of the transport Bradley that Prentice was driving, anything to be doing besides worry. That antsiness saved them. As Tag looked back again at the grove of firs, to see whether the second Kommando vehicle had started yet, the wedge of MiGs dropped out of a cloud and dived screaming toward the ridge.

"MiGs! Six o'clock! Air defenses up!" Tag was dogging down the hatch and rattling through the crew compartment to his chair as he shouted simultaneously over the intercom and the TAC frequency for the convoy. His radio voice was drowned in a deluge of high-velocity cannon fire from the first MiG's strafing run.

The flight leader was disappointed when he saw the vehicles staggered so widely; his wingmen would get most of the targets. As he was lining up his sights on the axis of the ridge, he saw the open truck lurch to a halt and men pour out the back. The medium tank to his left also hesitated and began to wheel in a jerky turn. He would have to remember to report that he did not recognize the tank's profile.

The double rows of parallel fire from the MiG wing cannons stitched the bald ridge in a cacophony of ricochets and exploding rock, throwing dust up as thick as a smoke screen. Lacking a battle plan, each vehicle on the ridge took its own action. The men from the deuce-and-a-half jammed themselves into cracks along the stone lip of the ridge; Weintaub's Bradley rotated its turret and picked up speed; Prentice stopped his.

"Up top," Tag ordered his driver, and Wheels gunned the No Slack up into the cloud of dust on the crest of the ridge, just as the second and third MiGs triggered their cannons. Sensing more than hearing the heavy tattoo of the strafing, Tag locked his sights on the flight leader as he banked right, scattering flares and foil confetti to confuse radar-guided and heat-seeking missiles. Tag grinned maniacally as he touched off the wire-guided War Club and watched through his scope as its smoke trail fishhooked high in the sky, consuming the MiG in a silent aster of fire.

Immediately Tag was back at his screen, picking up the two blips of the other MiGs, waiting to see which way they would break. They wheeled in tandem to the left, and he launched a pair of War Clubs, guiding one by wire and the other by radar. In the confusion of flares and confetti dropped by the two jets, the missiles converged on the lead aircraft, ripping away the rear of the fuselage and sending the wings and cockpit into a terminal cartwheel. The third MiG kicked in its afterburner and climbed out of the War Clubs' range before Tag could lock on it. There was nothing else on the screen.

Dimly at first, Tag became aware of chatter over the TAC frequency, then he realized Holz's voice had not come on, asking for situation reports.

"Ham," Tag said to his gunner as he pulled himself up into the turret, "take the screens."

Tag popped through the turret hatch and at once smelled the smoke that was boiling from the rear of Prentice's Bradley. Between it and the No Slack, Tag could see Sergeant Dunn trying to drag Prentice to his feet. He heard Prentice scream.

Tag bounded onto the rear deck and off the back of the No Slack and reached the two soldiers in seconds. Dunn looked at him with wild, frightened eyes.

"His shoulders are broken," Dunn cried.

"Make a chair," Tag shouted as he dropped to one knee. "Here. Give me your hand."

Lieutenant Prentice held an elbow in either hand and rolled his head in a delirium of pain as Tag and Dunn locked arms beneath his thighs and behind his back and staggered to their feet. Tag noticed then that Dunn's face was red and swollen and that his nose was bleeding.

"This way," shouted Tag. "Straight over."

He and Dunn half stumbled and half ran over the rocky crest, carrying Lieutenant Prentice between them. A few rounds of small-arms ammunition cooking off like the first firecrackers on a string was all the warning they had before the fuel and ammo in the Bradley ignited in a roar of buckling armorplate as the vehicle disassembled in a storm of ordnance and whining shrapnel. The blast tumbled Tag, Dunn, and Prentice onto the sharp flints and swallowed the lieutenant's howl of pain.

Tag cleared his head, except for the ringing in his ears, and took quick stock. His feet were uphill and still seemed to work—he pushed forward with his toes. Pain shot through one elbow and tingled in his hand. He pushed up with the other and saw the arm still pinned beneath Prentice. Dunn was on his hands and knees, breathing raggedly, as secondary explosions continued to pop in and around the Bradley. Prentice lay rigid, still cradling his crossed arms and leaking a sustained, high-pitched moan. Below them, at the lowest navigable edge of the crest, Jan and Sergeant Betcher skidded to a stop in the trailing commando vehicle and in a moment were out and racing toward the three.

The Jagd Kommandos lifted the nearly unconscious Prentice and laid him as best they could among the rocks. Jan helped Tag clean the gravel out of his elbow and wrap it in a pressure dressing, while Betcher searched Dunn's injuries.

"How's he doing, Sarge?" Tag said as Jan tied off the dressing.

The big commando looked ruefully at Dunn and shrugged. "His breath knocked out, a broken nose, maybe a rib, beat to hell. He's okay."

"What about Holz?"

"Nothing. We are going forward to find out."

"Take the lieutenant here with you—can you? We've got to get everybody off this damned ridge, and fast. Pass the word and we'll cover the rear.

"Dunn, how about you? We can make room for you in the No Slack."

"Pass," said Dunn. "I had enough of armor for one day. I'll get with first squad in the truck and scrounge me a weapon off them. Thanks, anyway."

Jan and Betcher made a chair for Prentice with their arms, carried him to the gun buggy, and strapped him in the passenger seat. From behind it, Betcher pulled a jump seat that folded up and over Prentice's head. Seated in it, Betcher could brace his back and legs against the roll cage and operate the .50-caliber.

As the gun buggy sped away, Tag and Dunn moved at a stoop in the lee of the ridge in the direction of the halted No Slack as small-arms ammunition continued to cook off from the Bradley. They came over the crest in the cover of the tank, feeling the heat from the burning Fighting Vehicle close around them. Tag pounded on the driver's hatch and looked over the other side of the ridge, where Prentice's first squad were grouping behind the deuce-and-a-half, its motor dead.

Wheels Latta's heavy shoulders filled the hatch.

"Shit, boss," he said. "Just cain't get rid of you, can we?"

Tag then knew how tired he was; he wanted to laugh out loud, to slap Wheels on the shoulder and insult his ancestry. But all he would allow was a thin smile as he said,

"Mr. Latta, you Dixie dumbfuck, we have to get this man back to that truck and get same truck, one each, moving."

"And it wuz such a nice view too," Wheels said, closing his hatch.

Dunn was not happy about riding on the fender of the No Slack, clinging to a War Club rack and kneeling on the explosive blocks of reactive armor, but he wasn't about to get inside, where Tag was at the radio.

"Meat Grinder Two, this is Butcher Boy."

"This is Meat Grinder Two. Over."

"Two, we have a troop vehicle stalled and are going to assist. How are things there? Over."

"The Bradley is fine. A few injuries. I still do not have contact with Meat Grinder One."

"Roger, Two. Out."

Wheels pulled the No Slack to a stop between the stalled truck and the burning Bradley. Tag got out and walked with Dunn to the squad of soldiers gathered on the downhill side of the truck.

"Who's in charge of this detail?" Tag said at large.

A very young-looking soldier with E-5 tabs on his collar and the name White stitched on his fatigues stepped away from the passenger door of the cab and came to meet him.

"I'm White," the soldier said, "the squad leader." He was sweating a sheet. "You think we ought to trash this thing"—he jerked a thumb over his shoulder toward the deuce-and-a-half—"and get the hell out of here?"

"Anybody hit?"

"Two." E-5 White swallowed. "We lost two. MiG on that second run hit the rock they were behind. It . . . they . . . they're in the gully. I don't think we can get 'em out, Sarge."

No time, Tag thought. "Is the vehicle hit?" he asked.

"No," White said, "I don't think so. I mean, it is, but not the motor. I think it's flooded."

"Well, we don't have time to fuck with it. Reel about fifteen feet of cable off your winch and get your men ready to roll. We're gonna pull you for now, then you can jump-start the sonofabitch later. We not leaving anything we don't have to."

Tag directed the No Slack to the front of the truck, where the soldiers from White's squad secured the winch cable to the tank's towing hooks.

"Have your men stay under cover of the tank until we're on top," Tag told E-5 White. "Then load up and hang on."

In less than two minutes the No Slack, with the deuce-and-a-half in tow, was careening down the ridge at nearly half throttle. The driver of the truck rolled his eyes and sawed the wheel in terror as they twisted and bounced through boulders the size of bowling balls. In the rear there was too much gear for the squad to hold down; loose weapons and ammunition boxes pummeled their shins and knees. But in ten minutes they had reached the lead Bradley and the gun buggy, with still no word of Holz and Giesla.

"After the first plane," Weintaub was saying, "I saw 'em for just a second, as they crossed back over. One of them was shooting the .50-caliber. That's about all I could tell. Then those next jets hit us. By the way," Weintaub added, "that was some nice shooting, Sergeant. Thank you. I . . . Thank you."

"Miracles of modern science, Top," Tag replied. Wein-taub had three dead and three wounded from the back of the Bradley, and he wasn't taking it well. It was, Tag could tell, a deep sorrow for Weintaub, who was almost like a scoutmaster to his company of drivers and supply clerks.

"Listen, that tank buster couldn't fly, so it's either off in one of these gullies or it's already into the woods," Tag said. "And either way we've got to find it.

"Top," he went on, "leave me four men to scout the rim

on foot. You take the others and the wounded and get your vehicles moving. If Holz is at the end of the ridge or down somewhere along the way, you let us know ASAP, okay? I want to be off this mother."

"Let's do it," Weintaub concurred. He called out four names, and four soldiers fell in beside him to be turned over to Tag and Sergeant Betcher. He loaded the rest in the vehicles, making room for the wounded in the open truck, and jolted away around the bend where the ridge began to descend toward the forest again.

With Jan joining two of the soldiers, and Fruits Tutti the other two, Betcher quartered back and forth across the crest of the ridge, like a bloodhound sniffing a cold trail, while Tag kept the No Slack on the high ground and stood in the turret hatch, scanning the naked ridge and its steep shoulders for signs of the commando vehicle. Tag would not even consider the chance that Heinrich Holz was dead, despite Betcher's hangman air. Not just because Rick was his friend and brother in arms, nor because Giesla had been in the vehicle with him—Tag had never stopped thinking of that—but because without Rick, Tag calculated that their chances of getting out past the Soviets and back to the loving arms of Mother Menefee as about zilch point shit to nothing. But that wasn't something he could afford to think about. He was proud of his crew right now, of their coolness and toughness and humor, but Tag knew that a lot of it was in response to how he acted. If Rick were lost, he would have to be the glue to hold this party together.

Up ahead, Tag saw Betcher's vehicle suddenly skid to a halt and the Jagd Kommando in it leap out and run forward to kneel next to something among the litter of rocks.

"Gun it," Tag barked to his driver, and the No Slack leapt like a quarter horse from the starting gate. Seeing the tank accelerate, the six men on foot raced to follow it.

Wheels slid to a stop on the ridge above the gun buggy. Before the tank quit rocking, Tag was out of his hatch and skittering down the slope on his heels toward the Jagd Kommando, shouting, "What is it?"

"It is him," said Sergeant Betcher, looking even more sorrowful than when he had thought Holz certainly dead. The Oberlieutenant lay in front of him, sprawled as though he had no bones. Betcher was hunkered beside him, cutting the blood-soaked shoulder and sleeve off Holz's jumpsuit and holding the kit of field dressings over his arm.

"How bad?" Tag asked.

Betcher rolled his shoulders in something like a shrug. "Inside, who knows?" he said. "No bullet holes and no bones broken, I think. But look at this. "Betcher pointed to the eggplant bruise still swelling over Holz's left temple. The shoulder beneath it that he had exposed oozed from a dozen ragged lacerations.

All Tag could do was pray.

"The vehicle," he said, rising, "any sign of it?"

Betcher looked at him blankly for a moment, then cut his eyes toward the wooded lip of the ridge and nodded once.

Following his gaze, Tag saw the path of fresh scrapes across the rock, white scars in the weathered surface of the schist that led to a place where the rim was even with the tops of trees growing forty feet below. Tag was halfway there when the six men arrived on foot.

Tag's head rang in tempo with his hammering heart and throbbing elbow. He couldn't seem to move fast enough, even running downhill, his shins splinting in protest. Every breath was a labor. As he slowly came closer to the place where the skid path left the crest, he could see the top of one tree parted at unnatural angles and, within the vee, the dull glint of painted steel. Thank God. His racing heart choked him with unanticipated relief. He backpedaled, scattering loose rocks, and took deep, noisy breaths: "Aaaah! Aaaah!"

As though in response, Giesla's voice, quiet and even, came clearly from the treetop. "*Alten!* Stop where you are!"

Tag stopped and called, "Are you there, in the car? I can see your car."

"Yes. Do not come any closer."

"Can you get out?" Tag asked, approaching the rim slowly.

"No," she said, letting Tag hear fear in her voice. "If I move, the vehicle begins to shift."

He could see what she meant now. The commando vehicle had split the yoke of a tall, stout oak and was wedged precariously between the branches of the fork, suspended almost nose-down by its rear tires and twisted gun tubes. One of the main branches had broken away at the bole, showing the hard, white meat of the oak, almost as deep as the heart. There was six feet of nothing between the lip of the crest and the rear towing hook on the wrecked vehicle.

"Okay," Tag called, trying to keep his voice calm. "We're going to get you out. It's just going to take a few minutes."

"Not your tank," Giesla pleaded. "It will shake—"

"No," Tag cut in, "no tank. Just stay still and trust me."

"Sergeant?"

"Yes?"

"My brother."

"We found him. He's hurt but he's alive. Now wait."

The adrenaline was working right for Tag now; he saw exactly what he had to do. In a matter of minutes he had it explained to the men, who were now paying out cable from the winches on the No Slack and Betcher's gun buggy. Tag carried the looped end of Betcher's cable to the rim of the ridge. The No Slack, parked nearly at the crest, anchored the Jagd Kommando with its own cable. Tag signaled both winches to take up slack while he taped the looped end to a section of cleaning staff for the No Slack's main gun and kept saying reassuring things to Giesla.

"Okay," he said. "We're about ready. How are you doing?"

"Hurry!"

Tag lay on his belly, stretched out with the cleaning staff, slapped the looped eye of cable through the self-locking towing hook, and felt the vehicle move in its perch. Giesla gave a small gasp.

"It's okay," Tag said. "We've got you now." He signaled Betcher to begin.

Tag guided the staff back as the cable drew taut. The first bump against it caused the vehicle to lurch and sag on the broken branch.

Tag waved a hand-and-arm signal, shouted, "Pull," and jumped aside.

Both winches engaged at once, and both the No Slack and the gun buggy engaged their clutches in reverse. Giesla's vehicle rode up in the split crotch of the oak, then suddenly jerked down and to the rear, its oversize back tires crashing airless onto the rock rim of the ridge. The front end began to rear when a wheel caught on the solid branch of the yoke. Tag gave the signal to stop, and the weak-side branch gave way, letting the gun buggy crash down heavily on its frame and totter, balanced, on the edge of the gully. Tag let Betcher take up just enough slack to settle it.

"Okay," Tag said. "Get out of there."

"I can't. I . . . I need your help."

Tag crawled quickly over the possibles box and the motor shroud, both ripped by cannon fire, until he could lean across the main roll bar behind the seats. All he could see of Giesla was her helmet and shoulders as he reached down and said, "Unstrapped?" before hauling her up by her armpits. She gasped through clenched teeth but made it off the rear of the vehicle without his having to carry her.

Fruits Tutti and the Jagd Kommando Jan were there as Tag helped Giesla to the ground.

"Cripes, Sarge," Fruits exclaimed. "Lookit her, her . . . leg."

Tag had already seen it, the dark stain on the crotch and down one leg of Giesla's jumpsuit, the blood-sodden scarf she had wrapped high around her left thigh.

"One minute," she said, holding her eyes shut and rising to one elbow. "I'll be okay."

But Tag had already kicked the lid off the ruined possibles box and had the kit of field dressings out on the ground beside her.

"C'mon," he told her, cradling her shoulders and reaching for the zipper on the jumpsuit, "we'll get you patched up."

Giesla exploded in his hands. The extended thumb she aimed at his throat grazed his neck, and the blow beneath his armpit sent fire through his injured elbow. In a wild flurry of hands he somehow ended up with both of hers trapped in his.

"I'll kill you," she howled.

Tag spoke with quiet intent. "Lieutenant Ruther, these soldiers don't have time to sit here and watch you bleed to death, and you're not the only problem we have right now. So you either shuck that suit or I'm gonna have these two men hold you while I cut it off. Either way I'm going to dress that wound."

He felt her relax and let go his grip. She ran a hand across her face and looked at him. There was no sullenness, no rancor in the gaze. "Of course," she said, and began unstrapping her shoulder holster.

She did not look as Tag peeled the soaked material away

from the wound and pulled her jumpsuit down past her hips. Her cotton briefs were stained dark red and pinked the water Tag poured from Jan's canteen to cleanse the ragged gash that a piece of flying rock or shrapnel had torn on the inside of Giesla's thigh, two inches from the top. Tag smeared the area with antibiotic salve and wrapped it tightly in a pressure bandage, then wrestled with the jumpsuit to pull it up.

"Help me to my feet," Giesla said.

Tag steadied her as she found the sleeves and zipped herself into the jumpsuit. She tried the bandaged leg gently and winced at the pain.

"Easy," Tag said. "You'll need that sewed up. Give me your arm, and let's get moving."

Fruits and Jan slipped the cable and toppled the wrecked gun buggy easily into the gully, while Tag supported the limping Giesla up the ridge.

"What happened?" he asked her.

"We didn't see the second planes," she said. "Foolish. Heinrich was firing at the first one, when suddenly we were hit. We rolled, and he was thrown out. When I came to, well, you found me."

"Lucky," Tag said.

"Yes," she said. "Lucky. Sergeant?"

"Ma'am?"

"Thank you."

Tag felt a sharp twinge of pain in his elbow and in the lymph node beneath his arm.

"My pleasure," he said grimly.

6

The column climbed up the fire trail at little more than a walking pace. There was a battle somewhere near enough to mask the sounds made as they parted the leaves on low-hanging limbs. On the rear deck of the No Slack, between two bandaged American GIs, Giesla rode with her unconscious brother's head cradled against her good leg. One of the GIs kept a cold pack against Holz's temple; the other held a foil IV packet of blood expander that drained into Giesla's arm.

They had first halted in the wooded hollow at the end of the ridge, to regroup and better tend their wounded. Prentice's shoulders—separated but not broken—were taped and slung and numbed with morphine. Two of Weintaub's men wounded by the MiGs were ambulatory. The third had a sucking chest wound and was going into shock. Giesla had lost some blood, but the pressure dressing was holding. Except for Holz, everyone else would do to cross the river with. Even Dunn—a tough little sonofabitch, Tag thought—had packed his nose, taped his ribs, asked for two aspirin, and declared himself fit.

The slow pace and close order Betcher said they would need to follow through the grades and switchbacks of the forest allowed Tag to soften the No Slack's suspension and make the tank's rear deck the best ride in the convoy. That's where Holz, with his head trauma, would go, along with Giesla, who would not leave him, and the two walking wounded to assist. Prentice rode in the cab of the deuce-and-a-half, and the chest wound rode in the Bradley.

Tag felt more concealed by the battle noise in the middle distance than by the trees overhanging the disused track that wound out of the watercourses and through those hills that resembled the bellows of a wrecked accordion. The hills offered the relief of shade, the womblike reassurance of the forest canopy, but the sounds of tank cannon and heavy artillery so nearby—Tag guessed no more than four or five kilometers; it was hard to tell in these hills—meant that Ivan had bigger fish to fry than their motley mess. Tag relaxed enough to shake a pint of water in a foil-lined bag labeled "Milk Shake, Chocolate" and gulp it down while he stood in the open cupola. He knew it would make him fart, and he didn't care. Tutti needed something to bitch about. Tag dropped the empty bag into the turret and leaned over the rear.

"How's he doing?" he said to Giesla.

She spoke without looking up at him. "He moved his feet once," she said, "and he's breathing easily."

The tank rolled over an exposed root and jolted the rear deck. Tag saw Giesla cushion Holz's head in her hands and heard her suck in her breath sharply.

"What about you?" he said. "You want something for the pain?"

"No," she said, looking up at him with the blank expression she had worn since he'd dressed her wound. "It is what keeps me sharp-set."

Sharp-set. It was not an expression that Tag had heard for many years, not since Oman and McBrien, the former British brigadier he worked with who was enthralled with falconry.

"You always hunt them hungry," Brigadier McBrien had told him. "Sharp-set, what? Rather like our woggies here, don't you think? Or don't you?"

McBrien mystified Tag at first. The retired brigadier had spent many years on the Arabian peninsula, most of them in Oman, on loan from the British Army. Yet he never missed a chance, when among non-Arabs, to turn a racist blade in the ribs of his hosts, never failed to disparage them as incompetents, inverts, ingrates, and ignoramuses. McBrien groused about the weather, the food, the housing, even the royal posturings of the Omani rulers, which Tag thought especially strange from a subject of one of Europe's last monarchies. Tag eventually came to accept it as McBrien's hobby.

McBrien was at that time the third-highest-ranking officer in the Omani Army, and Tag was the ranking NCO in an American advisory group sent to Oman to test a new series of desert-warfare gear and to instruct the Omanis in the revolutionary tactical theories of tank warfare espoused by General Ross Kettle, then thought to be something of a gadfly of military strategy and tactics. It was those theories, in fact, that had brought Max Tag to armor.

Tag had already distinguished himself as a recruiting-poster soldier (for which he had, in fact, once posed) in an increasingly trimmed-down U.S. Army, when he first read

Kettle's books. At the time Max had just won the second of his two Best Ranger awards and was trying to decide between becoming a permanent instructor at the Ranger School or requesting a Special Forces billet. Neither of them really appealed to him, because he, like most well-read professional soldiers, knew that the next war would not likely be one decided by counterinsurgency. Europe would be the theater, with tanks and mechanized infantry the means. But the traditional idea of tanks as heavy armor, little more than ultramobile field pieces, was disenchanting to a soldier of Tag's aspirations and inclinations. Kettle's theories—even the more speculative ones, based on nonexistent designs and materials—changed that for him.

Regardless of the hardware, Kettle's theories all stemmed from an impulse to treat tanks again as light cavalry—in organization, deployment, and tactics. He turned aside snide critics by openly embracing the idea that his Cherokee-Viking-Sioux ancestry made him genetically predisposed to "amuscade, rapine, and the best guerrilla virtues," as he put it in one preface.

The Omanis, Tag was pleased to find, came naturally to those same traits: They were sneaky, ruthless, and quick to strike. Fire discipline, in fact, was the only real snag he had hit in their training, once Brigadier McBrien's doubts had been overcome. Tag did that, even more than the officer in charge, by his encyclopedic knowledge of Kettle's theories and his clear enthusiasm for them. The brigadier took to Tag and mentioned that he had met Ross Kettle.

"Odd ones, you Americans turn out," McBrien had said, smoothing the feathers of a hooded saker falcon that sat on his wrist as he stood with Tag on the sand hills outside their field compound, combing the sky for bustards. "Looks almost pure aborigine but for those eyes and hair—both pale as moonlight, don't you know. Impressive sort of fellow all the same."

It was just three days later, while Tag was in the field with six Omani tank crews on their final live-fire exercise before the war games the following week, that Iran's mad mullahs and the fanatical Marxist regime of Oman's neighbor, South Yemen, attempted their disastrous invasion of Oman.

The rationale and politics of the affair remain muddled, but it is fact that, using a converted and disguised oil tanker to get close to shore, the Yemeni–Iranian force landed fifty amphibious tanks on the beach at Ras al Hadd and drove north toward the capital at Muscat, arcing inland through the hills, unaware of the military training exercises going on there.

News of the landing reached Tag's group even before the Omani air force was off the ground. He lay the six Omani tanks in ambush and fell on the double column of invaders from the rear, destroying fifteen of them before scattering to leapfrog along the columns' flanks.

When the invaders attempted to regroup, Tag took three of his tanks and drove like a wedge between the columns, throwing them again into confusion and dispatching another dozen of the Yemeni–Iranian tank crews to Allah, while the remaining Omani tanks struck at random from whatever quarter they chose.

Oman's F-16s reached the battle in time to take aerial photos of Tag's tankers accepting the surrender of the remaining crews from the invasion tanks, shortly before Brigadier McBrien arrived with the commanding general of the Omani Army and what looked like a division of tanks, rockets, and infantry.

True to Andy Warhol's predictions, Tag enjoyed his small share of fame in the aftermath of what came to be known as the Battle of Ras al Hadd. The Omanis awarded him an honorary rank and title, as well as a medal; the U.S. Army gave him another medal and a promotion, along with a transfer to the XM-F3 project at Ft. Hood; and every periodical from the *Teton County Times* to *Soldier of Fortune* to *Harper's* wanted his story. General Kettle even wrote him a letter of congratulation.

When Tag was leaving Oman, the last thing Brigadier McBrien said to him was "Look here, Sergeant Tag, a good piece of work you've done here, what. Just remember, lad: Hunt them hungry. And give my regards to that Kettle of yours. Odd duck, but a damned competent man, I'd say."

Tag had carried that message with him ever since, with no expectation of ever delivering it.

As the crow flies, the column had covered less than a mile from the ridge when Betcher halted them at 1640. They had been hugging a nearly sheer rock face for twenty minutes and, as far as Tag could tell, without benefit of any trail. Betcher seemed competent, if a little gloomy, and surely Giesla would know the location of the rendezvous —but Tag could not keep his own thoughts from nagging him. He scrambled down over the fender of the No Slack and walked forward to Betcher's vehicle.

"What gives?" Tag said, leaning into the roll cage.

Betcher was punching buttons on the radio with slow deliberation, pausing to rehearse patterned sequences with his fingers before entering them. "One minute," he mumbled.

When he finished, Betcher looked at Tag with a bearish but genuine grin. "We are here," he said.

"Where?" Tag said, looking around him at the steep forest and the blank face of the cliff.

Betcher's grin widened as he keyed the handset.

An electric hum, a metallic clank, and the jaw-aching sound of scraped gravel froze Tag to the roll cage as a wall-size section of the cliff in front of him fell in at the top, then rose out of sight in the dark ceiling of a tunnel.

"A miracle of modern science—*ja*, Sergeant Tag?" Betcher actually puffed his cheeks to keep from laughing.

"You," Tag said, "are a strange sonofabitch, Sergeant Betcher."

"It is from serving under your friend," Betcher said, jerking his head toward the rear of the column. "How is he?"

"Alive and, you might say, kicking. No worse, anyway. What is this?" Tag waved at the opening.

Betcher rolled his shoulders. "Landscaping?" he said. "That is the word?"

The tunnel entrance was a tight fit for the No Slack, and Wheels Latta had to juke the tank around in the scree and brush several times before he was square with the hole. Standing just inside, in the roomier space of the tunnel itself, Tag watched as a squad of GIs tromped flat the furrows he had left and spread them with leaves. Behind him, he heard something stir on the deck of the No Slack.

Turning, Tag saw Giesla throw her arm across her brother's chest and heard her call to one of the soldiers, "Hold his legs! He's convulsing!"

Tag leapt over the turbine hatches and onto the rear deck in one vault. He brushed away the soldier attempting to hold Holz's legs and straddled his friend at the waist. Tag took the flailing arms and held them aside as he smothered Holz's spasms with the weight of his body. The fit subsided, then Holz twice went rigid, as though a current had passed through him, made a *clock*ing noise in his throat, and ceased to breathe.

Tag leapt to Holz's face and forced open his jaw, found the tongue with his thumb, pinched the dead man's nose shut with his other hand, covered Holz's mouth with his own, and blew. He waited. He did it again. He waited.

"Hit him!" he said to Giesla. "Hit him in the heart."

He blew, and she hit the chest with the heels of both her hands.

"Harder!"

Again.

Again.

Heinrich Holz took a breath.

Again.

Another.

Tag put his fingers below Holz's jaw.

"Neck pulse . . . I think . . . yes. Yes."

Giesla took her brother's wrist and concentrated.

"Yes," she said. "Here too."

They both waited and after a while realized that they were staring at each other, and that the two GIs were staring at them. Giesla was the first to speak.

"Again I thank you, Sergeant Tag."

"Thanks for the backup," said Tag, his voice tight.

Giesla gave him a humorless smile.

They choked by fog lamps for almost a half kilometer through the dark, unvented shaft before they reached the spartan rock warren of the rendezvous site. Tag had worked a gold mine one summer in Montana, and he recognized the marks of pneumatic chisel-drills on the face of the cavern. It was like the inside of a Swiss cheese. There were three main chambers, each about the size of a basketball court and separated from one another by honeycombed rock partitions, and tens of smaller galleries. Dappled sunlight fell into the chambers through three large camouflaged openings on this, the west side of the hill.

Betcher halted them in the empty middle chamber. Through the pierced wall of stone Tag could see the three Jagd Kommando vehicles, with their towed racks of anti-tank missiles, parked beyond. In addition to the two Kommandos who were here to meet them, he could see one more in the chamber with the cars, tinkering with a motor. In one corner Tag could also see a canvas-covered pile of what he took to be supplies. From somewhere came the internal combustion hum of an electric generator.

Homey, he thought.

The sound of the battle was less intense but closer to them now. Tag felt the shelter of its lee as a quiver of exhaustion, a relaxation like letting out a long breath. He thought of his first being under fire, standing in the butts at the rifle range, pulling and pasting targets on the known-distance course, just inches beneath a withering swath of rifle fire, excited by the safe—even companionable—presence of death. Hunger hit him for the first time since dawn.

Weintaub fell his men out of the Bradley and the deuce-and-a-half and asked Betcher where they could set up an infirmary for the wounded. Tag ordered his crew to break out the remains of the rations lashed to the No Slack, then climbed onto the rear deck to check on Holz, while the commandos set up cots from the supply cache for the wounded and the GIs pitched their gear in the empty third lobe of the cavern.

Giesla looked like hell, worse even than her brother, whose bruise in the dim light stood out black against the clammy pallor of his face.

"He still okay?" Tag asked.

Giesla nodded dumbly, letting limp strands of hair fall across her cheeks, not bothering to push them away. She was hurt, dirty, and, Tag suddenly realized, very scared.

"Look, Lieutenant," he said, "we're okay now. Get yourself a cot and let the medic have another look at you."

Tag nodded toward the adjoining cavern, where the Jagd Kommandos were assembling canvas cots beneath a pair of gas lanterns and the GI medic was setting up a treatment station on a wooden ammo crate.

"Go ahead," he said. "We'll take care of Rick."

Giesla nodded again. "I want him next to me," she said.

Without another word she released her brother and scooted across the rear deck. Her weak attempt to climb one-legged over the blocks of reactive armor on the side ended in Giesla's falling into the arms of Fruits Tutti, who had left his work detail to help her. They both grunted when he caught her. His hand flattened one of her breasts.

Giesla regained her balance on her good leg and spun to face Fruits as he released her. Her face was that of a wild thing.

"Easy, Geese," Tutti said. "You're gonna be skatin' on dat one pin for a while. I remember when I got dinged in Honduras," he went on nervously, "hell, I's as stiff as loan sharks' interest for a month. Yeah, a month."

She let her face go blank again. "Yes," she said, "it is stiff, Fruits. Give me a hand."

Fruits took Giesla's arm across his shoulders and helped her limp to the aid station.

Wheels and Ham helped Tag roll Holz onto a poncho and carry him to a cot. Giesla was sitting in her T-shirt, bloodstained briefs, and boots on the edge of the cot by the treatment station, her jumpsuit a soiled pile on the floor between her feet. She gripped the canvas-covered frame and stared at the roof of the cavern as the medic poured peroxide over her wound and swabbed it with gauze. Tag and his men eased Holz onto the adjacent bed.

"Wheels, Ham," Tag said, "I want you guys to go over every inch of the No Slack, inside and out, all the systems, and give me a sitrep. Fruits"—Tag turned to his loader—"I want you to get on that radio again. Maybe you can scrounge parts from the Bradley or something. Just get it working, if you can. And get me an ammo report too. Shit, I wonder whether they've got any fuel stashed here?"

"Talk . . . to . . . Sergeant Betcher," Giesla said through clenched teeth. The cords on her neck stood out as the medic tied off the sutures in her wound.

"You better let me have another look at that elbow, too, Sarge," said the medic.

"Okay, you guys do it," Tag said to the crew. "I'll be along.

"What about Rick and your man with the chest wound?" he asked the medic.

The medic secured a pressure dressing on Giesla's leg and looked up. "Krebs isn't going to make it," he said. "He's bleeding too bad inside. This one"—the medic swung his head to indicate Holz—"I just don't know. I mean, that knot on his head looks bad, but you never can tell."

"You know he had a convulsion?" Tag asked. "Quit breathing on us for a while?"

"Yeah," said the medic. "She told me." He swung his head in the direction of Giesla, who was hobbling toward a corner that the Jagd Kommandos had curtained off with the supply tarp. "She said you saved his life."

"Anything you can do?"

"Let him rest for now, and keep the cold pack on. That's about all."

Tag watched for several minutes while the medic checked Holz's vital signs and resettled the sandbags that immobilized the commando leader's head.

One of the two walking wounded sitting on the cot next to Prentice's called out, "Hey, Bones. The lieutenant is hurting, man."

Prentice sat propped against two rucksacks, his arms double-slung, looking feverish, loony with confusion and pain. He swung his head and glared at Tag.

"*I said*," Prentice bellowed, "*where the fuck are we?*" He hooked one leg over the side and struggled to get up from the cot.

"Hey, easy, Lieutenant," said the medic as he grabbed his bag and stood. "Don't let him get up, guys. He needs another shot."

"Get ba-aack!" Prentice dragged the last word out in a scream as he lurched to his feet and sagged against the edge of a window-size perforation in the rock wall. "What are you trying to do to me?" he demanded. "I'm in command here."

The medic and the two wounded GIs stopped where they were. "Lieutenant," said the medic, "it's me, sir, Bones. Please, sir, just get back in bed and let me give you something for the pain. We're okay here."

Tag had turned and was watching from the first cot.

"You're trying to drug me," Prentice said. "That's what you're trying to do. What have these people done to you?"

"Lieutenant," Tag said, rising, "take it easy. We're at the rendezvous. Safe—"

"Stop!" Prentice shouted. He uncrossed his slung arms so that his hands were together in front of his chest. In one of them he held a fragmentation grenade, its spoon against his palm. Prentice worked the middle finger of his free hand into the ring on the pin and pulled. Pain burned through his shoulders, nearly toppling him.

Tag took a step forward. Through an opening in the wall

he caught a shadow of movement in the periphery of his vision.

"He's got a grenade," one of the wounded men said breathlessly, and he and the other began inching from between the cots.

"Oh, please, sir," the medic said in a small voice as he backed away. "Please, sir, no."

Prentice braced his back against the rock and worked the pin with his wrist. He yelped like a frightened pup when the pin came free, dropping it at his feet and clutching the grenade with both hands. Bullets of sweat stood on his face.

Tag came to attention and coughed in his best parade-ground voice, "Sir, Staff Sergeant Max Tag, at your orders, sir."

Prentice looked at him quizzically. "What are you trying to pull, Sergeant?"

A miracle?

Tag said, "Sir, nothing, sir. Does the lieutenant have any orders, sir?"

"Are you too afraid to run from me, Sergeant—or Comrade, or whatever the hell you are? Don't you think I'll kill you?"

"Sir, no, sir."

"I will."

"Sir, with all due respect, sir, the lieutenant is too good a soldier. That would be destroying Army property without proper authorization, sir."

Prentice blinked. "The Bradley," he said. He looked at the grenade he held, then at Tag. Prentice's face began to crumble. "Oh, my God," he said. "Oh, Lord. I . . . I was driving, and . . . and I just stopped, and . . ."

Prentice couldn't go on, as all that had happened and what he was now doing at once became real to him. He couldn't even call out for Tag to take the grenade he felt slipping from his sweaty grip, could only look at him in helpless horror.

Tag was coming toward him, still five steps away, when he saw the grenade shift position in Prentice's hand. Hold on, Tag prayed, meeting the lieutenant's stricken gaze.

The grenade slipped up half the length of its spoon.

Tag was in mid-leap over two cots when he saw a long, brown arm strike like a cobra from the opening in the stone wall next to Prentice. The hand closed around the grenade, thumb over the spoon, and plucked it from Prentice's hands.

"Gotcha!" said Ham Jefferson, moving into the part of the opening lit by one of the gas lanterns.

Tag skidded on his heels as he landed, already looking for the pin on the rock floor. Prentice double-flinched, staggered sideways, and sat heavily on his cot. Tag knelt and lifted the lieutenant's feet and saw the pin next to a leg of the cot. He handed it to Ham Jefferson through the opening.

"How about it, sir," he said to Prentice, "you want Bones to have a look at you?"

"Yes, yes," Prentice choked, gulping for breath. "Thank you, Sergeant."

"No problem, sir," Tag said. He moved aside to make way for the medic.

"Hambone," he said to his gunner, "that's one I owe you."

Behind Ham in the dimmer cavern, Tag could see Wheels and Fruits with their CAR-15s still at port arms. "I guess now you murderous bastards are gonna ride shotgun while the doc fixes my boo-boo?" Tag said. "What did you want—to watch ricochets chase each other around inside here? Jeez, I've got a dumbfuck crew."

Fruits, Wheels, and Ham all grinned.

"Proud of us, ain't he?" Wheels said.

"Yeah," Fruits affirmed, resting the collapsible stock of his carbine on one hip, "and really knows how to show it, ain't dat right, Mr. Jefferson?"

"Indeed, indeed," said Ham, "but it's his sense of gratitude that I like. Why, I expect he'll even let me keep this here play-pretty." Ham bounced the repinned grenade in his hand; Tag's almost phobic prohibition on explosives inside the No Slack was a standing joke. "I could keep it as a good-luck charm, a reminder of how appreciated I am."

"What I'd appreciate from you slackers is a sitrep," Tag said, sitting on the treatment cot.

While the medic picked the last of the rock splinters from his arm and dressed it with a fresh bandage, Tag listened to his crew's report. With the loss of Prentice's Bradley, they were left with only the five War Clubs in the racks and the main-gun ammo in the carousel. With the 75mm they were luckier; Weintaub had stashed fifty extra rounds in his Bradley. All the computer systems had checked out, and the Jagd Kommandos could let them have another hundred gallons of fuel, maybe more.

"Any luck on the radio, Fruits?"

"Yeah. All bad," Fruits said flatly. "I think I could make it go with parts from de Bradley, but dat Top Weintaub, he says no soap."

"I'll see what I can do," Tag said as he rose from the cot. "Thanks, Bones. Keep me posted on the Oberlieutenant's condition, okay?"

"You bet, Sarge," said the medic.

Near their vehicles, the Jagd Kommandos had set up a couple of alcohol stoves to heat coffee and hot water for the men to mix with their freeze-dried rations. The frozen moments during which Prentice fumbled with the grenade now passed, movement picked up again in the cave as soldiers, talking among themselves in groups of three or four, moved toward the coffee urns, as soldiers always will. Each man put one or two opened foil packets of dried rations in his canteen cup, mixed hot water in the packets, then filled the cup with coffee to keep it all warm.

Tag ambled toward the urns with his crew, looking for Sergeant Betcher. He rounded the rear of one of the gun vehicles and met Giesla, holding two steaming foil packets in her helmet and a canteen cup of black coffee in her other hand. She had pulled her hair back and put on a fresh uniform, but her face was still a mask and her eyes bottomless. Pulse thundered in Tag's ears like the sporadic booming of the nearby Soviet guns. Damn, damn, damn, went through his head. Why did this woman make him feel accused? Guilty of having seen the rust on her armor?

"You were very composed over there, Sergeant," she said without preamble or inflection. "Interesting psychology."

"When a man gets scared like that," Tag said, "it's like he's in a car on a bad hill with no brakes. Everything is out of his control. The lieutenant just needed something to get a grip on."

"You?" she asked, narrowing her hollow eyes.

"It's something he was trained for. It's not important. I'll come check on Rick in a little while. And you need to be off that leg."

"I'll be with him," she said.

Tag watched as she pegged gamely across the cave, then he caught up with the crew and drew his chow. After ten years in the Army, Tag still marveled at the secret process by which field rations made reconstituted chicken tougher than range-raised beef.

"Shoot, let me tell you how tough chicken can be," said

Wheels Latta as they all sat with their backs against the side of the No Slack, belching off their meal. "Once down at Charlotte, I took a run of my Uncle Octavius's best two-year-old white-oak whiskey to the big chicken-fight derby outside town there. Well, we wuz unloadin' jugs outa the back of my Chevy early, before they was hardly anybody there, when up shows the po-lice. Now, the ol' boys that run the cockpit weren't no lintheads. Naw, they told the po-lice, ain't no chicken fightin' goin' on here. This here's the Dumpling Cookoff.

"There's too many laws around for me to bust out, so I just kinda hung out with the rest—there's maybe a dozen there—tryin' to act like I's hired help or somethin'. Damned if that shèriff didn't say that he sure was sorry, but seein' as they was there and hadn't had no supper, chicken and dumplings sure would be good. Pluck enough for all my boys, the sheriff said, and he musta had fifteen deputies with him.

"Them deputies never laughed out loud, but they sure was grinnin' while they stood around and watched while the owners rung the necks on them beautiful birds and plucked 'em in piles of feathers that looked like fall leaves, I'm telling you.

"Well, they was a kitchen under the bleachers around the pits, where they used to fix beans and sandwiches and such to sell at the fights, and that's where they singed all them cockbirds, with ever'body gaggin' and spittin'. And then they cut 'em all up and took to boilin' 'em in the big bean pot. 'Course, they wadn't enough flour in the place to make a cobbler top, but they fixed up what they was for dumplin's.

"Now," Wheels said with closing emphasis, "can you tell me how tough a conditioned fightin' chicken is? Boys, the only consolation those chicken men got was seein' that sheriff break off three of his teeth on a drumstick!"

Tag threw back his head and laughed, more from fatigue than amusement.

"You dumbfuckin' cracker," Fruits said, bouncing a wadded ration bag off the driver's chest. "Dat ain't funny."

"I'm telling you, Tutti," Ham said languidly, "it's the religious influence. All the best bootleggers are Baptists in North Carolina. If you'd been weaned on hellfire and moonshine, you'd be simpleminded too."

"Okay, people," Tag said, gathering himself to his feet, "police our area. I'm going to go check on Rick and talk to Betcher. We need to know what's going on in the real world, so I'll see about an outside antenna for the command set and try to convince Weintaub to let you *borrow* a few parts, Fruits."

"T'anks, Sarge," Fruits said.

Tag passed through the opening to the infirmary area and saw Giesla sitting immobile on the cot next to her brother's, staring vacantly into his face.

"Any change?" Tag asked, sitting beside her.

Before Giesla could answer, Holz emitted a low groan and raised one hand to his chest. He smacked his lips dryly. Giesla wet a wad of gauze from the canteen on the floor and pressed it gently to her brother's mouth. He sucked weakly.

Tag moved to the other side of Holz's cot and knelt. "I think he's trying to come around," he said. "Wipe his eyes."

Giesla wrung out the gauze and wiped carefully, dabbing his cheeks and brow. His lids flickered; he sucked the gauze thirstily. Giesla paused to wet it, and Holz opened his unbruised eye, turning it glassily on Tag and muttering something in thick German before visibly relaxing and letting a loopy smile draw across his face.

"What did he say?" Tag asked.

Giesla looked at him, her eyes bright with tears, her voice husky with relief. "He said he must be alive, because hell couldn't hold two of you."

It was so right, so Rick, that Tag could only grin himself—and he found Giesla returning it.

"He will be all right, won't he?" she said, her voice hopeful as a child's.

"Yeah," Tag said. "Yeah, he will. I'll send the medic over."

Tag located the medic, then found Sergeant Betcher, who was ordering that plastic blackout curtains be hung over the camouflaged openings.

"You have time to fill me in?" Tag asked him.

"*Ja,*" said Betcher. "Here, come with me outside while it is light still, then we will at the maps look."

The steep hill above the cavern beetled several feet over its mouth. The camouflage covers hung from the outcropping to look like the wall of ivy and forest creeper that covered this side of the hill. Tag and Betcher slipped out one side of the camouflage and crouched beneath the low branches of a gnarled fir that grew against the hill. In front of them was a narrow, disused track that ran parallel to the hill. Beyond it, a gully broke steeply down to a watercourse; rose in a rugged, lower ridge; and finally climbed to a curving, tree-studded horizon perhaps two kilometers away. From it Tag could see the orange flashes of heavy guns, but no incoming fire.

"What you see is the Soviet line," Betcher said, indicating the distant line of trees. "Tonight we will scout the positions, try to listen to their radio communication, and then make our plan."

"I want to go with them," Tag said.

"No, my friend," Betcher said to him, "not tonight. Six fresh men I have. Two of them will go."

Tag felt the fatigue and tension of the day. He did not protest. He discussed radios and security with Betcher, told him of Holz's improvement, and grilled the commando on the rendezvous site, learning that it had been a bogus silver mine abandoned more than thirty years ago. As the last blue sky darkened toward black, they rose to go.

"May I have a word with you, Sergeant Tag?" Giesla said from the shadow of the camouflage cover.

Betcher looked ready to speak, but she cut him off with a wave of her hand. "I will be fine," she said to him. "You don't need to mother me, Mathias."

As Betcher reentered the cavern Tag and Giesla sat beneath the ground-sweeping branches of the fir. Tag could see no detail of her face, only the proud profile, as she spoke without looking at him, stripping a fir cone and filling the air with its rough attar.

"I have thanked you enough today," she said, "but I still owe you an apology."

"Not a bit of one," Tag said.

"Let me finish, please." She shucked a row of scales off the green cone. "Heinrich has spoken of you many times. I knew of your meeting him, your 'exploits together against virtue,' as he used to call it." Tag thought she smiled in the dark. She went on: "I also knew of your exploits in Honduras and—was it Yemen?"

"Oman," he said woodenly.

"Oman. And Fruits said that you refused a commission."

"No," Tag said. "Not refused, *resigned*."

"I didn't want to like you, and that was one of my excuses—that you lacked the character to command and the discipline to serve. I had already decided this before. Before today. I was wrong, and even after I knew that I was wrong, I continued to treat you as though it were true. You are a good soldier, and I have been a fool."

"Look," Tag said, "for almost everyone here, this has been the worst day of their lives."

"Yes," she said, holding the cone very still. "For almost everyone."

"I know about that," Tag said. He had not intended to bring it up.

"It is history," she said. "I was driving then too."

"It *is* history," Tag said roughly. "And you didn't make it happen. Now"—he cleared his throat and softened his voice—"for my part, I've never thought too highly of women as soldiers, and you may not make one, either. But you've made me believe in women warriors. You are uncommon."

"And now today is history as well." Giesla took a long breath and tossed the fir cone aside. "I am glad you are my brother's friend," she said.

"Friend, hell. He owes me money."

Giesla chuckled deep in her throat. "The things," she said, "that men find funny." She put her hand on Tag's sleeve. "Give me a hand," she said.

She slid a comradely arm across Tag's shoulders and let him help her through the camouflage cover. She stopped in the dark before they reached the blackout flap and kissed Tag warmly on the jaw.

"Max," she said, "that never happened, but you call me Gies now, okay?" and she went quite ably inside.

Tag's cheek burned like camphor where she kissed him. He slept through until his radio watch at 0400 without a thought of Fruits Tutti's radio parts.

7

Tag awoke exhausted. He was sore from dozens of bruises that had stiffened during the night, his elbow throbbed, and his deep, adrenaline-tossed sleep had given him little rest. Twisted in his sleeping robe, half off his air mattress on the gritty stone floor, he flipped up the cover on his wristwatch and illuminated the dial: 0345.

Tag kicked his way out of the bedroll and sat up, rubbing his shoulders and face. His tongue tasted of powdered aluminum, acrid and dry as sandpaper as he ran it over his lips. As his eyes adjusted to the darkness of the cave, he could see Wheels Latta sitting on top of the turret with his feet through the hatch and his CVC on his head. They exchanged a silent greeting.

Tag drew his boots on and fished a mini-flashlight from a pocket of his jumpsuit. He poked through the dark to one of the smaller galleries, where the Jagd Kommandos had set up a lister bag and a canvas sink outside a chemical latrine. Tag used the latrine, washed his face and rinsed his mouth with water from the lister bag, then made his way along the length of the cavern to the mess area.

There was still hot coffee in the urn, and someone had laid out bread, margarine, and black-currant jam. Tag made himself a sandwich with three slices of bread and ate it standing, washed down with a canteen cup of black coffee. In a moment of déjà vu Tag recalled those still mornings in Montana when he would be up early with his father and brother before a hunt or trout-fishing trip, too early for his mother to make breakfast, and the three of them would eat butter-and-jelly sandwiches and drink boiled, bitter coffee. *That's why I'm here*, he thought. *Just to be able to do that.*

Tag refilled his cup.

On the turret, he found the warm spot Wheels had left on the edge of the hatch and settled down with his coffee. Aside from running the ComNet scanner every few minutes, there was little to do now except think.

The events of the previous day seemed almost unreal to Tag as he recalled them. Even the term *World War Three* was still an abstraction to him. He had no doubt that it was happening, but without radio contact and HQ intelligence, Tag's only image of what was taking place was from Holz's crude sand table back in Bamberg. If things were going according to the Firebreak scenario, the potato plains to the north were already overrun, with Soviet columns striking for the Low Countries and the ports of the North Sea. Hamburg and Bremen and Hanover were likely lost already, and Tag had no confidence that the Red tanks would stop at the River Weser.

On the other hand, here in the southern sector, things were not going to go so smoothly for Ivan. The terrain and the combined French and American forces were expected to halt the Soviet advance well before it reached the Rhine. The danger here, as Tag had heard many times, was that Warsaw Pact frustrations might lead to an early use of NBCs—nuclear/biological/chemical weapons. To Tag that prospect was far more chilling than even a hand grenade in the crew compartment.

Tag ran his hand across the smooth finish of the armor on the top of the turret. He had a lot of confidence in this tank. He ought to, for Tag had been in on the XM-F3 project from the beginning, critiquing armaments, electronics, crew compartment design, even before Honduras. He had seen the slick-skin armor turn 155s, and he had put the first prototype through some antics at Ft. Hood that would have been court-martial offenses anywhere else. It was a plum job, he reflected, had it not been for the pot about to blow its lid in Europe. This was where he needed to be, not back at Hood jawing with the engineers.

But that was another crazy thing: He wasn't, in fact, even supposed to be in Europe. When the orders came down from the Pentagon sending the No Slack to Germany the previous winter, the field evaluation officer, the commander of the tank, was specified as one Captain Max Tag, because the paperwork on his voluntary resignation of a reserve captaincy in favor of his regular army rank had not caught up with the orders. The only galling thing was that he now owed one to Colonel Roger "Satin Ass" Menefee, who had ignored the discrepancy and brought Tag, anyway.

Now it had happened, what he had come for, but it was nothing like what he had expected. Still, it was where he should be, and with the very tank that could prove out even the most speculative of Ross Kettle's theories.

And not just with the tank itself, Tag thought. The No

Slack would be all potential if it weren't for the crew, that misfit trio of idiot savants. They had served together and been friends before Tag met them in Honduras, during the so-called "support-and-deployment" exercise that turned into Operation Golden Spike—a thirty-two-day war unmatched in its ferocity since the Spanish conquest. Tag remembered it well.

"*Spanish*, you fuggin' rube. It's *Spanish*, an' I'm fuggin' *Italian*. You unnerstan'?"

Tag stopped in the steaming heat of the Honduran foothills and swung his duffel to the ground as he leaned against the nose of the Sheridan light tank to eavesdrop on the crew he had come to join, who were hunkered under the shade of the camouflage cover at the rear, trying to haggle with a boy of about twelve who was selling watches, Mesoamerican "antiques," and pornographic playing cards.

"Aw, hell, Fruit Loops," he heard a Southern voice drawl, "that's close enough. I reckon he'll understand more of what he don't know in English in Eye-talian than not."

"You're fuggin' nuts," the first voice whined.

"Now wait a minute," said a third voice, this one a resonant baritone rumbling in the cadences of the black inner city. "Tell me, Wheelman, can you repeat what you just said?"

"'Course," said the Southerner curtly. "I know what I's sayin'."

"Much as I feared," said the baritone.

"I told ya, he's fuggin' nuts," said the first.

Tag walked softly around the side of the Sheridan, until he could see the boy but was still hidden from the crew. He recognized the kid as one he had shooed away from HQ a couple of days before.

"Hey, Juanito," Tag said casually. He stepped to the corner of the crew cover and leaned lightly on a post.

"Sergeant Tag!" blurted the boy, who then looked sheepishly back at the three tankers.

"What the hell are you still doing here, Juanito?" Tag asked wearily. "You want to make me tell your father you're out here peddling smut?"

"No, Sergeant Tag, *por favor*." The boy made no move to go but began stuffing decks of cards and "Mayan" carvings back in his Pony shoulder bag. "It is all sport, Sergeant Tag," the boy said. "No one was buying. It is all just for fun."

"So you think it's fun to listen to what other people have to say, when they think you can't understand them?"

"*Sí*," Juanito said brightly.

"Well, Johnny," Tag said, "you know that's what spies do, don't you?"

It took only a second before Juanito's bulb popped on and his eyes widened.

"And," Tag went on, pressing the boy's panic, "you know what we do to spies, don't you?"

Tag whipped his hand off the lean-to post and slapped the Beretta 9-mm in his shoulder harness, but Juanito was already a blur of blue jeans, T-shirt, and sneakers.

"Howdy, fellas," Tag said, turning to the crew. "I'm Sergeant Tag from HQ, come over here to replace Sergeant McAvery and teach you conscripts how to be a tank unit."

"Hey, yeah," said the whiny one, a short, dark E-3. "You're de one, dat hero guy, right?" He stood and dusted off a hand for Tag to shake.

Tag took it. "That's right," he said. "I'm hell on tracks. Who the hell are you?"

"Why, don't you know?" said the freckled corporal with the Carolina drawl.

"Sarge," said the mellow-voiced black PFC, "we are the crew with the brew—off the duty sheet and out of the heat. A cold can for our main man, please, Mr. Tutti."

So, on a sweltering off-duty afternoon, sharing cold, contraband beers, Tag got to know the crew that would follow him into Golden Spike, and into the apocalypse.

With a couple of remarkable exceptions among the cowboys, Tag had never known any black people while growing up in Montana. And even after eight years in the Army he was sometimes still put a little off his stride by the facetious humor and lazy cadence of their speech. He made a special effort to sound out Hamilton Jefferson first.

Ham. Hambone. Hamhand. *Hand grenade*. That was the one he finally picked. Hamilton "Hand Grenade" Jefferson, 47–4 as an amateur, 8–0–1 as a middleweight pro. He was good: good feet, a stiff left, and a right with real pop. He was hard to hit and could take a punch. What he couldn't take was a dive; it just wasn't in him.

Hamilton was the fifth of seven children and spent most of his childhood living with an aunt two doors down from his mother and stepfather on a street of small, drab wooden houses in East St. Louis. The yards were bare of grass, littered with old tires and broken tricycles and other discards of hope. From the single window in his room in the attic loft of his aunt's house, Hamilton Jefferson could see the St. Louis Arch. Watching it at night, etched by electric lights against the sky, Ham imagined it as a triumphal arch, imagined himself passing through it and into a world of realized dreams, not dreams deferred.

Ham took up boxing as a way to stay out of fights. Out on the summer streets at night, never drawn to join one of the gangs or delinquent cliques of East St. Louis, Ham found that a skinny eleven-year-old was fair game. He fought, and even then he had long arms and quick, bony hands, but he dreaded it. Ironically it was in the Boys' Club boxing gym that he found refuge.

Matched against boys his own weight and age, wearing leather headgear and oversize gloves, Ham also found a game he was good at. By that fall when he turned twelve, Ham would come in from school each afternoon and do his homework to the tinkling, dissonant accompaniment of his aunt's piano students, then leave after dinner for the gym. It was two more years before she found out he wasn't playing basketball.

Boxing gave Ham poise and confidence, but he insisted on covering his shyness with a line of rap banter and a humorous aloofness. He didn't join clubs at school or run for student council, so his good grades went largely unnoticed by all except his teachers and counselors. They had him thinking seriously of college the spring before he turned eighteen, when he won the Regional Golden Gloves welterweight title, and his whole world came apart.

The night he won, his aunt died. Ham didn't know that when he talked to a professional fight manager after the bout, a smiling, sweating white man named Brady. He didn't know it on the plane from Chicago or on the city bus that he took to his neighborhood. The house was locked and empty. He walked, with his suitcase and his trophy, to his mother's. She and his stepfather were drunk, so drunk that the conjured sincerity of their apologies and condolences made Ham almost physically ill. He went to bed with his youngest brother in another room—another world, it seemed.

Within a week Brady had shown up. But aside from coming to the gym to watch Ham work out and spar, he paid more attention to Ham's parents, even taking them out to restaurants and bars. He was around for about two weeks, only occasionally hinting to Ham about turning pro, when his mother began with her wheedling about money, and his stepfather began his awkward, avuncular attempts to give Ham advice. Within days it turned to screaming and threats.

Brady—"This family's savior," Ham's mother said—came to his friends' aid with a contract for Ham to sign, making Brady his sole personal manager in the professional boxing game.

Ham saw that he had been set up, but his loyalty to his mother and his self-delusions about making the big money and then getting out conspired to unseat his teenage resolve. He signed with Brady, who put him under the eye of Dinty McGinty, St. Louis's once-legendary fight trainer and coach.

When Ham debuted as "Hand Grenade" Jefferson three months later, he made a big stir without even winning the fight. He was in a six-round prelim bout against a onetime title holder who had never been beaten on points in all his nine defeats. Ham used the ring well through the first three rounds, moving and jabbing and backing up his opponent with hard rights. By the fourth round, the veteran was on to him, sliding under the jab with heavy body shots, clinching, then beating Ham to the punch after the break. Round six had the crowd on its feet. Ham fought a smart fight, picking up his lateral movement and avoiding the clinches while keeping his man off with a stinging left. The final thirty seconds saw the two fighters toe to toe in the middle of the ring, causing more action than damage.

The draw was a moral victory for Ham, who thought he had lost. He, in fact, became so keen on his skills that he soon had McGinty furious at him for winning two fights by decision that the trainer said he should have won by KOs. If he ever wanted a shot at some real money, McGinty told him, Ham was going to have to show that he could put men away.

Over his next five fights Ham put three men away inside four rounds, stopped another with cuts, and won a unanimous decision over a boxer nicknamed Iron Head, who just wouldn't go down. Then he started to see even more of Brady.

Ham had made some money in his last two fights—the bout with Iron Head was nationally televised—and had settled his mother and stepfather in a new house across the river in a suburb of St. Louis. Things were looking good, and Brady was promising him a fight with a ranked challenger, and from there a shot at a title.

The short of it was that Brady did indeed get him matched against the current third-ranked middleweight in the WBA. The only catch was, Ham couldn't win. The big payoff would be in cash, and his time would come. Ham said no. Someone shot all the windows out of his mother's house. Ham agreed, took half the money up front, and disappeared into the ranks of the U.S. Army.

"And to tell you the truth," Ham said, cracking another beer and passing it to Tag, "it was a kind of relief. I'd see those old punched-out pugs pushing broom at the gym or passing out towels or talking to something on their shoulder that you couldn't see, and I couldn't keep from seeing myself in a few years. It is one ugly business, I tell you, Sergeant Tag."

In time Tag would come to know Ham Jefferson as one of the best natural tankers he had ever met—cunning, resourceful, and vicious in combat, he also had a head for strategy, tactics, and gunnery. But at that first meeting Tag was only sure he liked the man, liked his intelligence and his humor, liked the way he struck the balance between his two crew mates, siding sometimes with one and sometimes with the other in their ceaseless, comradely banter. He also knew how to get cold beer.

Robert Edward Lee Latta and Francisco Gregorio Tutti, despite being poles apart in upbringing, were more alike than not. Each had dropped out of school from boredom, to pursue some personal interest, and each had run aground on the reefs of reality—that is, the police.

Wheels Latta was the sort that Tag took to instinctively. He was of average height but looked shorter because of his long torso and broad shoulders. He had sandy hair, freckles, and a Huck Finn grin—the sort of boy you'd love to have your daughter marry but would hate to see her date. His eyes shone with the lights of intelligence and mischief.

Latta came from Grandmother's Gap, in the mountains of North Carolina, just off the Blue Ridge Parkway and not far from the rattlesnake wilderness of the Linville Gorge. He grew up in a family whose traditional occupations were the making and selling of illegal whiskey and the preaching of the Southern Baptist gospel. In their spare time Wheels, his brothers, and cousins also built and raced NASCAR stockers, cars that were otherwise used between races to run Grandpa Latta's prime two-year-old white-oak whiskey to bootleggers and club owners in Tennessee, the Carolinas, and Virginia.

Wheels learned to drive before he was ten, and by fifteen was making regular runs to Greensboro and Durham and Charlotte. He was a lively boy who once slipped a skunk under the skirt of a revival tent, but he didn't have a reputation as a fighter or a thief and so was generally admired by his elders in Grandmother's Gap. He sawed fiddle with a rockabilly band but atoned for it by playing revivals with a bluegrass-gospel group. In his heart, though, Robert E. L. Latta wanted nothing except to make a name on the stock-car circuit. To that end, he quit school and became a full-time blockade runner, hoping to earn the $50,000 he would need to field a car by the time he turned eighteen. He almost made it.

It was on a return trip from Knoxville, while driving the narrow highway that is hemmed in between the mountainside and the turbulent Virgin River, that Wheels Latta finally got caught, trapped between a roadblock and the unmarked cruisers that had been tailing him since he'd crossed back into North Carolina.

There was just enough whiskey residue in his tanks to get Wheels charged and held, but little enough to make the case against him shaky. Wheels let some of the money from his savings change hands and got himself a plea bargain that included the option of the Army. Wheels would later claim it was his work ethic that made him decide to be an employee of the government instead of its guest.

Fruits Tutti's story had some of the same earmarks. Fruits was the essential city kid. His family was working-class Italian, from one of the last surviving "decent" neighborhoods in the Bronx. Less typically, he was an only child. He sometimes worked in his parents' small grocery or helped his mother with maintenance on the three apartments they also owned. But once his flair for math and computers emerged, both doting parents urged him on.

By the time Fruits was fourteen, his room at home had more computer capability than the offices of most Fortune 500 companies. At fifteen, he had copyrighted two extremely successful video games, written a Grand Master chess program that only he could beat, and developed a series of "inoculation" programs against computer viruses. He even designed and built a working mini-mainframe based on bubble-memory chips, then refused to let IBM have the plans.

In fact, as Fruits advanced into adolescence, he became increasingly eccentric and intractable, obsessed by computers and sex. ("Pussy," he would say later, "pussy was all I could think about, if I wudn't workin' on somethin'. But dat's normal for a Catholic, ain't it?") But Fruits' solitary pursuits had left him socially awkward, and his adolescent ego made him a troublesome employee, even as a free-lancer, and an even worse student. Like many prodigies, Fruits thought he was above common morality and standards of behavior.

At sixteen, already a high-school dropout, Fruits Tutti was earning more than his father doing part-time troubleshooting for computer-based businesses. After a year Fruits was bored with making money. So what he thought was a simple hacker's prank with the New York municipal computer files turned out to be Fruits Tutti's ticket to the Army.

Using illustrations scanned from the magazines he bought on Forty-second Street, Fruits planted pornographic "land mines" throughout the city's computer system, causing several attacks of the vapors among older female employees who, expecting to call up property-tax records, were treated to a five-second montage of every human perversion possible without the use of major household appliances.

The judge, a severe-looking woman who wore lace-up shoes—"A bull dyke in boots," Fruits called her—was not amused.

Tag smiled in the darkness. Fruits Tutti probably talked more pussy than any man in the U.S. Army, but he would throw himself across an open sewer to let a hooker pass.

Tag brushed absently at the place on his jaw where Giesla had kissed him. The last thing he needed to be thinking about right now was a woman, even one who was a soldier—hell, *especially* one who was a soldier.

Tag tried instead to concentrate on what their next moves might be, trying to second guess what the Jagd Kommandos might have learned on their night reconnaissance, wishing he had radio contact—the radio, shit.

Finally he remembered the parts he had promised Fruits Tutti.

8

At 0500, incoming artillery began to shake the folded hills. In minutes it was answered by Soviet guns on the ridge. The exchange was intense for about a half hour, then slackened to a steady pounding. That was when the first of many long rounds from the Allies that day crashed into the hollow beneath the cave, moving the rock and sending fine cascades of dust from every ledge and outcrop in the cavern.

Someone lit a lantern in the Jagd Kommando chamber, and Tag could hear Weintaub making his way among his troops, obviously rousing some of them. *Good*, Tag thought. *Let's get 'em out of the dark and give 'em something to do. This is bad enough on the nerves as it is.*

As more lanterns came on, Tag could see that Weintaub had organized a KP detail, and in a few minutes he could smell fresh coffee and the smoky bite of frying sausage.

At 0615, the crew of the No Slack could no longer pretend to be asleep and let the smells drag them from their bedrolls.

"Okay, my sleeping beauties," said Tag as they stood, stretched, and scratched themselves, "you guys hit the latrine and get back here so somebody can go draw my rations."

"Uh-huh!" Fruits grunted. "Smells sweeta den 'tang, don't it, Wheels?"

"Baptists don't eat pussy, Fruits," Ham said. "You know that."

"Yeah? I always heard dat about spades."

"That," said Ham, "is a foul canard, Mr. Tutti." He tapped Fruits smartly on the head and then, smiling, stepped away from the loader's ineffective flurry of hands and turned toward the latrine.

"C'mon, Fruits," Wheels said. "If Hambone gets to a place where he can sit down to shit, we may be waitin' all day."

Breakfast smelled better than it tasted. The canned sausage was bland and soggy, and the cooked cereal was like a concoction of powdered milk, sugar, and sawdust. Still, it was hot and hadn't come out of a foil sack. Most of the men ate in silence, and those who did speak, did so quietly, as though fearful of being overheard by the thudding artillery. Even in so large a cavern, the atmosphere was already tense, claustrophobic.

Tag finished his chow, told the crew to prepare personal weapons and gear for inspection, then went to check on Holz.

He found him sitting up in bed, with Giesla beside him. Holz's one eye was swollen beneath the bruise; his other was bright but not entirely focused.

"Hey, Rick," Tag said casually as he lowered himself to a crouch beside the cot, "how are you doing?"

"Good," Holz said thickly, essaying a crooked grin that caused him to wince.

"Oh, yeah," said Tag. "And you look great too."

"*Ja*," Holz said, closing his eyes and resting his head on the rucksack behind him. "And you are still two of you too ugly too." He breathed shallowly through his mouth.

Tag questioned Giesla with his eyes.

She looked at her brother and touched his hand. "He is tired. He's been awake since the shelling started. Maybe now he can sleep."

Tag nodded and rose and stepped over to Prentice's cot, where the medic was touching up some of his cuts and one of the walking wounded was spooning sawdust cereal into the lieutenant's mouth.

"Looks like the royal treatment, sir," Tag said.

Prentice made a face and swallowed hard. "You're a witness, Sergeant. This man"—he jerked his head in the direction of the soldier holding the mess kit—"is trying to poison me. And this other one is inflicting gratuitous bodily pain on a superior."

"I'll have them both shot, sir." Tag grinned.

"No. Wait until I'm well and I'll do it myself."

"Sounds like you're on your way there, sir," Tag said. He turned and saw one bunk empty.

"Krebs didn't make it, Sarge," said the wounded soldier. He lowered his voice and added, "Hey, Sarge, what about that German guy? That woman of his won't hardly even let Bones get near him."

"That 'German guy' is an officer, soldier—a Jagd Kommando officer—and 'that woman' is his sister. Also an officer. Got it?"

The soldier shrugged and spooned up another glob of the cereal.

"No," said Prentice, looking at Tag. "Sergeant, I need to see Weintaub. Can you find him for me?"

"I need to see him, too, sir," Tag replied. "I'll find him

and Sergeant Betcher and get back to you, as soon as I've inspected my crew."

"Thanks. Oh, and, Sergeant, about last night . . ."

"Mox nix, Lieutenant. *Nada*. Forget it, okay?"

"Forget what?" Prentice asked ingenuously.

Tag started away, then paused by Holz's cot.

"How are you doing?" he asked Giesla.

She wagged her head. "Stiff," she said. "Thirsty, a little weak. I'll be all right. And you?"

"Fine as frog hair."

"Pardon?"

"I'm okay," Tag amended.

"Good."

Tag squeezed Giesla's shoulder, shot her a reassuring smile, and went back to the No Slack.

The crew's gear and weapons were in good shape, considering the past twenty-four hours. And to show their own high spirits, Ham, Fruits, and Wheels were sporting the personal side arms that Tag allowed himself to overlook. Wheels had his Ruger Super Blackhawk .44 Magnum slung in a cowboy rig on his right thigh; Fruits, who thought anything smaller than a 75mm was bullshit, anyway, carried an antique .30-caliber Luger in a flap holster; and Ham packed his 9mm Colt Commander in an elegant, hand-tooled black leather shoulder harness, with spare magazine pouches that hung beneath his right arm.

Tag told them to clean the bores and receivers on all the No Slack's guns, then stand down to radio watch until he had further word.

Betcher walked up as Tag was finishing.

"I am going now to debrief our patrol," said Betcher. "I thought you would want to be there."

"Yeah," said Tag, "thanks. I do. And I think we should have Weintaub and Prentice in on it too."

"Prentice?" Betcher said. "The American lieutenant?"

"Yeah. I just talked to him. He had a bad patch last night, but he seems to have his shit together now. He's got to at least know."

Betcher, wearing his customary look of inscrutable gloom, merely grunted.

"I'll find Weintaub and meet you," Tag said.

Betcher had already assembled the four men from the patrol at Prentice's cot when Tag arrived with Weintaub. Giesla rested on a five-gallon jerrican while the others arranged two more cots in a vee, its open end toward Prentice, and all sat to look at the maps, while Karl, the Jagd Kommando who had led the patrol, gave his report in English.

As Karl described it, the Soviet disposition along the ridge consisted of two companies of T-80s—twelve in all—and a battery of 152-mm self-propelled howitzers. The tanks were strung out at more or less regular intervals for about a mile along the ridge. The howitzers had been divided into three two-gun platoons and stationed at arbitrary locations where it was flat enough for good artillery positions. Karl penciled in the tanks and guns on the map acetate.

What really got Tag's attention, however, was Karl's report that there was no infantry pulling security for the ridge. The foot troops were all staged in BMPs at either end of it, where the westward slopes were less steep, allowing faster deployment for them into the flat land, once the assault was under way.

"When will that be?" Tag asked.

"I cannot say," Karl replied. "They are not digging in their positions, but they have put up camouflage nets."

"See anyplace where we might sneak through?" said Tag.

Karl shook his head. "No, not here. Perhaps farther south."

Tag chewed the insides of his cheeks. "I want to go have a look," he said to no one in particular.

"But why?" Giesla said.

"I'm not sure," Tag admitted. "But as little G-2 as we have now, any more can't hurt." He looked at Sergeant Betcher. "What about it? Can you loan me Karl? I can take Jefferson and Latta with me too."

Betcher looked as mournful as a hound. "*Ja*," he said after a long pause. "Karl and one other. You leave two here to man your tank. Just in case."

"Mathias," Giesla said, "how long can we stay here?"

Betcher hunched his shoulders in a shrug. "No longer than we must," he said. "The longer we wait, the more difficult it will be to help our friends here break out. As soon as our wounded can travel, I would say."

"But where?" Prentice asked. "Where do we go?"

"South from here we go," said Betcher, pulling the map between his feet and pointing at it with a blunt finger. "We look for a break in their line. Here, maybe, in this wood— it is no good place for armor—or here." He jabbed at a delta of roads converging on the Mannheim highway.

Tag turned to Weintaub. "Listen, Top, if we can get our ComNet radio working right, we might be able to get some decent intel from HQ, at least enough to tell us where we stand on the board."

"Your man already talked to me about that," Weintaub said. "No way is he going to cannibalize my Bradley."

"Give it to him, Top," Prentice said, an edge of command in his voice.

"But, sir—" Weintaub began.

Prentice cut him off short. "Top," he said, "listen to me. The Army's first priority among this bunch is to get that tank back safely to our lines. We are the Army here, and that makes it our job. Got me? You give Sergeant Tag whatever he needs."

"Yes, sir," Weintaub said stoically, too good a soldier to let his irritation show.

Tag checked on Holz and found him snoring softly and evenly in a deep sleep, then rejoined his crew.

Tag made a superfluous inspection of the guns, knowing they would be spotless, then gathered his men to brief them on the meeting.

"Fruits," he said, "you got your radio parts. Go talk to Weintaub when we're through here. Wheels, you stay out of his hair and baby-sit the tank. And you, Mr. Jefferson, my favorite son, you and I have patrol tonight, so you cop some zees early. Meanwhile"—Tag spread out a map on the fender of the No Slack—"all of you have a look at this."

When he had finished going over the strategy session and the plans they had made, Ham Jefferson gave a low whistle. "Man," he said, "it's gonna be like feeling our way down a dark hall looking for an open door."

"Yeah," Fruits added, "and hopin' the mothafucker don't open on an elevator shaft."

"I just love an optimist," Wheels said.

For the rest of the morning Tag busied himself with an inch-by-inch inspection of the No Slack and with updating the performance-evaluation log. In it he detailed the damage from each hit the tank had sustained, its fuel consumption over various terrains, and the performance of everything from the suspension system to the War Club missiles.

Silently Tag cursed himself for being so damned efficient. Chances were that he'd have to torch the log and the No Slack before it was all over. It was, he knew, something closer to superstition than a sense of duty that kept him at it, as though keeping the log and all the pretenses of normalcy would somehow pull them through—and he could chap old Satin Ass's hide. Wouldn't it be just like Menefee to gig him for failing to keep the log?

At noon Tag passed up the sausage sandwiches in favor of freeze-dried chicken teriyaki. He carried the steaming bag in his canteen cup and went from the mess area to look in again on Holz.

The Jagd Kommando leader was awake and sitting up, drinking something hot from a collapsible metal cup that he held in both hands. Giesla sat on the next cot—the one between her brother's and Prentice's now empty one—resting her injured leg and also drinking from a metal cup.

"What happened to our lieutenant?" Tag asked.

"He said he was rejoining his troops," Giesla replied.

"Didn't like your company, huh?" Tag grinned at Holz.

"You won't believe this, Max," Holz said, "but he said he was going to inspect them."

"I'll be damned," Tag said, shaking his head. "You don't suppose he's gonna make a soldier, do you?"

"You did, didn't you?" Holz said.

"Sounds like you're feeling better—that is, like a horse's ass," Tag said. "How's the head?"

"*Ach,*" Holz said weakly. "It only hurts when I'm awake. But that's not much. After a few minutes I get dizzy, and sometimes I cannot tell whether I am asleep or awake."

"He is eating," Giesla said, "and keeping it down. That, I think, is a good sign."

"Okay," Tag said. "Get all the rest you can, both of you. I don't see how we can stay here more than another twenty-four hours, so you've got to be able to move."

"What of your radio?" Giesla asked.

"Fruits is working on it now, and Betcher has a man stringing us an antenna outside. I'll let you know."

Tag ate his cooled teriyaki as he walked back to the No Slack, where he found Fruits Tutti sitting in the commander's chair, his lap full of electronic parts and bundles of colored wires.

"How's it going, Fruits?" Tag asked as he scrambled into the crew compartment.

"Dis is a goddamn cluster fuck, Sarge. It's like tryin' to fix a computer with typewriter parts."

"But does it work?"

"Yeah, sorta. I mean, I got no schematics, no solder—nothin' but by-guess an by-golly and a buncha alligator clips. You want I should give it a try?"

Tag thought for a moment. "Can you send a distress burp?"

"If it'll work at all, yeah."

"Okay, do this. Send out to Queen Bee. Give our grid coordinates and request instructions. You can get that in a one-second burp, can't you?"

"Sure."

"Anything coming in that we can use?"

"Nah, but it sure sounds like our guys are takin' a poundin'."

"All right. Do it."

While Tutti muttered and fiddled with the wires, Tag sucked his teeth and wondered what he would do if there wasn't a headquarters anymore. *I can't believe*, he thought, *that I'm actually worrying about Satin Ass. The guy who said politics makes strange bedfellows never went to war, I guess*.

"Message sent," Fruits announced.

Tag pulled a CVC over his head and waited, listening to the static hiss and pop on the jury-rigged radio.

"Butcher Boy, Butcher Boy, this is Queen Bee Actual." The signal cut through the interference clear and strong.

"Copy your burp. Be advised, the eagle is at roost two. From roost one, go left five-zero klicks and you can fly the coop. You have blackbirds for company beyond that. Good luck. Queen Bee Actual out."

Tag removed his helmet and reread what he had copied on his message pad. Something was not kosher here.

"Fruits," he said, "find Betcher and ask him to come over here, and Lieutenant Prentice, too, if he's up to it."

Tag got out of the tank, spread his maps on the fender, and studied them until Fruits returned with Betcher, Prentice, and Weintaub. They gathered around Tag, along with the rest of his crew. Prentice was still pale, with a light sheen of sweat on his face. In him Tag recognized a man who was fighting pain.

"I've just received a message from our headquarters, and I may need some help to sort out what it means," Tag began. "The U.S. Seven Corps HQ has withdrawn from Nürnberg to Mannheim, and Ivan apparently has control for at least fifty klicks up the highway toward Mannheim. If that's right, it puts our position here almost twenty miles behind the lines. But I know that those howitzers on the ridge have a maximum range of about eighteen klicks, and they're damn sure not burning all that powder for drill. Also, as of right now, anyway, we can get under our own air umbrella for the last hundred or so klicks on the road into Mannheim. Any ideas?"

"Can you get any clarification?" Prentice asked.

"Nix," Tag replied. "We made contact with a message burp, but I don't want to press our luck. Ivan wouldn't be able to get a fix on us, but if he even suspected we were here, it could get hairy."

"What is it exactly that you're thinking?" asked Weintaub.

"Well, Top," Tag said, "if we knew where we stood on the board, we could hot-rod it to a likely spot along the line and try to sniff out a gap. If we don't know, we'll have to go slow, make sure we don't run up the six of a bunch of bad guys. But that could kill us too. We haven't got time to fuck around. Every hour is an hour that Ivan has to firm up his line. Right now he's not organized, probably as confused as we are, and not too concerned about one tank, a Bradley, a deuce-and-a-half, and four gun buggies. It's like being taken prisoner: The sooner you can make an escape attempt, the more likely you are to get away. You have any guesses. Sergeant Betcher?"

Betcher could make his smile look like a frown, and did so now. "Max," he said, "I am Mathias, *ja*? I am not a Gypsy card reader. Tonight you will try to find out something. Tomorrow we must go. That is all I know."

"Well," Tag said, folding his maps, "you sure read my mind."

After this inconclusive session Tag managed a few hours of much-needed sleep and awoke to the shuffle of boots on the floor of the cave as the troops began to make their way to the mess area for a last hot meal.

Tag went to the latrine and then to the mess area, where he was eating the tinned stew and black bread that the Jagd Kommandos had provided when Betcher found him.

"You and your *schwartz* soldier come see me when you are finished," Betcher said.

In a half hour Tag had collected Ham Jefferson, and together they joined the Germans gathered around the gun vehicles.

"You will need some things for this patrol, I think," said Betcher. He gave Tag and Ham grease sticks to camouflage their faces and hands and a roll of green tape to wrap the loose legs and sleeves of their jumpsuits, as well as a pair of black silk watch caps.

"Max," Betcher said as Tag and Ham streaked their faces with the green-and-black camouflage, "do you want weapons?"

"We have CAR-15s and side arms," Tag said.

"Not good," said Betcher. "Here." He turned to a wooden crate and took out a pair of suppressed Walther 9mm submachine guns, each with two thirty-round magazines taped end to end. The suppressors, themselves as long as the guns, were covered in black sponge rubber to serve as handgrips.

"These," said Betcher, handing Tag and Jefferson the guns, "are like little birds farting."

Ham disengaged his magazine, checked its load, and snapped it back in the receiver. "Right rare teeth in these birds," he said.

"*Ja*," said Betcher fondly. "They are my pets."

"Who else will be with us?" Tag asked.

"Besides Karl, I will send Jan with you," Betcher said. "At 2100, I think it will be dark enough to begin."

"Did Karl report any sentries, electronic ears, anything like that?" Tag asked.

"Nothing," Betcher said, shaking his head. "And you will need to move quickly in and out."

Tag nodded in agreement. "At the latest, 0200, 0300, okay? I'm like you; I'd like for us to be out of here before daylight."

They were joined by Karl and Jan, both of them already greasepainted and armed with silenced, wire-stocked Walthers.

The four men of the recon team reviewed the maps and picked Karl's brain again for details of the Soviet deployment, then all went outside and hunkered against tree trunks while their eyes became accustomed to the dark.

* * *

The scraps of cloud that had been scudding across the thin sliver of moon since it rose at 2000 hours were beginning to pile up, and the air smelled of rain when Tag gave the order to move out.

With Karl at point and Jan at drag, they went in single file, keeping a five-meter interval as they zigzagged down the steep hollow into the watercourse and up the far side to the forested benchland that sloped more gently to the base of the ridge occupied by the Soviet armor and guns. A light, windless mist was beginning to fall as Karl halted them in the trees at the foot of the ridge. They had been moving steadily for nearly an hour, and Tag felt a pleasant burning in his thighs that reminded him of how casual he had become about staying fit during the previous six weeks of evaluations of the No Slack. Still, in the silence that gathered around them in the misty forest, he could not hear anyone sucking wind, and his own pulse was as steady as a metronome. It was Karl who spoke first.

"From here," he said softly, "it is maybe five hundred meters to the top. But there is no low cover, only the trees." He looked at Tag.

"Okay," Tag said. "Karl, you move out again at point, and I'll shadow you. Jan, Ham—you two flank me and pick your own cover. We'll all guide off Karl, until we have visual contact with the top. We can regroup there, or play it by ear, whatever comes up. If we get separated, I want everyone off this hill by 0100. But remember: We're just here to eavesdrop. Karl, go."

The litter on the forest floor was spongy beneath Tag's feet. Stretches of the climb were little more than fissured rock studded with teeth of evergreens and carpeted by a mossy humus of lichens and fallen needles. Even in the mist that was slowly rising to a drizzle, blanketing both sight and sound, Tag felt exposed and vulnerable as he moved from tree to tree, using his peripheral vision to keep track of the wraithlike forms of the other three men moving around him. He kept the battle sling of the Walther looped over his neck and held the gun close in both hands to prevent it from accidentally catching on a limb or clattering to the rocks if he fell. He could feel the light rain running off his watch cap and down his greased cheeks.

After every second or third move Karl would stop, and they would all pause to listen. Tag judged they were no more than a hundred meters from the crest when he first caught a sound from there: a hatch being opened against armorplate and a grunt that might have been a curse or a greeting. Ahead, he saw a ghost of movement as Karl moved laterally into a shallow gully. Jan, flanked to the right, saw it, too, and began angling toward him. Tag blinked water from his eyes until he made out Ham Jefferson's form off to his left and signaled him to close with the others.

As Tag low-crawled through the last twenty feet of wet compost, approaching Karl's position from below, he twice thought he whiffed the stench of shit.

When the four were lying together, Karl whispered to them all, "This is the center of their line, almost. Up there"—he tilted his head to indicate the gully—"is a latrine, about thirty meters from the nearest tank. A good place to listen, *ja*?"

The dime dropped in Tag's mind. He showed his teeth. "Not just to listen, gentlemen," he said. "I think we need a friend to take home with us. And I think it should be an officer."

Ham and the two commandos returned Tag's wolfish grin. He was liking these German boys more and more.

"What's the setup at the latrine, Karl?"

"Just a log across this low place to sit on, at the edge of the trees. Some brush beyond that."

"Anyplace I can get close, really close?"

"*Ja*," said Karl. "One tree the log rests against."

"All right, then, let's keep it simple," Tag said. "I snatch one; you guys take out any buddies he has with him; and then we all hiako. Got it."

The men all nodded, and Tag waved Karl forward.

They moved at a crouch from tree to tree until the smell from the latrine was unmistakable. Then they low-crawled to within twenty feet of the log seat. It was empty. Tag motioned all three of the others to take positions in the trees to the left while he slithered up the gully, trying without much success to stay on the high side and out of the effluents that had begun to trickle downhill in the rain. Tag made it to the base of the tree that Karl had described, its roots exposed by erosion on the downhill side, where he settled in the shadow not three feet from the log seat. The stench was ripe, stirred by the rain. Tag slipped the Walther's battle strap off over his head and had to make an effort not to breathe through his mouth.

It was nearly silent along the Soviet line as Tag waited in the gathering rain that kept the tankers inside their hatches. Somewhere farther along the crest he heard one, then two engines start. Charging their batteries, Tag thought. He hoped it also meant that the watch was changing—a good time to go take a dump.

All ears and eyes, Tag lost any sense of time. It might have been ten minutes or an hour that he waited before he heard the movement on the slope directly above him. The footsteps stopped. A voice said something in Russian, and two others responded. Tag could hear the scratch of plastic against the brush as the footsteps came closer. Then he could see them, approaching from his right front—the silhouettes of two soldiers in ponchos, carrying AKs, a third man empty-handed, wearing a cloth cap and raincoat. The two ponchos stopped and faced away from the latrine as the raincoat approached it. Tag leaned a fraction farther back in the shadow.

The Russian in the raincoat stepped down to the log, turned his back on it, and began hoisting the skirts of his slicker.

In a single blur of motion Tag stepped out and around the tree, his foot sinking into something soft, and whipped the Walther's battle strap over the Russian's head, twisting the weapon as he turned to pull the man backward and down, back to back with him.

As the Russian clawed at the nylon webbing that bit into his throat and kicked ineffectually at the backs of Tag's churning legs, the two soldiers in ponchos turned toward the noise, only to be met by a silent volley of 9mm fire from Ham and the two commandos. All Tag heard was the clatter of their AKs and the heavy sound of men going down with no effort to break their falls. Even as he ran broken-field through the trees with the struggling prisoner on his back, he thought he had never heard a sound so loud before.

Tag ran as far as the place in the gully where they had hatched their plan before he realized that the man on his back was growing weaker, flopping more than fighting, and that he himself was blowing hard, adrenaline beating like thunder in his ears.

Tag slung the man off his back and into the gully and was on him at once, untwisting the sling and jabbing the suppressor muzzle against the Russian's upper teeth. The man gagged and clawed his throat. Ham Jefferson slid in beside Tag, a Lyle fighting knife at once at the prisoner's jaw, just below the ear.

"Slick as owlshit, Sarge," Ham said, sucking rain off his upper lip. "Those dudes were buttoned up so tight, they didn't hear squat."

Tag stuffed a battle dressing in the Russian's mouth, wrapped the ends tightly around his head, tied them off, then turned him over and lashed his wrists together with another.

"Where are Karl and Jan?" Tag said.

"They're stashing our two KIAs in the woods."

Tag rolled his prisoner back over and pulled him up into a sitting position. Tag read anger and amazement in his eyes but no sign of fear. Tag grabbed the man to pull him to his feet. The Soviet went limp.

"Fuckin' passive-resistance bullshit," Tag sputtered, and drew back a fist. "If we carry you, Ivan, it's gonna be unconscious."

"Sarge," Ham said quickly, "let me show you a little trick."

Faster than Tag could follow, Ham had his knife back out, its point digging into the Russian's crotch at about the base of his balls. Ham held his face close to the Russian's and increased the pressure on his knife hand. This time Tag saw fear in those widening eyes. The Russian jackknifed to his feet as Jan and Karl rematerialized in the rain.

Tag motioned them all to move out, while Ham stroked the Russian's buttocks with the point of his blade.

"Let's boogie, Boris," he said quietly, "or I'm gonna carve me some red meat."

Even with the prisoner to slow them, the recon party was back in the cavern in little more than an hour. Betcher and three of the Jagd Kommandos met them coming up the slope.

Betcher looked at the trussed Russian, sniffed, and wrinkled his nose. "Any problem?" he said to Tag.

Tag mimicked Betcher's characteristic shrug. "If you're catching pigs," he said, "you have to get a little shit on your shoes."

Once inside, Betcher took charge of the prisoner, and when Tag returned from changing into a clean uniform,

Giesla was sitting on an ammo crate, facing the Russian, who squatted on the floor drinking coffee from a canteen cup.

Tag knelt beside her. "What have we got here, Gies?" he said. "Anything Ham can help with? Seems that Ivan here gets nervous around black men with knives."

"No, Max," she said matter-of-factly. "This one is very talkative. Do you know who he is?"

"Just the first one we could snatch. An officer, right? Anybody special?"

"Sergeant Tag," she said in mock formality, "I would like you to meet Colonel Yegevny Goudonov, commander of the Lenin Regiment of the Eleventh Guards Tank Division."

Tag whistled softly. "Or so he says."

"His documents confirm it," Giesla said.

The Russian on the floor saluted Tag with his cup and spoke to Giesla in Russian.

"What's he say?" Tag asked impatiently.

"He says," Giesla replied, "that you and the others are daring soldiers, and that he will see that you are treated well after you surrender."

"Surrender!" Tag snorted. "The sonofabitch has gall, I'll say that for him. Why does he think we will surrender?"

"He says that after tomorrow—I think he means today —that when the 'bubble,' as he called it, of resistance collapses in this sector, it will be impossible for us to reach our lines."

"A bubble," Tag mused. "Sure, a bulge. That explains it. Most of their advance *is* past Nürnberg, maybe even waiting for this bunch to catch up."

He faced Betcher, who stood glowering at the Russian. "What does all this tell you, Mathias?"

"Enough," said the big commando. "I hope 0400 is not too early for you."

9

Tag only catnapped, and when he did, he dreamed maps. On one of them he plotted the No Slack's route in red, through the gap between Scheinfeld and Neustadt an der Aisch, and from there toward Mannheim, crossing the Tauber at Bad Mergentheim. In his dream he could see the names in German but could not say them. His red line strayed to canals and railroad tracks, searching for a word he knew.

Tag awoke and checked his watch—0335. He was weary—not truly tired but feeling the effects of an adrenaline hangover simmering in uncertainty. With all he had had to think about, he had, he knew, been blocking a lot out of his thoughts, especially concerning Prentice and his men. Like it or not, Tag felt annealed to them now, forged by combat. Holz and his bunch were pros—they knew the score and they knew the odds—but he couldn't shake a nagging sense of responsibility for the scant platoon of clerks and ordnance men under Prentice's command. Nor could he stop his cock from beginning to swell when he thought of Giesla.

Tag got up and went to the latrine, and when he came back, the rest of the crew was stashing their gear and giving the No Slack a final once-over. Flashlights were bobbing among Prentice's platoon, and from the Jagd Kommandos came sounds of belts being jacked into machine-gun receivers, and of recoilless rifle breeches locking their lugs behind armor-piercing rounds. No need for reveille before a battle, Tag quoted to himself, all the while praying it wouldn't be that, not a fight, not with this ragtag and unattached detachment.

At 0415, Tag was standing in the mess area, eating a cold sausage sandwich and appreciating the last of the fresh coffee, when Betcher found him.

"Max," the commando sergeant said to him, "I'm having the wounded put in the Bradley, except Lieutenant Ruther. She will ride with Jan in the lead, in my vehicle. Next the Bradley, then the truck and the rocket stands. I will be with them, and you will cover the back."

"Fine with me," Tag said. "What's the rendezvous if we get split up?"

"The wood I showed you yesterday. At the south end it narrows into a farm valley. After that we must wait until dark."

"I'll have my crew ready."

"Good. We will use the same tunnel we came in. There is a way to the top from that side, where we are out of sight."

In a half hour Tag sat with his head through his open hatch, watching the last of the missile racks disappear down the dark tunnel. He gave Wheels the order and felt the clutch engage. At last they were moving.

When they emerged through the false-rock opening into the dark before the dawn, Betcher was there to seal the cliff behind them. Tag followed the Jagd Kommando up the trackless ridge until they reached its humped crest and halted on their side of it.

Betcher got out and walked from his idling vehicle back to the No Slack. "Max," he said, "I have sent Jan ahead with Lieutenant Prentice and his people. But I am a sponger, *ja*? I cannot leave all those tanks on the ridge with my missile tubes still full. *Ja*? But you, you must go. I know your orders."

Tag stood in the hatch. "I got orders, and I got orders, Mathias," he said. "One order I have is to engage the enemy; the other is to get this tank back intact or not at all. If they smoke me, I've fulfilled both my orders. No, mister, you don't get these ducks all to yourself."

Betcher grinned largely.

"You got a place we can fight from?" Tag asked.

Betcher led the tank past where the crews of the other two gun vehicles were deploying their unhitched missile racks along the upper edge of the military crest, their vehicles parked farther down, protected from direct fire. About seventy-five meters beyond the second missile stand, Betcher stopped again and motioned the No Slack to pull abreast of him.

"Max," he said, "I fight from here. You will find a flat place there"—Betcher pointed down the ridge—"where the woods come over the top. Shoot the cannons first, Max."

Betcher and Tag both froze, as at the same moment they heard the incoming whine of artillery, then the ground-jarring explosions of the allied barrage on the Soviet positions shuddered through the earth beneath them.

"Wheels, go," Tag ordered, and the No Slack moved

forward at a fast idle. Tag directed his driver higher up on the crest. With the distraction of the artillery barrage, he was not concerned about their profile moving across the dark horizon, only with getting to a place where they could join the fight.

Tag halted the tank at the edge of a thicket of small firs that spanned a flat saddle of the ridge.

"Too dark," he said through the mike in his CVC. "Load HE and stand by; I'm going naked."

Tag slid down over the glacis of the No Slack and darted into the thicket of evergreens. A half minute of slapping around in the dark told him that the thicket was all saplings—no heavy trunks—and there was just enough slope to protect the tracks and, he hoped, keep the turbines' heat signature below the crest.

A salvo of return fire from the Soviet positions flickered through the thicket a second before Tag heard the thunder. He broke from the thin timber and shouted to Wheels, "In here, Hot Rod. Guide on me."

Wheels jammed the No Slack through the firs, juking it around at Tag's hand signals until the tank was set. Tag leapt back in his hatch.

A salvo of incoming counterbattery fire fell long into the valley beyond the Soviet howitzers' reverse-slope positions. The Communist 152s responded.

"Target!" Tag barked as the muzzle flashes from the nearest platoon of self-propelleds blossomed digitally on his thermal sight.

"Confirmed!" Ham responded.

"Shoot."

"Shot."

Tag did not bother to "splash" the round: a fireball erupting on the Soviet ridge did that, washing out his thermal scope in a sea of VDT green. He panned right and found the second platoon of guns, just at the limit of the 120-mm's maximum accurate range, twenty-five hundred meters away.

"Target one, mark," Tag ordered his gunner.

"Mark."

Tag moved the turret a fraction. "Target two, mark."

"Mark."

"Target two, shoot."

"Shot."

Even as the green heat signature of the explosion blazed across his screen again, Tag called, "Target one, shoot."

"Shot."

The image on the thermal scope throbbed, intensified, and grew. "Spa-lash," Tag pronounced. "Oh, yes, a splash."

He leaned into his IR periscope. Through it he could see missile trails like tracers arcing across from ridge to ridge and crashing into the Soviet tank positions, wave after wave of them, as Betcher seemed intent on emptying his tubes.

Another volley of incoming long rounds momentarily confused themselves in Tag's mind with the impact of an AT-8 Songster missile, tube-fired from one of the Soviet T-80s, that detonated against the face of Betcher's number-two missile rack, killing both the Jagd Kommandos manning it. He heard Betcher break radio silence in German, then Ham shout, "Target, Sarge. We're taking counterfire."

"Target," Tag confirmed, reading his own screen. "Sabot." He heard the loading carousel whir, and the sabot locked home.

"Shoot!"

"Shot."

The sabot separated from its core projectile, struck the slightly downward-sloping rear deck of the T-80, and tore through to the ammunition well, causing a downblast that lifted the Soviet tank tracks over turret and sent it crashing in flames down the ridge.

An HE round from another T-80 blew a gout of rock and dirt from the slope opposite the No Slack, peppering its skin with a harmless shower of dust and stones.

"They see us, boss," Wheels said, idling up the turbines.

"Steady," Tag said over the intercom. "Target." A .50-caliber spotter round from one of the gun buggies spat like a meteor across his IR scope.

"Target," Ham responded.

Between Tag's "Shoot!" and Ham Jefferson's "Shot!" there was time for Tag to see the streaks and afterimages of two 106mm recoilless rounds converging on the same target. The almost simultaneous impact of them with the 120-mm sabot ruptured the T-80 like a rotten piñata.

A horrendous concussion blasted the No Slack from its fighting position as two cassettes of reactive armor detonated a shaped-charge armor-piercing round fired from one of the surviving Soviet tanks. Inside, the crew were thrown against their seat harnesses, cracking their CVCs against hatches and breeches and 300mm slick-skin armor.

"Well, kiss mah money-loving ass," Wheels bitched, spitting blood from a split lip.

"Report," Tag called.

"Strack," Ham said.

"Okey-fuckin'-dokey," Fruits confirmed.

"Wheels?"

"Ah, shit, boss. Number-one turbine ain't revvin'. Throttle's dead."

"Butcher Boy, Butcher Boy," Betcher's voice came over the tactical radio, "run with me."

"Wheels," Tag ordered, "go with what we got. Hard left, and hit it."

Wheels Latta jammed the No Slack into a tight, track-spinning maneuver that turned them in place, then let the tank lunge forward as one gun vehicle tore past towing a missile rack, followed by two more with empty hitches. In the east, the dawn was red beneath the last, lingering clouds of the previous night's rain.

The tank and the three commando vehicles raced through the woods in the rising light until they finally broke over the watershed's divide and into a heavy forest that spread south and west toward the dairy farms and vine-yards that marked the fall of land toward the River Tauber. Ten minutes into the forest, Betcher called a halt.

Tag came out of his hatch and walked ahead. In the first vehicle he passed, a young Jagd Kommando sat slumped over the wheel, either gasping or sobbing, and in the second vehicle Karl sat alone and mute, his eyes locked in a thousand-meter stare. Betcher was standing behind the lead car, leaning against its full rack of unfired missiles, his face a mask of impassive sadness.

Tag was overwhelmed by a flood of grief, shock, and understanding, abashed that he had been calling the engagement a victory in his mind. He stopped five feet from Betcher.

"Mathias," he said. Betcher did not move.

"How bad?" Tag said this time.

"There was not enough time for me to fight my missiles, even," Betcher said, his voice high and hollow. "My best crew, they were the first, and they die for it," he droned bitterly.

"They got them, though," Tag said. "I know they must have hit at least three."

"Yes," Betcher said, and he shuddered and looked levelly at Tag. "Yes, we hurt them, but they were better than I thought."

"A missile?" Tag asked. "A Songster?"

Betcher nodded.

"How many hits did you count?" Tag asked.

"Seven, maybe eight tanks; three or four of the guns."

"Yeah," said Tag. "Three, I think. And we got their CO. We hurt them bad, Mathias."

"*Ja*," the burly commando agreed, "but many victories like that, we do not survive. Come."

Betcher turned, walked to the passenger side of his vehicle, and unclipped the radio handset from the dash. He punched a sequence of the numbered buttons in its handle and keyed the handset twice. Tag stood by in silence, until the handset hissed against Betcher's ear so loudly that Tag could hear, repeated twice, the opening chords of Beethoven's Fifth Symphony—boom-ba-ba-boom, boom-ba-ba-boom.

Betcher replaced the handset and turned toward Tag.

"The others are safe," he said, "one half hour from here. But what of you? Your tank took a hit, *ja*?"

"The reactive armor took most of it; we just got slapped around by the blast. But we've got no throttle to one turbine, and the radio Fruits rigged was all in the floor around my feet, last time I saw it."

"But you can go?" Betcher asked. "You are still—how is it you say—in the team?"

"Still on the game," Tag said, deadpan.

"Okay," said Betcher briskly. "We go."

Within the half hour that Betcher had promised, the No Slack and the three commando cars had crawled just over three miles through dense woods, trackless save for game trails, and come to a stand of old hardwoods with room enough among the trunks to hide a battalion of armor.

Tag directed the No Slack to a spot near the American vehicles and the gun buggie in which Giesla rode, and told Wheels to kill their power. "All right, shade tree," he said to the driver, "you wiggle some wires and get that turbine working. Fruits, you reassemble this goddamn Heathkit of yours. And Ham, I want you to check all systems and survey the damage from our hit. Replace those cassettes, if you can. Now move, we may not have much time here."

As the crew took up their orders, Tag walked toward where the Bradley sat with its rear ramp and hatch yawning open. He arrived a step behind Betcher.

Betcher walked to the rear of the Bradley and nodded to Weintaub, Prentice, and Giesla, who stood by the ramp. Inside, Holz lay on one of the folding bench seats, his head resting on a nylon rucksack. Colonel Goudonov sat on the opposite bench, trussed, gagged, and impassive.

"How is he?" Betcher said.

"He is not traveling well, Mathias," Giesla replied.

"What happened?" Tag asked.

"Nothing," Prentice reassured him. "He's just badly hurt, Sergeant Tag, and in a lot of pain. He passed out on us an hour ago, but Bones says his pulse is good. What happened back there, anyway?" Prentice worked his left hand in a fist, squinting angrily at the pain.

"Targets of opportunity," Tag replied. "Sergeant Betcher lost two men, but we really pounded them, Lieutenant. Half a battery of their guns and more than half their tanks. We took a hit on the No Slack, but we're still rolling." Tag caught the eye of Goudonov inside the Bradley and gave him a breezy two-finger salute.

They all turned at Holz's voice coming from inside the Bradley: "Who, Sergeant Betcher? Who did we lose?"

Holz was up on one elbow, and Betcher sat on the ramp to talk to him.

"*Lund und Schmieding*," Betcher said. "First Battery. We recovered their vehicle."

But Heinrich Holz had slipped back into unconsciousness.

"Mathias," Giesla said, "get us your maps."

With the ad hoc command staff gathered around the maps spread on the fender of the Bradley, Giesla leaned on Tag's shoulder to take the weight off her stitched leg, as they brainstormed possibilities about the Soviet deployments between themselves and the NATO air umbrella. East-west fire trails through this forest could allow the Soviet forces to traverse it, and they might now be deploying anywhere along its western edge, past it, or have bypassed the area altogether.

When they had all stood in silence for a ten-count, Tag said, "My whiz-kid loader was right: It's just like feeling down a dark hall for an open door that you hope isn't an air shaft."

"Sergeant Tag," Prentice said, "we are in an escape-and-evasion mode, are we not?"

Tag wished he wouldn't talk that way but said, "Yes, sir."

"Then we put foot recon out front and flank."

"Trip wires," Tag said.

"Exactly," Prentice agreed. "We can't move fast in these woods—Holz couldn't take it, anyway, and I need another . . . another shot myself, before I get back in there."

"Lieutenant," Tag said, "we can't ask your guys to do that. They're ordnance and supply people, not a Ranger platoon."

Prentice squinted at him, then relaxed into a thin smile. "Hell, Sergeant," he said, "there's nothing about this outfit that's TO. I've got twenty soldiers and Sergeant Dunn I can put out."

"Can Dunn make it?" Tag asked, reassured by the idea of the tough little NCO being in charge.

"He can make it," Prentice said. "I'll give every man two LAWs and keep two Dragon teams staged in the truck."

"Communications?" Giesla said.

"We have a half dozen of the new PR-Ms."

Tag and Betcher exchanged a glance.

"Mathias?" Tag asked.

Betcher pointed with his shoulder toward Giesla. "I am not in command," he said.

Giesla increased her weight on Tag's shoulder. He looked at her uneasily. She grinned like a cat.

"I think," Giesla said, composing her face and looking down at the map, "Lieutenant Prentice has a sound idea. Now, what will be our options if we make contact?" She pushed off Tag and leaned forward on the fender.

It took them another half hour to plan, organize, and equip the patrol. Aside from the walking wounded, Prentice held back just the Dragon crews and drivers for the Bradley and the truck, giving Dunn two eight-man squads. In addition to their M16s and LAWs, every man carried a two-hundred-round drum of .223s for the four Squad auto weapons issued among them. Tag helped one soldier settle a twisted patrol harness on his shoulders.

"Bullets and Band-Aids, water and a weapon," he said quoting a boot camp litany. "Looks like you're light to fight, soldier."

"Yeah, and quicker on my feet," the soldier said seriously. "Thanks, Sarge."

Tag felt better about the patrol after going through the briefing with the men and helping them saddle up. They were keyed up, sure, but not fidgety or playing grab-ass. Some of them were probably playing war at Fort Polk six months ago, Tag reflected. Chances are they remembered more about weapons and tactics than Weintaub. The thought was a poor consolation.

Tag rejoined his crew, to fill them in and check on the status of the No Slack. Ham had replaced the reactive-armor blocks, but the scorched ones around the point of impact marked it clearly. He also showed Tag where the explosion had warped the flange around the base of the turret, causing them to scrape together but not quite bind. Wheels calculated that this same hit had transferred its force through the one-piece armor, damaging the turbine.

"I got the throttle working, boss," the driver told Tag, "but there's some kinda bad vibration in the lower fan shaft. Can't get to that without a shop."

"Will it still run?" Tag asked.

"Till it stops," Wheels said noncommittally.

Fruits Tutti's luck was equally mixed.

"There's nothin' broke, Sarge," he said, holding up a radio module trailing wires and clips like some cybergenic octopus. "But it ain't gonna stay dat way if ya leave it hooked up. I can wire it in anytime ya need it, but ya better just monitor on de AUX." The AUX was the auxillary command monitor, with no sending capability.

Tag shook his head. "Tutti," he said, "I thought you had to speak English to get in the Army."

"Yeah," said Fruits, wrapping the wires around the module. "Dat or Bronxese."

"You're lucky you got me, Sarge," Ham Jefferson said, speaking through the hatch. "These two gray-meats need a translator just to talk to each other. Southern-bred and city-born, I am. The worst of all possible worlds."

"Okay, everybody," Tag said, "saddle up. We've got a

little while before our infantry calls in its first checkpoint, and we need to have our column formed."

Betcher took point in his own vehicle, with Jan, followed by Weintaub in the Bradley—along with Holz, Giesla, the two wounded, and the Soviet colonel—then the deuce-and-a-half towing the remaining missile stand, and finally the No Slack. The two other commando vehicles were split out on the flanks.

The forest was a nightmare and the pace of advance excruciating. Unthinned stands of second-growth timber would not allow them through; briars hid stumps and ditches. It reminded Tag of illustrations from his childhood copy of the Brothers Grimm—a perfect spot for trolls and ogres. But there was no running here. They moved at a crawl for fifteen minutes, then waited for the recon report before moving the next stage. Start. Stop. Wait. Go. And listen—always listening—to the trees, the wind, the radios.

At noon Dunn sent a runner in to report that they had crossed the first fire trail. It had been heavily traveled by both tracked and wheeled vehicles, all headed west. It was the only sign of Soviet activity they had found in the forest. So far.

Twice they heard fixed-wing aircraft whistling past somewhere above them, and at 1440 they began to hear the boil of battle coming from near their old position in the hills. The Soviets had obviously regrouped after their bushwhacking that morning and were now mounting their offensive on the allied bulge. Going over the maps in his mind, Tag could see no reason the Soviets should have stopped here. The line had to be ten or fifteen klicks to the west. And most of that was open dairy land and fruit orchards, all hatched with rock farm roads and a pair of macadam north-south highways. It was good country for a fight, and a bad one in which to hide.

They crossed the second fire trail, also well and recently traveled, then halted for a quarter hour while Weintaub, in the Bradley, winched Betcher's scout car off a rotting deadfall. The recon patrol reported it was halting at its next to last checkpoint.

At 1715, the convoy assembled with the patrol at the top of a steep ridge where the forest ended abruptly and the land fell away into a cultivated valley and hills of fruit and cattle. Directly below them, on a tier above the floor of the valley, sat a timber farmhouse, and below it a stone barn, a silo, and a concrete milking shed. A rock road led west from the farm. Following it with his binoculars, Tag passed from the splintered top of the silo and the two cows and a calf grazing near the house, to the flattened fences and torn hedgerows, then into the hills that themselves looked bruised by the treads of Communist armor—gaps in orchards and, here and there, a dark plume of heavy smoke twisting behind a rise—and farther still, to the saw-toothed horizon of wooded hills where Tag now felt certain the Soviets had halted. It was smelling again like rain.

Betcher sent Jan and Karl down to scout the farm on foot, and in minutes they radioed an all-clear. The vehicles, with the GIs from the patrol aboard, circled east into the head of the hollow and approached the farmstead from its highest pastures, following the gouged path of Warsaw Pact armor.

As they drew nearer, Tag could see that, except for crushed fences and the shell-shattered cornice of the silo, the place was practically untouched. The plain wooden house with its brightly painted gingerbread facade looked like a quaint tourist shop. Geraniums bloomed in boxes by the door.

In the barn, where Tag pulled the No Slack up behind the three gun vehicles, there was even a single light bulb still burning in a metal reflector hung above a partially disassembled tractor that stood beside a greasy tool bench.

Jan and Karl had directed the Bradley and the truck into the concrete milking shed. After a quick word with Betcher, Tag left the crew to scrounge for tools and fuel, then walked across the barn lot to the milking shed to look in on Holz. The first fat raindrops from the gathering clouds splattered on the hard-packed earth.

Inside the shed, a concrete aisle with a drainage trough down the middle ran between two rows of milking stalls equipped with electric stainless-steel milking machines attached to a network of clear plastic hoses that carried the milk to the refrigerated warehouse at one end of the shed. The place smelled of sour milk and disinfectant.

Tag edged around the missile stand and the deuce-and-a-half that carried the footsore soldiers from the recon patrol and walked to the open rear of the Bradley. Goudonov was still hog-tied in one corner. Holz was sitting up next to Lieutenant Prentice on the other bench. Weintaub, Bones, Giesla, and the two wounded men stood by the ramp, stretching. Holz and Prentice each wore a sloppy grin—the one from concussion, the other from morphine, Tag guessed. In any other situation they would have been a comic pair, and even now Tag had to suppress a smile.

"How's casual company doing, Top?" he said to Weintaub.

"Loose and light," Weintaub responded, rubbing his lower back. "But we've got a couple of officers here that could stand being still for a while. I don't think adding four feet to these Bradleys has done a damn thing for their ride."

"They made sure of that when they put that heavier turret on for the 75mm," Tag said, "and added the extra armor."

"Sergeant Tag," Prentice said deliberately, like a drunk choosing his words, "when you get back to Fort Hood, you tell them to put on a little more, just for me."

Tag grinned at him and turned back to Weintaub. "Okay, Top. I had a word with Sergeant Betcher just a minute ago, and I think we all agree. Let's hole up here for a few hours, get some rest, and try to get some intel from my head-quarters. Depending on what we find out, I want to be across that open country before it gets light. My hunch is that our time is running short. Not to mention fuel and ammo."

"Max," said Giesla, "can we move the men into the house? This place smells like baby puke."

"Yes," Weintaub said before Tag could reply. "I'll leave a couple of men with the vehicles. Let's get out of here."

"Okay," said Tag. "I'll meet you all there."

10

The first thing Tag and Weintaub had to do was keep the men from turning on the electric lights in the house, although they left on those that were already burning in the kitchen. But even with this nod to discipline, Tag could see it was going to be hard to stall a party. Whoever ran this dairy farm must have a big family or a lot of hired hands, for the refrigerator was chockablock with eggs and hams and sausages. The pantry was bursting with canned fruits and vegetables, preserves, pickles, homemade sauerkraut, even two one-pound tinned loaves of French pâté, a whole ripe cheese, and a dozen sticks of hard rye bread. But the real problem was in the cellar dug into the side of the hill, where Dunn and an ambitious Italian corporal found the wine and beer.

The single calf that Tag had spotted earlier could not give sufficient relief to the swollen udders of the two cows, so Tag now watched from the porch as Wheels—who had been left to look after the No Slack—and two of the GIs tried to milk them into their helmets, while the cows jostled at the door of the milking shed with the single-minded bovine intent of standing content at the electric machines inside.

Fruits Tutti joined Tag on the porch. The rain was not yet hard but was falling as heavily as scattered grapeshot on the flagged walk that ran to the farm lot. Tag took a long pull on his first bottle of the local beer with the unpronounceable name.

"Whadda fuck's he doin' to dat cow?" Tutti said in shock.

"He's milking it, Fruits."

"Jeezus," Tutti whined, "no. That's disgusting. *Milk* comes outa dem wax cartons. Dat's sick, Sarge. Buncha fuckin' animals."

"You just come out here to deliver an editorial, Mr. Tutti?" Tag asked.

Tutti broke his gaze away from the grotesque spectacle of the driver leaning his head against the side of a Brown Swiss cow while he manipulated her privates with both hands.

"Da fuel oil for dis place," Fruits said, "it's a number-two diesel, and dere's two hunnerd gallons of it in the tank out back."

Tag drank from his beer and nodded. "Good," he said. "The Bradley can probably use it too. And there's got to be gas for that tractor in the barn somewhere. You want to rewire the ComNet now or grab some chow first?"

"Yeah, let's do it," Fruits said. "Dat Geese, she's puttin' dem legs to work makin' some kinda friggin' banquet or somethin'. Fuggin' milk," Tutti shivvered, flapped his lips, took a swig of beer, and stepped off the porch into the rain ahead of Tag.

Tag paused just inside the barn to shake the rain from his hair before he slid into the driver's seat and started the port turbine, while Tutti sat in the commander's chair hooking up the makeshift ComNet module. Tag turned on the VDT maps, recorded their coordinates, and encoded a brief message on his pad.

"Anytime you're ready, Sarge," Tutti said.

Tag handed him the message sheet. "Burp this," he said.

Fruits punched in the code and keyed the handset. They both waited.

"Butcher Boy, Butcher Boy, this is Queen Bee. Receive you five-by-five. Wait."

Tag listened to the open-channel static through his CVC, feeling an unexpected relief to be in contact with HQ. "Butcher Boy, this is Queen Bee Actual," Colonel Menefee's voice grated over the headset. "From your position, left one-zero klicks, you have a high fence to jump. Blackbirds are down to seven-five klicks from roost two. Sorry, Max. Queen Bee out."

"Fucking great," Tag muttered.

"What's dat, Sarge?" Fruits asked.

"Satin Ass tells me everything I already know and nothing that I need to know. The air umbrella is shrinking, Fruits, and there are bogeys in those far hills, just like I thought. But we've still got no idea where their line extends from there to the south."

"So, what's da drill?"

Tag sighed. "Eat, drink, and be merry, Mr. Tutti, for tomorrow, early, we sky."

"I always knew you wuz a reasonable man, Sarge."

Fruits rolled up the wires to the module, put the whole affair in a sock, stashed it in Tag's cubbyhole, and hauled himself out of the hatch.

Wheels Latta came in the barn, swinging a helmet full of frothy milk by its chin strap. "Hey, Fruits," he called, "y'all want a slash of fresh moo juice?"

"Aargh!" Fruits Tutti croaked, making the sign of the cross with two fingers held in front of him. "Get away from me, you fuggin' pervert." He backed out of the barn door and kicked it shut behind him.

Wheels took a long draw from the helmet and wiped away the milk mustache with the back of his hand. "What's ol' Tutti Fruity's problem, boss?" he asked.

"Personal problem," Tag replied. "His mama was scared by a milkman. You want a beer?"

"Naw, just give me some relief later; I hear they got real groceries up at the house."

"That's affirm. I'll come down and relieve you in a bit, Wheels. Sure you don't want a beer?"

"I *never* drink and drive, Max. That's how come they never caught me."

"Later," Tag said as he left.

He sprinted through the rain up the hill to the house, pausing on the porch to slap water off himself and scrutinize the dark distance for any signs of activity on the far ridge across the valley.

Nothing.

In the light and warmth of the sprawling kitchen, Giesla stood by a massive iron stove, stirring the pots on top of it with a long wooden spoon and ordering GIs around like a drill sergeant: "You, find us some bowls, and tell your friend there to wash his filthy hands. Bring me the pepper. If you can't carve a ham, soldier, find someone who can."

Sergeant Dunn stood guard at the cellar door, rationing out bottles of beer with the help of Fruits Tutti, who kept glancing apprehensively at Giesla. Tag drew another bottle of beer from them, then joined Betcher, Weintaub, and

Prentice at one end of the long trestle table that dominated the kitchen. Next to them, Holz sprawled on an easy chair and hassock that someone had dragged in from another room. He was awake, looked comfortable, and had a ghost of his old, wolfish smile playing across his lips as he looked down at Colonel Goudonov, who sat on the floor with his hands bound.

"I just received a message from my HQ," Tag said.

"Any news?" Prentice asked. He looked less comfortable than Holz, but had none of the morphine haze about him.

"Nothing really good, sir," Tag said, straddling the bench. "As best I can tell, Ivan is sure enough setting up in the hills across the valley. They've pulled in the air support to seventy-five kilometers around Mannheim. But still no word on where the Soviet line extends, how fast it's moving—nothing."

"Max," Holz said, shifting in his chair, "that does not change our plans. We are going to get you out, and it does not matter where we do it. Only when, *ja*?"

Tag nodded. "But that 'when' has got to be now, tonight. If the Russkies have control of that next network of feeder roads, we will be in really deep kimchi."

"Maybe we can shake a little more out of our guest here," Weintaub said, nodding toward Goudonov.

"I think not," said Betcher. "Anything he knew is changed now; for us it is no good."

"He's probably right, Top," Tag said. "My call would be to eat, rest, and run. Maybe this rain and the element of surprise will give us the edge. But we'll lose it for sure if we don't do something."

Lightning flashed outside, followed by a long roll of thunder.

"Okay, Sergeant," Prentice said, "I'm convinced. Let's

feed, give the men a little rack time, and be out of here by—what?—0300?"

"Unless the rain fails before then," Holz said from his chair.

"And no more than three beers per man," Weintaub growled.

"A done deal," Tag said, saluting them all with his bottle.

Giesla came to the table and laid her hands on Tag's shoulders as he drank. "Before this becomes a drinking contest," she said, "all of you eat. Ham or sausage, Heinrich?"

The meal that Giesla's shanghaied KPs had concocted was a wonder. On the table were platters of sliced ham, sausage, cheese and bread, crocks of butter, and emerald jars of pickles. On the sideboard by the stove stood steaming bowls of corn, peas, beans, sauerkraut with caraway seeds, and heaps of boiled, buttered potatoes.

Tag filled a plate with some of everything and joined Ham and Fruits to eat standing up around a massive chopping block, its top concaved by decades of cleavers and knives. Pot liquor ran off their plates and collected in the hollow.

"Mmm-mmm," Ham Jefferson hummed in pleasure. "Now this is what I call the spoils of war."

"Yep," Tag said, sopping his plate with a hard heel of bread, "rape, kill, and plunder, the unalienable rights of guerrilla forces since the beginning of time."

"So when does da rapin' start?" Tutti mumbled through his full mouth.

"Soon as you put your hand under the covers," Ham said.

"Aw, fuck you," Fruits said.

"Huh-uh," Ham said to him. "I promised my mama I wouldn't be despoilin' no virgins."

Tag popped the last crust of bread in his mouth. "I'm going down to relieve Wheels," he said.

"Wait one, Sarge," Ham said. "Got something I want to show you."

"What's that?"

"Ah, he just found him a dry place to shit," Fruits grumbled.

Ham led Tag down the hall, using a mini-flashlight to guide them. He stopped outside a closed door and faced his tank commander. "For your delectation, my fearless leader," he said, opening the door and playing the light around inside.

"A bathroom!" Tag exclaimed. "So Tutti wasn't lying."

"I suggest," Ham said in a conspiratorial whisper, "that we be cool about the hot water. I don't know how much we got."

"Jefferson," Tag said, "you are a scoundrel, a thief, a sneak, and a man after my own heart."

"I'm flattered," Ham replied, "'cept for that last part."

"Okay," Tag said. "I'll be quick. But, listen, Gie . . . Lieutenant Ruther gets a crack at the shower before any of you scumbags. Got me?"

"I'll wash her myself," Ham said.

"No, Mr. Jefferson, I don't need a gunner with broken thumbs."

Tag took a navy shower, turning off the water while he lathered with the sweet soap from the dish, then scalding the suds off himself with a long blast from the spray head. He dried with a hand towel in the dark, stuffed his dirty skivvies and socks in his pockets, and tried to slip nonchalantly through the bustling kitchen. Sergeant Betcher stopped him near the door.

Betcher sniffed twice and almost allowed himself a smile. "I see," he said, "that you found the ladies' toilet. Such a nice smell for a soldier."

Tag could only grin sheepishly.

Betcher slapped him on the shoulder and slipped something hard and flat into Tag's jumpsuit pocket. "A little schnapps," he said, "to sweeten your breath as well."

"Okay," said Tag, "but it's my gunner you need to bribe."

"Bribe?" said Betcher, his eyes widening. "Who do you think told him?"

"Thanks, Mathias," said Tag as he went out the door.

Tag sent Wheels and the Jagd Kommando on duty in the barn back to the house. Then he stripped, found fresh socks and underwear in his duffel, redressed, and was sitting on the tractor seat beneath the light, updating the evaluation log, when Giesla came through the barn door.

"Hello," he said.

Giesla came and stood beside the tractor, the light falling hard on her face from the unshaded bulb. She had twisted her still-wet hair into a knot beneath her cap. Her skin was smooth as unveined marble, though no statue, however beautiful, ever possessed eyes like hers—intelligent, self-assured, and as blue as the big Montana sky, Tag thought.

"Hello, Max," she said, sitting a vacuum bottle and a knotted napkin on the engine cowling. "You left before the coffee and cake. I thought you might like some."

Tag shut the log and stepped down from his seat. "Thanks," he said, "but that dinner you rustled for us was too good. I'm stuffed. Coffee sounds good, though. Or"—he felt the weight of the flask in his pocket—"perhaps I could offer you a drink." He took out the flat, leather-covered bottle.

"Ah," she said appraisingly, "and do you invite me to your penthouse for this?"

Tag waved at the ladder to the loft. "Only to see my stamp collection," he said, uncertain how far the game would go.

Giesla ran her tongue over her lips. "Do I get to lick them?" she said, her voice either mocking or inviting, Tag could not tell which.

"Uh." He stalled dumbly.

Giesla's face lit with a girlish, impish grin. "Come," she said, taking up the vacuum bottle, "and I will show you my tattoos also."

Do I get to lick them? Tag thought as he followed her up the ladder.

One wall of the loft was pierced high up with a row of small windows, their shutters open, through which came the odor of rain and the ragged illumination of lightning. The freshly baled fodder in the loft still smelled of green, and Tag made a couch for them in one corner out of loose hay and broken bales.

Giesla sat beside him, holding her wounded leg out straight, and unscrewed the cap on the thermos. "A very nice penthouse," she said, "but I see you have no cups or glasses. Do you mind if we share?"

"No," said Tag, drinking in her profile as he leaned across to put the flask of schnapps on the bale beside her.

She poured a large measure of the clear liquor into the thermos cap, filled it with coffee, and handed the cup to Tag.

"After you," he said.

Giesla shook her head. "No, Max," she said. "This is something I like doing."

He took the cup and drank, letting the peppery vapors rise through his head as the liquor spread warmly through his belly and chest. Tag said, "Thanks," and returned the cup to Giesla, who also drank and set it aside.

"Another?" she asked.

"No."

"It would please me to make it for you," she said.

"I think you've already pleased a houseful of men," Tag said, regretting it almost at once.

But Giesla only laughed. "That," she said, "that was only necessary, what a good officer would do. Now they are not so pleased; now they are washing dishes."

"Guess I'd better make the best of this, then," Tag said. "Yes, another, please. Only this time I mix."

He reached across her to pour the coffee and schnapps into the cup and felt her breath against his neck. This is nuts, Tag thought, straightening slightly with the cup held between her lips and his. "Ma'am," he said, offering her the drink.

Giesla took the cup and Tag's hand in both of hers and looked at him over the rim as she drank and let her fingers play across his knuckles. Still holding on, she put the cup to his mouth. He drank. She set the thermos cap aside.

"Max," she said as she turned toward him, "what did Heinrich tell you about . . . about Africa?"

"That you were there, that they killed your husband."

"And that is all?"

"A little more, not much."

She slid into the circle of his arm and put her head against his chest. "I want to tell you all of it, Max. Can I tell you all of it?"

"Do you want to?"

"Yes," she said, holding tightly to the fabric of his suit. "It is something you can do for me.

"We were leading in the rally, Bobby and I, but we had drawn a late start that day. If we had been not so good, a little slower, we would have missed the ambush. We knew something was wrong at the checkpoint when we approached it. There were other cars sitting empty and no one at the roadside. I should not have stopped.

"Suddenly there were black men with scarred faces and rifles all over the car, tearing open the doors and hitting us. One of them hit Bobby in the face with a rifle, and a piece of skin fell over one of his eyes and blood poured out. Two others were trying to drag me from the car. Then I heard someone with a Russian accent say in French, 'Take them; take them.' Then the three black men got in the back and grabbed me by the hair and held rifles to my head and grunted and pointed into the bush.

"I don't know how I drove or how far. We came upon two Land Rovers, and I followed them until after dark, until we came to their camp. All this time Bobby sat with his head in his hands, and I thought he was dead. Now I am sometimes ashamed that I prayed for him to be alive.

"The worst part was not just what they did to me. They tied Bobby and poured water and whiskey on his open cut and laughed at him when he cried out. I screamed. I begged them not to hurt him. I said I would do anything they wanted if they would not hurt him. I even said it in Russian.

"Then the one, the Russian, came over where I could see him in the fire. He said, 'Yes, I know you will,' and then something in another language I did not know. And then . . . then there were hands on me everywhere, tearing my clothes, hitting me again.

"At first they raped me, lying there in the dirt beside the fire, one after another, except the Russian. Then someone took the backseat from the Audi and put it down. I thought it might be over, but instead they held me over it and raped me in . . . in the other place and made me take them in my mouth. They poured whiskey on me that smelled like vomit. They urinated on me. And then I passed out."

Giesla paused, took a tighter grip on Tag's uniform, then went on. "When I came to, I was tied to the seat, with my arms spread. They had tied my ankles to a long stick to hold my legs apart and pushed one of the whiskey bottles inside me. I was facing Bobby. They had been beating him some more, but when he saw I was awake, he began to curse them and call them cowards. The Russian said, this time in English, 'Now you can have back your German whore, if you still want her.' Then he spoke to the African men again in their own language.

"One of them took the rope that tied Bobby's hands behind his back and jerked him to his feet, pulling his hands out behind him. Another one took out a cane knife and he cut off Bobby's hands. I saw the one with the rope hold up the hands. They twitched, like crabs on a string. Then I saw Bobby looking at his arms, where his hands had been. They laughed as he ran to the fire and pressed them against a burning log and screamed.

"Then the Russian shot Bobby in the back of the head and he fell in the fire. Then he aimed the gun at me and I looked him in the face and he laughed again and shot the bottle between my legs.

"After that they all left, and left me there. All night I smelled Bobby's flesh burning in the fire. Finally I freed myself. They had not even taken the keys to the Audi. I drove back to the road alone; I could not look at Bobby, not even at the funeral."

Tag was no psychologist, but he knew enough to keep his peace and hold the woman with both his arms as the lightning forked and thunder boomed outside.

* * *

Giesla, dry-eyed, looked up at him. "I hate those men, Max, and not just the black men. What they did was savage and terrible, but it was not something they thought about. The other, the Russian, he knew he was being cruel, and he enjoyed it. But I am the one I have never completely forgiven. 'Survivor syndrome,' I think it is called, like those poor Jews who lived through the Nazi death camps but were still haunted by a sense of guilt, because they had not died too."

Tag had seen men under his command die, and he had accused himself for it. It was not the same, for he had had the chance to fight and purge those feelings, but he did understand what Giesla felt, how much worse it was.

"Why are you telling me?" he asked.

"I do not hate men, Max, I only wanted to feel clean again. Somehow, with all that is happening now, all of that past seems, I don't know—personal, petty. I think now it would be a luxury to despise myself. Now I have duty."

"But why me? Am I like your husband?"

"In some ways that are only American, yes." She held him close. "Max," she said, "I am going to cry now."

And she did, with racking, wretched sobs.

When she had stopped, she sniffed, wiped her eyes on Tag's shoulder, and looked again at him.

"Max," she said quietly, "there is one more thing you can do."

"Make you another drink?" he said.

"Make love to me."

Whatever Tag had hoped, thought, or expected, he was caught unawares. "Now?" was all he could manage.

She slipped from his embrace and stood in the dim light of the loft. Without a word she unzipped her jumpsuit, shook it from her shoulders, and stepped out of it naked, except for her boots and cap. Her smile was one part mischief and one part brave front, but there was no mistaking the nervous anticipation in her voice. "Am I," she said, "an old war-horse yet?"

Tag stood and took her face in both his hands and kissed her eyes, her cheeks, her lips. Her mouth opened hungrily as she stripped the zipper of his jumpsuit down the front and pushed it back over his shoulders. He tried to kick his legs free; she peeled away his T-shirt. They sank together on the couch of hay, and Giesla winced as Tag's hand brushed the bristled ends of her sutures.

She relaxed and pulled his hand back between her legs. "Carefully, Max," she whispered.

Giesla held his cock, so large that she needed both her hands, while she grew wet beneath his touch and his tongue. Keeping a hand on him, she turned away and raised one leg, bracing her foot against the knee of her wounded leg.

"Like this," she said.

And then Tag found her from behind, found the hot, wet lips of her sex with the dry wedge of his own, found her breast with one hand and her belly with his other. He held her still and entered her slowly, as a high moan emptied from Giesla's throat. She began to move, and he with her. He bit her shoulder, and she twisted to kiss his lips. His hand slipped down her belly, past the blond delta of her pubis, and into the wet course of their delight. He could feel himself in her, and he could feel her tiny shoal of pleasure swell beneath his touch: a seal rolling in oil. So they touched and moved until the touching and the moving were all there was and the world did not exist except as feeling and motion and the green smell of fresh hay. And then the lightning strobed again and froze them for the applause of thunder that ran through every stone of the old barn's walls, every moment of their being.

They lay together like that for a while, still breathing in
unison. Then Giesla moved away from him and made a
soft *ooo* of regret at they parted. They settled themselves in
the scattered hay and lay side by side, their fingers en-
twined.

"What do you think, Max?" Giesla said.

"Soul of eagle, heart of feather," he said.

"What is that?" she asked languidly. "What does it
mean?"

"An Indian saying," he replied, "from my home in
Montana. It means you are the sexiest thing in combat
boots I've ever seen."

"But only at this time, in this place. You understand
that, don't you, Max?"

"What do *you* mean?" he asked, rising on one elbow.

She turned toward him, her cap comically askew, spilling blond hair from its rim. She smiled. "Max, I have not
used you," Giesla said. "Another time, another place . . .
who knows? But today we may both die. We are both soldiers, Max. I did not want to die thinking I was a cripple.
This has been a happy accident for us."

"Well," he said, "who knows? Maybe when we get to
Mannheim, we'll have another accident, or two or three."

"No, Max. I know what you are thinking, but no. No
matter what you say or think, I am a soldier, a 'sponger,'
you say. You and the other Americans, we will get you out.
But our orders are here. This is my country, Max. That, at
least, you can understand, can you not?"

Tag did not believe women were any smarter than men,
but almost always wiser, capable of being terribly practical
even about sex. And in the case of this woman, he knew
her fiber, her toughness. This grappling had been transient
but not casual. Like her, he had to separate it from his duty,

keep it locked and hidden, like gold kept in a well in time of war.

"You want that other drink now?" he asked.

She squeezed his hand and stood, seeming to glow in the dark. "After we dress," she said, stooping to pick up their jumpsuits and dropping his across his middle.

They were back below, sitting in one of the gun vehicles and finishing the schnapps and coffee, when Ham Jefferson and the Kommando Karl came in.

"Hey, Sarge," Ham said, "they want you back at the house. You want me to fuel up?"

"Okay," Tag said, dismounting from the car. "You coming too?" he asked Giesla.

"Yes," she said. "If there is a bed, I am sleeping in it."

"Ham," Tag said to his gunner, "you grab some rack when you're finished. We could be pulling out anytime."

"I heard that," Ham said.

Once outside, Tag and Giesla took hands and ran through the rain and puddles, laughing like children, toward the lights of the house, where they stopped, composed themselves, and Tag held the door for her like a batman.

11

Tag sent Fruits and Wheels back, and after settling some details with Weintaub and Betcher about their order of march and contingency plans in case of an ambush, he returned to the barn to sleep with his tank and his crew. The men had the No Slack fueled and the guns cleaned. Ham was standing at the tool bench under the light, running a shell game on Karl and Jan with three grease cups and a ball bearing. Wheels was peeking through one of the turbine-access hatches with a flashlight, and Fruits sat on his bedroll, propped against the side of the tank, blowing the same note over and over across the top of an empty beer bottle.

"You better start blowing 'Taps' on that thing, Mr. Tutti," Tag said. "Ham, you look like a night owl. You take first watch; get me up in a couple of hours. The rest of you, into your fart sacks."

Tag spread his own bedroll and fell into a dreamless sleep. He awoke easily, to a feeling of great well-being, stretched in his sleeping bag, and looked at his watch. It was past midnight and Ham hadn't roused him.

Tag whipped the bag off his legs and leapt to his feet. "Ham!" he said sharply.

"Be cool, Sarge." Ham's voice floated down from somewhere above him. "They people trying to sleep."

Tag looked up and saw Ham's long brown face peering down from the loft. "I was supposed to relieve you more than an hour ago," Tag said.

"Oh, Sarge," Ham said. "I couldn't charge you for what time I spent in commerce, could I? But I'll consider myself relieved."

Ham climbed down, and Tag said to him, "What the hell are you going to do with Deutsche marks, anyway, Jefferson?"

"Shoot, I like this country, Sarge. I may wanna come back and buy me a piece of it."

Tag just shook his head.

"Oh, and, Sarge," Ham said, running his hand in the cargo pocket on the leg of his uniform, "I think these might be yours."

He pulled out a pair of OD-green boxer shorts and handed them to Tag.

"Well, thanks, Jefferson," said Tag. "I was cleaning these when they went off; didn't have any idea where they hit."

"I shot my wad off in the air, it came to earth . . ." Ham began to recite.

"Ham," Tag said seriously, "enough. Get some sleep."

Ham stopped short and cleared his throat. "Right, Sarge."

Tag tried to stay busy. He completed the entries in his

evaluation log, reviewed maps of their planned route, fiddled with his gear—anything not to think of Giesla. He didn't have much luck.

At 0200 he stepped outside to take a leak and saw that the rain was still falling steadily. Eager to be moving soon, Tag made a final, unnecessary systems check on the No Slack and roused the crew. After a few minutes Betcher, Giesla, and the other Jagd Kommandos came down from the house, bringing with them a pitcher of coffee, some cold meat, and bread. None gave any hint that he had noticed Tag's or Giesla's hour-long absence the evening before.

Tag said to Giesla, as she snapped the skirts of her slicker into coulottes, "Shouldn't you be in the Bradley with Rick?"

She gave him an irritated glance but said nothing.

"I mean," Tag said haltingly, "you could pop a stitch or something."

Giesla straightened and looked him full in the face, her own again a mask but with no hardness to it. "Don't you think I am well?" she said. "I am very well, Max, and now we have our duty."

Tag searched for words. "You're right," he said at length, and then held out his hand. "Shoot straight."

Giesla shook his hand with both her own. "And you keep safe," she said.

It sounded like good-bye.

Tag sent a final message burp to Menefee, to say they were on their way.

The column formed in the pelting rain, with Betcher leading, the No Slack next, followed by the truck, the Bradley, and the other two gun buggies. Once off the farmstead and onto the rock road that crossed the main valley, they accelerated to eighty kilometers per hour and ran in closed formation to the foot of the far hills, where they dispersed into a rain-blackened pear orchard, killed their engines, and listened for a quarter hour.

They reassembled and moved out at fifty-meter intervals, easing slowly through the open woods parallel to the road. At that pace it took the convoy nearly twenty minutes to reach the broad, flat back of the ridge that sloped away to the south and west. As the rain began to let up, they could hear distant reports of artillery.

Where the timber began to clear, Tag opened his hatch and stood in it. Ahead, he could dimly make out the silhouette of Betcher's gun vehicle, and behind, he could hear the laboring of the deuce-and-a-half. So far, so good.

Then they were hit.

Tag's skin tightened in the split second between when he heard the whoosh of RPGs and when explosions ripped the night around him. A block of reactive armor on the No Slack's flank blew, rattling Tag back inside his hatch; the cab of the deuce-and-a-half burst into flames, and men began spilling out the back; the Bradley's armor turned a fusillade of 25mm cannon fire.

The turret screamed against its warped flange as Tag swung their guns and screwed the focus of his IR scope.

"Half left," he ordered.

Small-arms tracers lashed Tag's field of vision. Then he could make out the profiles of BMPs, stationary, no more than a hundred meters away. They had sneaked into the rear of a motorized infantry-reconnaissance unit.

"Stop," Tag barked. "All guns, targets of opportunity."

As Wheels opened up with the coaxial 7.62mm, three shots from the 75mm sent hot brass clattering into the wire hopper, and Tag twisted up through the turret and threw back the hatch.

He hauled himself behind the faring of the .50-caliber,

released the mount, and turned the muzzle toward the burning BMP, as the turret moved around him, keening in complaint. Tag thumbed the .50-caliber's butterfly trigger and let the gun pound his shoulders like a jackhammer. He raked a long burst across the small arc along which the turret traveled, then began to pulverize positions where he saw muzzles flash. From his right rear he heard the roar of Betcher's 106s. The Bradley fired its 75mm, and Ham echoed with the No Slack's own. AK rounds crackled around Tag's head and shied whining off the faring of the gun. As they were hit two more BMPs squirted flames from their hatches, and the 25mm fire ceased. Two white trails from RPGs forked like phantoms out of the woods, bracketing Tag's head. He churned a hundred rounds into the crotch of their trajectories. Then the gas tank ruptured in the burning truck, lighting the No Slack and the Bradley and the thin skirmish line of GIs like a flare.

Tag slammed down the hatch and swung through the turret to his seat.

"Move it, Wheels. Hit the road and go."

As the No Slack juked and crashed through trees split and shattered by stray rounds and errant RPGs, Tag panned the forest with his IR and thermal scopes but couldn't read the jerking images.

The tank burst onto the road and steadied Tag's field of vision. He counted three—no, four—heat signatures approaching through the forest from the south. Shit, it must be a whole goddamn company, Tag thought. This was the chance they had planned for, the chance for the No Slack to break out, while the others drew the fire. But Tag knew that without the tank, the rest were, at best, a close match against what was probably six more BMPs, with infantry and at least one 73mm cannon, if not antitank missiles. But none of that would cut the brush like a 120mm sabot.

"Stop! Wheel left!" Tag barked. "Sabot! On my command."

At a distance of about three hundred meters, Tag tracked the profile of a turreted BMP as it flickered through the trees. No computer backup here; he had to look for an alley through the forest with no trunks large enough to deflect the sabot, then fire manually when the target entered the opening.

There!

"Shoot."

"Shot," Ham responded, and the main gun buckled back in its dampers and rocked the tank.

Tag was so intent on watching the BMP shudder to a smoldering halt that he was unaware of the two gun vehicles that careened past him, spinning their tires in the ditches to get around the No Slack, which sat athwart the narrow road and blocked it.

The TAC frequency radio cackled in Tag's CVC, as Weintaub's voice came through: "Butcher Boy, move it off the road. We're coming through."

"Wheel right and go," Tag told his driver. "Ham, stay on your sights."

As the No Slack made its turn the Bradley scooted through the far ditch around it, causing the Soviet RPG aimed at the troop carrier to strike the War Club mount on the left side of the tank's turret. The explosion ripped the rack from the turret in a confetti of twisted metal and battered the men inside.

"Nail it, Wheels!" Tag whooped as he hit the "fog" button and dense cubic meters of concealing smoke spewed from the rear of the tank. He shut it off when they broke past the military crest, and Betcher came over the radio, telling him to halt.

Wheels pitched the No Slack across a ditch and off the

road into the trees. Someone hammered on the hatch, and Tag came up for air.

"Max," Betcher said, "this is the time. But you need to take this with you." He motioned behind him, and Jan stepped forward with Goudonov.

"Why can't he go in the Bradley?" Tag said, instinctively not wanting a Soviet tank officer to see the guts of the No Slack.

"They are staying, Max. The lieutenant's order."

Tag silently and swiftly damned Prentice for a shavetail idiot, but there was no time to protest.

"Fruits, Ham," he ordered, "drag the sonofabitch in here and stash him somewhere in the turret."

A burst from a BMP's 25mm chain gun shredded the branches above them.

"Go now," Betcher said.

"We're history," said Tag.

The No Slack tore through the thinning forest, angling right until Wheels hit the road and opened the throttles. Tag elevated his seat pedestal a fraction so he could look over the lip of the open hatch as they drove for the southwest, toward the road that intersected the Mannheim Highway. The feeder road followed a stream and a strip of wooded valley—not the most direct route, and not one that would put them under air cover, but the only one that offered any concealment along the way. And they still had thirty kilometers of no-man's-land to cross before they reached it.

"All defenses up," Tag ordered. "Ham, you have any kind of damage report?"

"Lost one War Club rack, Sarge; we got three tubes still full and operational. Primary radar link on the 75mm is down again, but Fruits is working on it."

"Wheels?"

"The right-hand turbine is real funky, boss. It's only givin' me about sixty percent, and it's gulpin' fuel. Feels like there's some slack in the left track too. Maybe from that first hit, I don't know."

Tag felt it, too—the knock and vibration of something out of kilter, a gut-churning, syncopated shudder with every revolution of the treads. He made a quick time/distance calculation in his head.

"Wheels, run on the number-two turbine unless we need them both. Full throttle. We don't want to be in the wide open when the sun comes up."

"What happened to dose supply guys, Sarge?" Fruits Tutti asked nervously.

"They all got a change of MOs, Fruits," Tag told him. "That damn Prentice is either going to be making license tags at Leavenworth or be up for the CMH when this shit gets back to Seven Corps."

Wheels chuckled. "You gonna make the report, boss? Tell how he screwed things up?"

"Fuck 'im," Tag said. "He can do his own goddamn paperwork."

Tag scanned the rolling countryside through his IR scope, keeping the thermal sensors synchronized with its movement. The valley had been heavily populated and intensely farmed. The vineyards and orchards and fields of winter wheat were crowded across the landscape like a tight gingham plaid, with a house on every twenty or forty acres, it looked. He saw cattle and roaming pigs, stray dogs and loose horses, but no people. Neither, however, was there any sign of a battle. Gates were open here and there, but the stone walls and fences that gridded the valley were mostly intact. His thermal sensors detected nothing hotter than a fermenting compost heap. Tag called up his VDT maps.

"Wheels," he said, "you see this burg coming up on your map?"

"There where we cross the creek and turn south, boss?"

"That's it. Now listen. If Ivan has a forward position anywhere, it's gonna be in that vil. If we get hit in there, we're gonna run before we fight. Wheels, I want you to bring up both turbines and give us all you got until we're over the stream and into that flat country south of town. Got it?"

"Coming right up," Wheels said, urging the balky turbine to life.

The No Slack gathered speed to more than ninety kilometers per hour as they bore down on the village. Wheels swung through a right-angle turn onto the cobbled main street of the old town and held steady as their tracks knocked tops off the humped paving stones, scattering rock splinters like loose gravel. He made an open-field juke around a baroque fountain in front of the Gothic church in the middle of town, clipped an abandoned Volkswagen, took out an empty bicycle rack, and all but vaporized a plastic telephone kiosk, before he wrenched the tank back between the rows of two-story stone buildings, with their medieval balconies beetling over the street.

Coming from the direction it did, fast, and in the dark, the No Slack confused the four-man *spetsnaz* recon team, who had their listening post in the bell tower of the church. Their one glimpse of it was nothing they recognized. It gave Tag and his crew precious minutes of indecision, while the Soviet NCO in charge decided whether to break radio silence to ask for an identification.

Wheels shut down the damaged turbine and at seventy kilometers per hour ran roughly down the crown of a three-lane blacktop that hugged the wooded ravine of a creek and joined the autobahn just fifty miles from Mannheim. The rain had stopped, and the light fog that lay in the valley was just being grazed by the rising sun when the air-alarm horn squawked alert.

Tag killed the horn and keyed his radar link.

"I've got three at about five klicks and closing. Direction: zero niner hundred."

"Confirmed," Ham responded. "Too low and slow for fixed-wing."

"Okay," Tag said, "lock in the War Clubs. You have the 75mm on system yet, Fruits?"

"Just de backup, Sarge. Dat last lick's got all dese turret systems flaky."

"Do what you gotta, then. Wheels, you be ready to take us into the ditch. But if these birds are Hinds, they'll have thermals. So don't think you're gonna hide from 'em, got me?"

"I'll dazzle 'em with footwork," Wheels said.

"Suppose they're reading our radar, Sarge?" Ham asked.

"Not if our intel about their systems is even close," Tag said, double-checking a row of breakers. "Doesn't matter, anyway. Fifteen hundred meters is about tops for their AT ordn—"

"*Incoming!*" Ham shouted as the thermal signature of a launched missile separated itself from the superimposed radar image on his scope.

"Ditch it, Wheels," Tag said without hesitation.

The No Slack flattened a steel traffic retainer and went airborne for half its length, came down with a spine-crushing jolt, and rode over birch saplings with its glacis. Wheels worked the brakes and throttle, fighting for control of thirty tons of carbide, steel, and fighting men. The upper track caught, and the No Slack came up hard broadside against an immovable oak, throwing Wheels from his controls.

At the same moment a slender, two-meter long, heat-seeking antitank missile called the Tree Toad, issued for the first time by the Soviets for this invasion, looped once in confusion and augered in on the blacktop, burning through it like a water jet through mud and exploding six feet beneath the ground with a force that cratered two full lanes of the road.

"Give me a place to fight from, Wheels," Tag said urgently. Unless the Hinds gained altitude and slowed their assault, he knew the ravine gave him only seconds that he could hide beneath the helicopters' radar horizon. And what the hell had they shot at him? This was turning into a real quick-draw situation, and it wasn't making Tag at all happy.

"Too steep to go up, boss," Wheels said, spinning both tracks.

"Go to the creek, goddammit. Get me somewhere flat."

Wheels executed a perfect bootlegger's turn backward around the tree and rode low gear against gravity and the slope of the bank down to a creek swollen into the trees by the previous night's rain.

"Snorkels up, Wheels," Tag said. "We're going swimming."

On the rear deck of the No Slack, two telescoping snorkels rose from the turbine intake ports until they were level with the turret.

"Muzzles up," Tag reminded his gunner.

The tank's glacis nosed into the roiling, turbid stream. Water rose up and over the turret flange and to the base of the main-gun mantle before the tracks found the streambed. Wheels pivoted on the left track, letting the No Slack settle up to its guns in a haystack swell below a logjam, keeping the exhaust flutter-valves downstream, where the current carried away the bubbles.

"Radar down," Tag said, hitting the switch. "Let it idle, Wheels, and just hope this water hides our heat. Ham, let's try to get visual contact and shoot 'em on wires. Maybe we can ambush these suckers before they see what a trail we blazed."

"My favorite form of combat," Ham replied earnestly.

They waited, and nothing in the world—not the gurgle of the purring turbine's exhaust, not the nerve-grating complaint of the turret as Tag jockeyed it to position, not the surflike sound of flood rushing around them—was any louder to each man than his own breathing.

Tag increased the magnification on his commander's scope.

"Target," he said as a Hind, in its unmistakable attitude of attack, suddenly hovered like an armored dragonfly in the middle of his scope. "Range: one two hundred."

"Got him," Ham said.

"Shoot."

"Shot."

The top War Club in the rack made a popping sound, ignited, and launched itself from the mount in a hissing rooster tail of steam. Like Tag, Ham noticed the hesitation and felt his heart in his throat. Then he had the missile, had it on target, and saw the contrail bend in the wire-guided War Club's characteristic fishhook attack. It struck the MI-24D from above, just aft of the exhaust tube. The shock envelope of its explosion expanded through the Hind, blasting out glass and spiraling curled plates of smoking armor off its belly.

"Spa-lash!" Tag said wickedly, watching as the Hind twisted crazily on its free rotor then fell like a sack of smoldering slag. "Stand by. His buddies are going to be looking sharp now."

The fog that lay in the ravine was light enough that Tag could see clearly through it to the paling sky, just dense enough to blur the contours of the No Slack's gun and turret that protruded from the flood swell. But the fog would burn off, and the creek would subside, and they couldn't wait there forever.

"See anything, Ham?" Tag asked.

"Radar sensors!" Ham said. "Got 'em. They're circling high."

Tag homed his scope on the radar from the Hinds.

"Target. War Club."

"Confirmed."

"Shoot."

"Sh—" Ham mashed the launch button again. Nothing. "Won't fire, Sarge," the gunner said.

"Try the other one, Ham."

Jefferson threw the third toggle and again pressed the launch button. There was a hideous scream of rocket propellant boiling the stream against the side of the turret as the War Club fought the weight of the flood, then tore from its mount and veered sharply right.

"It's off the wire, Sarge," Ham said. "Oh, shit."

The missile executed a perfect barrel roll into the slope of the wooded ravine and went up in a mushroom of black and white smoke three hundred meters upstream from the No Slack.

"Stand by on the 75mm," Tag said. "Wheels, I'm gonna put the top down, and you're gonna get us out of here."

Chest-high in the turret hatch, Tag passed an image of a submarine captain coming onto his bridge. The spray off the guns wet his collar and neck. He scowled in disgust at the malfunctioning War Club mount.

"Come straight back, Wheels." There was no climbing the slope they had slid down, no point in going toward the Hinds. The tank came out of the swooping haystack into water that still ran fast and thick with leaves across the deck.

"They coming, Sarge," Ham said through the intercom.

Thirty meters downstream, where the creek widened in the ravine, the rear deck came up and cleared the water.

"Wheel right," Tag ordered, "and goose it."

The No Slack slewed in the shallowing water that broke straight up against its track skirts. Wheels engaged his lowest gear and locked the throttle. The tank lurched, found purchase, and clawed its way into the flooded timber, up onto a silted flat, where a culvert entered the stream.

"Wheels," Tag said, "put our six against the hill."

As the tank came to a stop with its rear wedged into the brush that grew along the culvert flow, Tag could see that he could not see through the forest canopy. Outside the tank, the roar of the swollen stream was deafening.

"Ears up," he ordered as he buttoned the hatch and activated the audio directional receiver. The sinister *whump-whump* of Hind rotors was recognizable at once. Tag swept for the strong signal and took a bearing.

"One coming at us," he announced. "Audio bearing, Ham. Stand by on the 75mm for a passing shot."

Like a predatory insect out of nightmare, the Soviet attack helicopter swayed through the air, banking back and forth across the width of the ravine as it ran its length. The Hind pilot saw the twisted guardrail and the crushed path of the No Slack's descent into the creek. He kept the nose of his aircraft toward the trail and swung out wide below it, sweeping the woods with his thermal sensors as the Hind passed directly over the No Slack.

Too close for radar or thermal sights, Ham took the 75mm manually and hammered out three rounds in four and a half seconds, the last one striking the Hind low on its midship armor and ripping open a ragged wound that trailed wires and cables like intestines from the belly of the aircraft, as it pitched, caught the air with its prop, and labored for altitude, rising above the 75mm's cone of fire.

"Goddamn, those ugly suckers are tough," Ham swore.

"Move us, Wheels," Tag said, throwing open his hatch. "Hard right just beyond that big willow."

The low-slung tank shot in a tight arc, slammed over the rise of the culvert flow, then moved gingerly on the steep face of the ravine. Tag heard the throb of the third Hind as it banked wildly above them, pounding the culvert with 37mm cannon fire. He tried to read the slope for anyplace where they could fight or maneuver. They broke through a leaning stand of small birches, and there it was: a revetment of loose limestone covering the lower half of the slope.

"Charge that rip-rap, Wheels," Tag said. "Give it all you've got."

Latta ignited the right-hand turbine and hit the stone retaining wall at a forty-five-degree angle, scattering limestone chunks in a clatter like the collapse of a mountain of bowling balls. Wheels fought the controls as the No Slack's rear end kept sliding downhill. He had to travel fifty meters to cover the thirty to the top of the revetment, knowing—feeling deep in his bones—how exposed and vulnerable they were each inch of the way. At the lip of the stonework, he drove the No Slack perpendicular to the rim, felt it hesitate for a heart-stopping moment as it hung on the edge and the ailing turbine guttered, then felt it groan forward and jerk into motion up an incline the No Slack could negotiate.

Tag could see the road, could see an angle through the woods that would put them on it, could see the wounded Hind hovering above it a hundred meters away. Somewhere behind him he could also hear the angry whine of the third, as it circled the culvert for another pass. Tag recalled a quotation from Bat Masterson that used to hang framed in a bar in Missoula: "The best weapon in a gunfight is a shotgun, preferably from ambush."

"Wheels, stay in the trees and get us as close as you can to that Hind—do you see him?"

"Got him," Wheels said, changing their direction in a series of small movements to test the slope.

"Ham," Tag said, "beehive."

"Beehive," Ham responded, then added, "What the hell are we doing, Sarge?"

"We're gonna jump-shoot the motherfucker, Hambone. Then we run and defend with the 75mm."

Fruits completed the reloading, and Ham got a thermal lock on the Hind to back up his optical sight.

Wheels accelerated through the woods just off the shoulder of the road. Less than thirty meters from the Hind, Tag gave the command: "On the road! Shoot on sight!"

Evergreens snapped beneath the tracks as Wheels jammed the pedals and gunned the No Slack out onto the blacktop. The turret screamed, its main gun canted at a forty-five-degree angle.

"Stop!" Tag said.

The split images in Ham's sight crossed once, twice.

The Hind saw the movement and pitched its tail high for attack, wheeling to face the No Slack.

"Shot," Ham said as thousands of one-centimeter, saw-toothed discs, spread in a trailing cone three meters broad, enveloped the nose and cockpit of the MI-24D, flaying the pilots in a blizzard of steel and glass.

The Hind reared like a shying hawk, dipped its rotor into the trees, bucked once in a desperate cavort, and crashed, bouncing and burning, down the slope of the ravine into the creek.

"Nail it, Wheels!" Tag ordered as he keyed toggles on his console. "Radar up. All systems up."

And then they were running again down the crown of the highway, the constant flat-shaft vibration of the off turbine punctuated by the loose slap of their stretched tread.

"Guns rear," Tag said. "Target."

The turret squeaked mildly.

"Yo' mama's fuckin' servo unit, Wheels," Ham muttered. "It's jammed, Sarge," he said more loudly. "Can't go to the rear."

"Wheels, one-eighty," Tag said. "Radar, lock. Shoot 75mm on sight."

Wheels dipped to the right shoulder, braked the inside track, and brought the No Slack to rest squarely in the middle of the road. The Hind was closing in an evasive approach at two hundred kilometers per hour from less than a klick away.

"I'm blind, Sarge," Ham said. "Radar's down."

"Laser, lock. Shoot."

At Ham's shot the Hind jinked, and again at the second. Two rockets shot from one of the Hind's wing pods, stringing their white vapor trails.

The first rocket passed inches over the No Slack's turret; the second struck the reactive armor on its glacis. The combined eruption of the missile and the armor drove the tank back, stalling the turbines and hammering the men inside like a colossal fist. Wheels yoked the joystick with his solar plexus; Tag cracked his CVC against the radio console; Ham was knocked unconscious in his gunner's seat; and Fruits Tutti whined over the intercom, "Oh, my fuckin' wrist."

No one inside the No Slack saw the three contrails that converged on the Hind from a troika of American AH-1A King Cobra choppers.

Fruits Tutti pulled himself into the auxiliary gunner's position just in time to find a fireball in his sights. "Sarge, Wheels!" he yelped. "Start us. Start us!"

"Butcher Boy, Butcher Boy, this is Blackbird One," said the voice over the ComNet receiver. "Butcher Boy, if you read me, come up on TacNet One. I say again, TacNet One."

Tag found himself keying in the frequency even before the radio transmission registered in his mind. Who was hit? Tutti?

"Yo," Tag said drunkenly.

"Butcher Boy, do you need extraction?"

Tag connected to the familiar drone of the KC turbine. "Wait one," he replied.

Wheels was arced grotesquely in his chair, hacking for breath. Tag hit the starters and got one turbine to respond.

"We're mobile," Tag radioed to the chopper.

"Follow me," the pilot replied.

12

With just one engine and the track slapping ominously, Tag calculated that it would take them almost two hours to reach Mannheim. They ran unmolested for the first thirty minutes of that under the cover of the circling King Cobras, until they reached the ramps and overpasses at the junction of the Mannheim highway.

From the moment they could first see the junction, they could also see the horrific remains of battle—or retreat. Concrete overpasses ended in midair, shattered and blackened and exuding bent tendons of reinforcing steel. Shell holes were dotted across the scene, which was all littered with infantry gear and blasted, disabled vehicles, some of them still smoking.

Back again at his controls, Wheels turned the tank up an entrance ramp and said, "Looks like Sherman's goddamn march to the sea out there, Sarge."

Tag opened his hatch and raised the pedestal of his combat seat. From the height of the autobahn he could see the crushed remains of a village to the south, the rolling countryside smudged by smoke and pocked by artillery craters. Loose hogs rooted and snuffled in charred barn lots.

They passed trucks, trailers, towed weapons, and APCs, all strewn as smoldering wreckage in the parkway and along the berm of the road. It was awful to see the toll levied by Mars for possessing this field. In the cipher of the aftermath, Tag read men's lives in the incinerated trucks and twisted howitzers. He recalled Ernie Pyle's quote about war existing only a hundred yards on either side of you—but here he felt that it went on forever.

Ham was groggy but conscious. Fruits's wrist was swollen and probably broken; Tag splinted it from the first-aid box. Wheels nursed a bruised diaphragm and drove in a stoop. Goudonov, although battered from being tossed inside the turret, was still conscious. He had pissed in his uniform, was wet to the waist, and lay knotted in fear on the steel plate.

"Butcher Boy, this is Blackbird One. Can you go any faster, Butcher Boy? We're burning a lot of gas up here."

"Blackbird," Tag said, "this is Butcher Boy. That's negative. Sorry guys, but we're crippled."

"Copy, Butcher Boy. We'll stay with you as long as we can. You should be okay from here on, anyway. People know you're coming."

"Thanks, Blackbird. Out," Tag said, thinking, *Hell, they can probably hear us*. Even in field trials and exercises, Tag had grown accustomed to the No Slack's almost noiseless operation, because there were always mechanics and logistics people—even engineers—on hand to tinker with every screw, every microchip. Now, after three—no, four—days of hard driving and direct hits, the once-sleek XM-F3 looked like a four-car collision, with its nose warped and sooty from blast burns, the bent fingers of one War Club rack twisting toward the sky. But it was the noise that was maddening. Even with a CVC clamped tight on his head, Tag could do little to dampen the arrhythmic, metallic din that roared inside the tank.

After an hour it was exquisite.

"Butcher Boy, this is Blackbird."

"Go, Blackbird," Tag responded through the din inside his tank.

"Butcher Boy, we have what appears to be movement in the woods to the south, about one klick down the road. You want to hold up while we check it out?"

Tag thought only a moment.

"Negative, Blackbird. We're still armed. You spot for us, and we'll cover each other."

"Roger, Butcher Boy. Stand by to copy."

While the KC pilot fed them coordinates, Tag entered them in the LandNav computer and called up a map enlargement of their area.

"Fruits," Tag said, "can you load?"

"Ain't gonna break no speed records, but yeah, I can load."

"Okay," Tag responded, "stack a pan in the 75mm, and man it yourself, then give us HE for the main tube."

The loading carousel hummed. Fruits locked home a round in the 120mm, then struggled with a magazine for the 75mm, finally having to give up and stack the rounds in the pan one at a time.

Tag could hear his driver grunting in pain with each breath.

"Wheels," he said, "you okay?"

"Uh-uh," Wheels replied, "but I'll do, I reckon."

"All right, then," Tag said, "throttle back a little. Leave yourself some pedal, in case we need to dance."

"Butcher Boy, this is Blackbird. We have that movement now at your niner o'clock, about two-zero-zero meters south of the road. You copy?"

"Roger, Blackbird. Butcher Boy copy. You going in after them? Over."

"That's affirm, Butcher Boy. Stand by. We may have a whole herd of Holsteins in there."

Tag ordered Wheels to turn down into the swale of parkway dividing the lanes of the highway, then halted the No Slack with just its turret above the level of the pavement, facing toward the woods to the south.

"Stand by your guns, gentlemen," Tag said. "I'm going up top with the fifty."

Tag paused in the turret to deliver a one-finger salute to Goudonov before he went through the hatch and swung the farings of the .50-caliber around in front of him.

"Fruits," he shouted back inside, "pass me up a can of .50-caliber."

Tag flipped open the breech of the heavy machine gun, disengaged the belt from the holding pawls, unhooked the half-empty can from the side of the receiver, and replaced it with the fresh one. All the while he kept one eye cocked on the three AH-1As as they swung wide over the suspicious movement, converging on their target cautiously. Tag double-cocked the .50-caliber and took the grips in his hands.

Suddenly the air was split by the ripping sound of chain guns from the KCs. Tag could see two of them hanging on their rotors, noses depressed, raking the heavy forest with arcs of 20-mm destruction, walking it toward the road.

"Butcher Boy, this is Blackbird. Stand by; we have an estimated six—I say again, six—unidentified vehicles scattered in the trees and moving toward your position. Copy, Butcher Boy?"

"Blackbird, this is Butcher Boy," Tag replied. "I copy. Are the vehicles wheeled or tracked?"

"Wheeled vehicles, Butcher Boy. We've nailed one recon car that looks like a Bravo Tango Romeo. Can't tell about the rest, except that they're headed your way."

"Thanks, Blackbird. Out.

"Look sharp now," Tag said softly to his crew.

"I have three confirmed heat signatures at about one o'clock," Ham Jefferson said.

"Roger, Ham," Tag said. "I've got some sort of movement over there in the—"

Tag's words were cut short by the sudden appearance of a pair of old model BTRs bursting from the trees behind a motorcycle that had a machine gun mounted on its sidecar.

"Fire!" Tag shouted, thumbing the trigger on the .50-caliber and sweeping it on the motorcycle.

The bike veered from the impact of Tag's rounds and flipped as it struck the far guardrail, spilling its dead rider and gunner on the scorched berm.

As Tag swung his heavy gun back toward the BTRs, Fruits cut loose with the 75mm, hitting the lead vehicle twice, separating its front end from the chassis and blowing men out of its open crew cab. Ham touched off the 120-mm, and the second BTR disappeared in a ball of flame and black smoke.

Inside the woods, another explosion marked a kill by one of the KCs.

"Butcher Boy, Butcher Boy," the lead pilot's voice crackled through Tag's CVC. "There's one at your ten o'clock."

Tag swung the .50-caliber and locked on another cycle in the notch of the gun farings. It was speeding up onto the road about two hundred meters to the east. Leading it the way he would a green-winged teal, Tag mashed his trigger and watched as the bike disintegrated under the fusillade of fire—wheels, sidecar, and crew all flying mangled to the roadside.

The rapid *whump-whump* and solid recoil of the 75mm brought Tag back around in time to see a third recon vehicle rocked by the cannon fire and, almost simultaneously, ripped by a long burst from one of the King Cobra's chain guns.

The choppers' guns then fell silent, as the birds tightened their searching circle.

After a minute, Tag radioed up to them. "Blackbird, this is Butcher Boy. See anything? Over."

"We've got nothing from up here, Butcher Boy. Are the targets near you neutralized?"

"That's affirmative, Blackbird."

"Okay, Butcher Boy, move out. We're going to hose the area one more time, then we've got to go. We're flying on fumes right now."

"Roger, Blackbird. And thanks for the company."

"Our pleasure, Butcher Boy. Out."

Wheels backed the No Slack up onto the pavement and pulled them a hundred meters down the road to watch the choppers pulverize the near woods with streams of 20mm fire that hacked through limbs and trunks like chain saws before dipping their rotors in salute to Tag and his crew.

The KCs left them, and for thirty minutes everyone was all smiles. They just didn't say much, because talking only added to the noise. They all felt like men on the last leg of a grueling relay—exhausted, with only the sight of the finish keeping them going. So it was a relief of sorts when the track finally snapped just twenty klicks from the headquarters outside Mannheim. It shelled off the drive wheels and lashed against the skirts with a sound like the hinges of hell.

"Shit patooie," Wheels spat as he ground them to a halt. "We slung that one for good and sure, boss."

"Yeah," Tag said slowly. "Okay, everybody, slowly, take five. No slammed hatches, please."

Tag and his crew were standing outside, stretching and trying to clear the ringing from their ears, when two Bradleys and a four-wheel-drive enclosed truck came tearing up the opposite lanes of the autobahn, dug across the parkway, and skittered to a stop around the No Slack. Dressed in class As, with a yellow ascot at his throat, Colonel Menefee sprang from the passenger seat of the four-wheel-drive.

Satin Ass! Tag almost shouted as the squat colonel with the overdeveloped physique advanced toward him in short, muscle-bound strides. Menefee looked past Tag to the tank, and his broad grin collapsed in shock.

"Ten-hut!" Tag barked, snapping a salute.

Menefee did a double take on the tank as Tag added, "Staff Sergeant Tag reporting as ordered, sir. All present, sir."

Menefee was simmering. He returned the salute and extended his hand.

"It's good to have you back, Max. But you better have some *goddamn* good excuses for me to give the eagles about the XM-F3."

"Maybe you didn't hear, sir," Max said innocently, "but there is a war going on."

Menefee dismissed the remark. "Finally found out how much it takes to break it, didn't you, Max?"

"It's all in the log, Colonel," Tag replied.

"All right, get your people. You're all riding back with me. We'll get a retriever out here to pick up your mess. You people get to chow down, shit, shave, shower, and be shining in my office at 1530 hours for debriefing. Got it?"

"I've got one man injured, sir?"

"We'll get him seen to," Menefee said irritably. "How bad is it?"

"Broken wrist, I think."

"Well, have him with you, then."

"One more thing, sir."

"What is it, Tag?"

"A little present for you, sir, since you think we played too rough with the new toy.

"Ham, Wheels," Tag called over his shoulder, "show Colonel Menefee what we brought him."

The driver and the gunner pulled themselves stiffly onto the rear deck and up over the turret. They leaned in through the hatch and hauled the Russian colonel up and out by his armpits, dragged him off the back, and deposited him in a pile at Colonel Menefee's feet.

"Colonel Menefee," Tag said, "I would like you to meet Colonel Goudonov, Commander, Lenin Regiment, Eleventh Guards Division."

Menefee's eyes widened—Tag could see stars in them, general's stars. "Well," Menefee said with satisfaction, "this is a different ball of wax. Where did you get this one, Max?"

"Picked him up hitchhiking," Wheels volunteered, "but he's acted real ungrateful, sir. Just pissin' and moanin' all the time."

Menefee wrinkled his nose. "I see," he said. "Well, put him in behind the rear seat. I want to deliver this one in person."

The crew collected some of their personal gear and weapons and in minutes were sailing smoothly along in a camouflaged Chevrolet Blazer, crammed happily together in the backseat, while Tag rode in front, sandwiched between Menefee and his driver.

"Tag," Menefee said to him, "I need to tell you right now that you and the No Slack have caused quite a stir. You and your bunch of outlaws are about the only things in that tank that aren't classified—and, of course, we're glad to have you back—but the eagles were having fits. You guys are under wraps, for the time being, until we've had a chance to pick your brains, anyway. Hope you don't mind staying in a transient officers' barracks. We've got one empty at the HQ compound, just across the quad from my office. You'll have to take chow there. Club's closed too. Meanwhile, you don't talk to anybody about what you saw or did behind the lines."

"Yes, sir," Tag said mechanically. He wasn't saying shit about anything until he'd had a bath and a meal.

They dropped Tutti at the base hospital's trauma/triage area, with special orders to the nurses and doctors to dispatch him directly to the transient barracks as soon as they were through, then drove across the bustling base to the headquarters area. Everywhere, Tag saw men and vehicles in motion, stacks of supplies. C-130s were coming on and off the airstrip as frequently as subway trains.

"How bad has it been, Colonel?" Tag asked.

Menefee looked straight ahead. "Bad enough. You've read the book. That's about how it's been, Max. If there's no push in the next forty-eight hours, they're going to declare Stage Two. I've still got to read some reports and let Seven Corps know you're here. I'll tell you everything I can at 1530."

Menefee put them in the junior officers' wing of the clapboard barracks—two-man rooms with showers, television, a game room with a refrigerator, and a private mess hall. The rest of the barracks seemed to be empty. It struck

Tag as very strange that Menefee hadn't even allowed them to pick up their personal gear from the warehouse where it had been moved. "I'll have it delivered" was the last thing he told Tag.

Ham Jefferson strode down the hall of the barracks, swilling beer from a bottle and carrying two others by their necks in his other hand. He kicked on the half-open door of the room Tag and Wheels were sharing across from his own.

"Patrol coming in from officers' country," he announced, toeing back the door. "Anybody want a Beck's?"

He handed out the beers and sat on the bunk next to Tag.

"I don't know what to drink to," he said, "but I think we need some kind of toast, Sarge."

Tag straightened and looked at his men—still unshowered, unshaven, still bright-eyed from adrenaline—and raised his bottle. "To the ones who stayed behind," he said.

They all drank long and in silence.

Tag broke the moment. "Ham," he said, "you find any food?"

"Better," Ham said, mopping his chin with his cuff. "Got a cook frying bacon right now. Unless you want to wait for Salisbury steak at lunch."

"Shoot," said Wheels, "I always like a little steak to help settle my breakfast."

They finished their beers and hit the showers. Tag scoured himself with a rough washcloth and changed cartridges in his razor twice. The face in the mirror looked gaunt to him, hollow as the feeling in the pit of his stomach when he recalled the wild night battle they had driven from, with Prentice and the Jagd Kommandos (and Giesla, *Giesla*) covering their escape. He knew now what she had meant about the guilt of survivors. That it was all part of his duty was cold consolation to Tag.

Fruits Tutti arrived with his left hand and wrist in a cast. "Ain't nothin'," he said. "Dem nurses just wanted to give me a handicap."

They ate bacon and fried potatoes and toast and eggs cooked to order. A pickup delivered their duffel bags and lockers, so Tag ordered fresh uniforms for their debriefing with Menefee—polished boots and no rank insignias.

An hour later, much to the surprise of the cooks, they ate lunch. The only others in the mess area were two lieutenant colonels eating together at a corner table, ignoring the crew of the No Slack, who kept asking each other the questions none of them could answer: What next? When? How goes the war?

At 1520, Tag led his men across the grassy quad to the headquarters building, where Menefee had been given a basement office for an HQ. Tag knocked and entered.

"Staff Sergeant Tag and crew reporting as ordered, sir," he said, saluting crisply. Flanking Menefee's desk in armchairs were the two officers he had seen in the mess area, one balding and wearing glasses, the other dapper and nondescript.

"At ease, Max," said Menefee, rising from his chair and returning the salute. "You and your men drag you up a seat." He pointed to a stack of metal folding chairs. "This may take a while.

"These officers are from SACEUR," Menefee went on, using the acronym for the Supreme Allied Commander Europe. "Anything they want to know, you tell them."

Tag nodded and sat.

"Let's begin," said Menefee, "with an account in your own words, Max. Just start with day one, and give us the rundown."

Speaking tersely in the emotionless language of an after-action report, Tag told the officers of the initial action around Bamberg, of their attaching themselves to the Jagd Kommandos, of picking up Prentice and his men at the depot, of the stealth attack and its results, of the flight to the rendezvous, of their strike against the rear of the Soviet line, and of their bizarre engagement against the three Hinds, and finally of the skirmish with the recon unit on the highway.

"The rest of it you pretty well know," Tag concluded.

"Any of you other men have anything to add at this point?" Menefee asked.

"Jus dat we owe dem commandos a big one, sir," Fruits said. "And dem ordnance guys. Ain't there anything we can do for dem? Any way we can get them out?"

"I appreciate your loyalty, Specialist," said Menefee, "but we've got a lot more to consider here."

"Sergeant," said the bald officer with glasses, "do you know what your little bit of heroics caused?" His voice was querulous, almost accusatory.

Tag swallowed hard. Here it comes, he thought.

"No, sir."

"Well, first of all, it caused us to think you were dead—or worse, captured. You did not have to engage those targets, did you, Sergeant, in order to effect a withdrawal?"

"Not absolutely. No, sir. At least not all of them, I suppose."

"As it turns out, Sergeant," the other lieutenant colonel said, "we're all damn lucky that you did. It played hell with the Soviets, Sergeant; stalled their advance for at least twelve hours and allowed us to get two regiments of the cav out of that pocket. I don't think the Reds know yet what hit them. But let me ask you—is this account of your kills really accurate?"

"I may have left something out, sir."

"May have left . . . indeed!"

"Sergeant," said the bespectacled colonel, "Colonel Menefee has told us that you managed to keep your evaluation log up-to-date. Is that right?"

"Yes, sir."

"Good. We'll have a look at it later. But is there anything you'd like to add or emphasize right now?"

Tag thought a moment.

"A couple of things, sir," he said. "The servo unit on the turret has got to be replaced, maybe redesigned. I don't know what the problem was with the radio— maybe Specialist Tutti can fill you in. But the big bugbear was in the radar link on the 75mm and the War Club ignition system."

"Explain, please," said the dapper colonel.

Tag told in some detail of their fighting the No Slack from the flood swell, of the electrical shorts and misfirings that they experienced with the antiaircraft missiles, as well as the radar breakdown that had forced them to fire the 75mm manually.

The colonel sucked in his teeth.

"Oh, yeah," Tag said, snapping his fingers. "About missiles, at least one of the Hinds had some sort with a lot more range than we thought, possibly radar homing too."

"That would be the Tree Toad, Max," Menefee said. "We've recovered a few of them and already heard plenty. You boys were lucky, if that's what they shot at you. We lost some armor to them pulling out of Nürnberg."

"I think that's all we need for now, sir," the bald officer said to Menefee. He and the other lieutenant colonel got to their feet. He turned to Tag.

"See you in Brussels, Sergeant—or, I should say, *Captain*—Tag."

Tag sat thunderstruck as they walked out the door.

"What's this captain shit," he said, twisting in his chair to face Menefee, "sir?"

Menefee sat back and grinned.

"And this Brussels shit?" Tag added for measure.

"The Army's not giving you a choice about it this time, Max," Menefee said. "Tomorrow at 0700, you and I and your gang and whatever you have left of the XM-F3 are going to be on a C-130. You're not going to bitch about orders from SACEUR, are you?"

"They're takin' the No Slack out of the field?" Wheels said in disbelief.

"And damned happy we are able to, Sergeant," Menefee snapped at him. "Why the hell do you think you were called in, anyway?"

"Okay, sir," Tag said, "orders are orders. But what's the drill?"

"Right now, *Captain*, you know as much as I do. But whatever it is, you've still got me. Nice, isn't it?"

"Just peachy, sir. Anything else?"

"Just don't leave the barracks. We'll have a truck to pick you up in the morning. And"—Menefee opened a drawer in his desk and withdrew a square bottle of Irish whiskey—"since the clubs are closed, I thought you might want to treat your men to a little nightcap. Congratulations, Captain."

Tag took the bottle and shook Menefee's offered hand as the rest of the crew got to their feet.

"Thanks, sir," Tag said. "We could all use some downtime."

"Well, you've got twelve hours, Captain. Use it well. You're all dismissed."

Tag turned to the crew. "Okay," he said, "you heard the colonel."

"Oh, Captain," Menefee said as Tag reached the door, "one more thing. You do have your log up-to-date, for me to look over in the morning, don't you?"

"It's in the No Slack, sir," Tag said, thinking: But you can't take the asshole out of the soldier.

Back in the barracks, the men sorted out their gear, read and answered some of the mail Menefee had delivered with their bags, swapped paperback novels—"I'll trade you two Clancys for a Steelbaugh." "Ah, fug a buncha war-games bullshit."—and generally tried to force themselves into the lazy familiarity of garrison. But it *was* forced; they joked and laughed and cursed each other without really meaning any of it or taking any pleasure in their respite. Each of them was already anxious for the next move, the next phase of their war.

At 1800, they went to eat again, alone this time, and had a choice of steak or lamb chops. Something about all this was making Tag uneasy.

"Hey," Fruits Tutti said to him through a mouthful of mashed potatoes, "cheer up, Sarge—I mean, sir. I mean, shit, bein' recommissioned ain't de worst dat could happen. Like Satin Ass said, you still got us."

"Yeah, Cap'n," Wheels said. "What could be worse'n we already been through? Hell, we're heroes."

"Sure, Wheels," Ham said, "they probably gonna bronze us and put us on display. Shit, boy, they just recycling us. You watch, you be back with a line company in a week."

"I'm not so sure about that, Ham," Tag said, pushing his plate away and sucking on a toothpick. "There's something fishy about this whole deal."

"Now that you're an ossifer again," Wheels said, "you know something we enlisted swine don't?"

"Just a hunch, Wheels. Listen, the way I see it, they're not keeping us all together just because we sing cute harmony. Putting us up here, in officers' quarters, keeping us isolated from everybody below the rank of light colonel, flying us to fucking SACEUR headquarters—no, there's something else. We may all be back in a week, but I think it's gonna be together, and not in any line company."

"And not in the No Slack, neither," Ham said with a shake of his head.

"Yeah," Tag agreed, "not unless Logistics Support Group has some mighty rare spare parts up their sleeve. But I don't care if they give us a goddamn Sherman. We've fought 'em and we've whipped 'em. We know how, fellas, and *that's* what's gonna get us sent back."

"Doin' what, you suppose?" Wheels asked.

"Why, we be kickin' ass, you ridge-runnin' redneck," Ham told him.

"Come on," Tag said, rising. "I'm buying drinks for the baddest tank crew in Germany."

Tag fetched the bottle and joined the crew in the recreation room. Ham liberated four more bottles of beer from the refrigerator, and Fruits found the BBC on a stereo tuner hidden in a cabinet. They drank boilermakers for a while, listening to Percy Cushy-Hassock (as Fruits called the BBC announcer) read the news, which consisted largely of quotes and paraphrases from world leaders.

What they heard did little to cheer up the men of the No Slack. Reading between the lines and adding to it what they knew firsthand, the situation in northern Europe looked more grim than any of them had guessed.

The Warsaw Pact's attempt to encircle West Germany from the north and south was clearly well advanced, especially in the north, where Communist forces were already occupying parts of the Netherlands and pushing south down the Rhine, where the British II Corps had taken a pounding around Wesel just that morning. Fulda had fallen. But as the battle went farther south, into the forests of Bohemia, the Americans and the surprising French had inflicted heavy damage on the Soviet assault and stalled it on a line from Würzburg down to Munchen, giving the Allies a deep cushion between the front and their support positions along the upper Rhine.

On other fronts, the Chinese had assumed their expected posture of neutrality. There had been a major naval battle in the Sea of Japan. A combined force of Cubans and African Marxists had attacked South Africa from land and sea, in a clear attempt to cut off its supply of critical materials to the West, but without a declaration of war on the NATO countries, with whom the South Africans had no military treaties.

The Middle East seemed to be simmering but not yet fully boiling. The greatest danger appeared to be that some of the Arab states might take advantage of the situation to launch an attack against Israel, and were deterred only by the Israelis' show of strength in neutralizing the Libyan oil and chemical facilities in a massive air strike just twenty-four hours after the first Soviet tanks crossed into Germany.

Tag got up and tuned the radio dial until he found the "soft sounds" of Armed Forces Radio.

As they neared the bottom of the bottle, Fruits said boozily, "Dose goddamn Jagd Kommandos, what a hell of a bunch. Goddamn, I'd like to see dose fuckas again. Wouldn't you, Sarge? Sir, I mean."

"Toots, I tell you," Tag said, realizing he was about one drink away from recklessness, "by God, we will. 'Cause wherever Satin Ass is, it's gonna be polishing a chair someplace. Just let him give us a goddamn tank and see what happens. Fuck 'im."

"Ain't no way to talk about a fellow officer, boss," Wheels said.

"Fuck 'im," Tag repeated. "Fruits, pass me that jug."

Tag was pleased with the hangover he had calculated. He didn't think about Giesla for the entire hour it took to fly to Belgium. All he could think about was what to say to SACEUR. At last he would be able to convey Brigadier McBrien's regards. At last he was going to meet Ross Kettle.

GLOSSARY

AH-1A—Nicknamed the "King Cobra," the AH-1A is a larger, faster, more heavily armed and armored version of the AH-1 Cobra attack helicopter

AP—Armor-piercing rounds

Av-gas—Aviation gasoline

BMP—A fully tracked Soviet infantry-fighting vehicle. Its armaments may include anti-tank missiles, a 73mm gun, a 25mm cannon, and a 7.62mm machine gun. It is similar in function and design to the Bradley Fighting Vehicle

BTR—Any one of several types of Soviet armored personnel carriers, the most common being the BTR-60, an eight-wheeled vehicle, either open or closed in armor, and mounted with heavy and light machine guns

CAR-15—Collapsible-stock carbine, similar to the standard M-16 automatic rifle

CMH—Congressional Medal of Honor

227

CVC—Combat vehicle crewman's helmet. This helmet provides both protection and communications links with the vehicle's radio and intercom

Deuce-and-a-half—a 2½-ton truck

Dragon—A medium anti-tank missile launcher. This man-portable weapon requires a crew of two and has a range of 1000 meters

EOD—Explosive Ordnance Demolition. EOD personnel perform a variety of tasks, including the destruction of unexploded bombs and artillery shells

G-2—Army intelligence, also used to mean any information or the presence or lack of intellectual capacity ("He ain't got no G-2")

Hind—Nickname of the Soviet MI-24D attack helicopter, a heavily armed and armored aircraft

IR Scope—Infra-red scope, used for low-light situations and at night

KIA—Killed in action

Laser Doppler Sights—Computer-assisted range-finding sights that measure the "red shift" or "Doppler effect" of a laser beam directed on a target in order to determine the target's range and position

LAW—Light anti-tank weapon. A disposable 66mm anti-tank rocket launcher with a range of three hundred meters

M-1A—The U.S. Army's Abrams main battle tank

MI-24D—Soviet attack helicopter. See *Hind*

152s—Soviet 152mm self-propelled howitzers

One-five-fives—155mm howitzers

RPG—Rocket-propelled grenade, similar in effectiveness to the U.S. LAW

Sabot (French for *shoe*)—A type of armor-piercing round consisting of a core or penetrator projectile surrounded by a boot the same diameter as the gun bore. The boot, or sabot, falls away after the round leaves the gun tube, and the penetrator continues toward its target

Stinger missiles—Shoulder-fired, wire-guided anti-aircraft missiles frequently in use by infantry and other ground units

TAC—Tactical, as in TAC radio frequencies

T-64B—Upgraded version of the Soviet T-64 main battle tank, armed with 125mm main gun and equipped with an array of the latest in Soviet tank electronics. The T-80 was developed from the T-64

T-80—Soviet main battle tank, designed to be the Soviet counterpart to the Abrams M-1A

WIA—Wounded in action

XM-F3—The "No Slack" is the third prototype tank (and first field operational model) built using monopolar ("slick skin") carbide armor and new designs, intended to fulfill the requirements of tank warfare outlined by General Ross Kettle

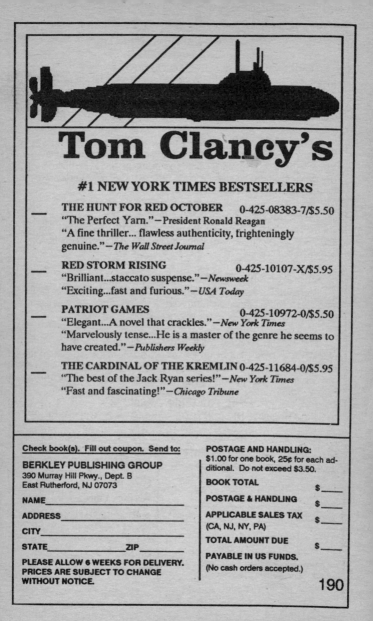

Tom Clancy's

#1 NEW YORK TIMES BESTSELLERS

__ **THE HUNT FOR RED OCTOBER**   0-425-08383-7/$5.50
"The Perfect Yarn."—*President Ronald Reagan*
"A fine thriller... flawless authenticity, frighteningly genuine."—*The Wall Street Journal*

__ **RED STORM RISING**   0-425-10107-X/$5.95
"Brilliant...staccato suspense."—*Newsweek*
"Exciting...fast and furious."—*USA Today*

__ **PATRIOT GAMES**   0-425-10972-0/$5.50
"Elegant...A novel that crackles."—*New York Times*
"Marvelously tense...He is a master of the genre he seems to have created."—*Publishers Weekly*

__ **THE CARDINAL OF THE KREMLIN**   0-425-11684-0/$5.95
"The best of the Jack Ryan series!"—*New York Times*
"Fast and fascinating!"—*Chicago Tribune*
